LOVE IS A
BATTLEFIELD

ANNALISA DAUGHETY

LOVE IS A BATTLEFIELD

A WALK IN THE PARK – BOOK 1

BARBOUR
PUBLISHING

Scripture quotations are taken from the *Holy Bible*, New Living Translation, copyright © 1996, 2004. Used by permission of Tyndale House Publishers, Inc. Wheaton, Illinois 60189, U.S.A. All rights reserved.

This book is a work of fiction. Names, characters, places, and incidents are either products of the author's imagination or used fictitiously. Any similarity to actual people, organizations, and/or events is purely coincidental.

Cover Model Photography: Jim Celuch, Celuch Creative Imaging

Published by Barbour Publishing, Inc., P.O. Box 719, Uhrichsville, OH 44683, www.barbourbooks.com

Our mission is to publish and distribute inspirational products offering exceptional value and biblical encouragement to the masses.

ecpa Member of the
Evangelical Christian
Publishers Association

Printed in the United States of America.

DEDICATION/ACKNOWLEDGMENTS

To my dad, Stephen Daughety,
who has been coaching me since I played tee ball.
Thanks for a lifetime of good advice.
I love you, Daddy!

In loving memory of my grandparents, Stephen and Dorothy Daughety.
Special thanks to: Vicky Daughety, Christine Lynxwiler,
Rebecca Germany, Kristy Coleman, Vickie Fry, Kelly Shifflett,
Katherine Bennett, Dawn Branablett, and all my former co-workers at
Shiloh National Military Park—especially Stacy Allen and Joe Davis.

Have I not commanded you?
Be strong and corrageous.
Do not be terrified; do not be discouraged,
for the Lord your God will be with you wherever you go.
JOSHUA 1:9

CHAPTER 1

If someone had told Kristy O'Neal that the battlefield at Shiloh would see another casualty nearly one hundred and fifty years after the battle ended, she'd have thought they were crazy.

Yet two weeks ago, one last soldier had been injured on the majestic field. And Kristy had the battle scars to prove it. Admittedly, her wound was emotional, not physical, but she still wondered if the splintered pieces of her heart might be tougher to knit back together than a bullet-shattered bone.

Whether she was ready or not, her recovery time was over, so she squared her shoulders and headed back onto the hallowed ground. Never let it be said that Kristy couldn't soldier up with the best of them. Ranger hat firmly in place and gold badge glinting in the May sunlight, she marched briskly to the visitor center.

"Morning, Kristy." Ranger Owen Branam stopped putting money in the cash register slots long enough to nod in her direction. "You have a nice trip?" He closed the drawer, finished with his preparations for the day's visitors.

Nice trip? A cruise spent faking allergies to explain away tears. Who wouldn't enjoy that?

"Lovely." She managed what she hoped was a convincing smile. "The weather was great." Scooting past him, she attempted to make it to her office without further questioning.

"Um, Kristy?"

The apprehension in the older man's voice made her stop in her tracks. She slowly turned to look back at Owen.

He ran his finger around the neck of his shirt as if he had a little too much starch in the collar. "The chief asked me to have you go straight up to his office when you got in." He motioned toward the counter. "You can leave your things here. I'll keep an eye on them while you're upstairs."

Only five minutes into her morning and her plan to fly as far under the radar as possible had already gone out the window. So much for the low-key first day back she'd hoped for.

"Thanks, Owen." Kristy put her hat on the counter and tucked her purse underneath the desk.

As she got to the top of the stairs, an unfamiliar voice called out a greeting to Owen. Twisting around, she peeked over the railing. *Wow.* A Johnny Depp look-alike was helping Owen straighten the brochures. The second thing she noticed about him, after his movie star resemblance, was the park service uniform he wore. Surely he wasn't a new employee. She'd only been gone a few weeks. Things didn't usually happen that quickly at Shiloh National Military Park.

"Glad to have you back."

The gruff voice of Chief Ranger Hank Strong made her jump and turn around.

She felt her face grow hot. Had he been watching her ogle Ranger Depp? She cleared her throat.

"Glad to be back." She followed him into his office and perched on one of the uncomfortable plastic chairs in front of his desk. Her gaze skimmed over a hodgepodge of furniture, maps, and historical books. None of the furnishings matched, except for

Hank's oversized desk and equally oversized chair that had always reminded her of a king's throne.

"Good, good." Hank settled himself behind the desk and peered at her over his round bifocals. "Look, Kristy. There's no easy way to tell you this." For a moment, an expression that looked like uncertainty flitted over his weathered face.

Uh-oh. As befitted his name, Hank Strong was always sure of himself. Whatever he was about to say, she wasn't going to like it.

"I told you before you left on your trip there'd be a job waiting for you when you got back." Hank paused.

Kristy could tell he was choosing his words carefully.

She nodded. "Yes. And believe me, I'm so grateful." When she'd turned in her two-week notice, it had felt like she was letting him down, letting the park down. After all, she'd begun working at Shiloh while she was still in college. It was the only place she'd ever worked—or ever wanted to work, for that matter. After her plans had abruptly changed, she'd been relieved when Hank stepped in and told her there was still a place for her at Shiloh.

"Well, there was one thing I didn't mention."

"Oh?" *Why do his words sound so ominous?*

"By the time I found out you weren't moving and were still available to work, your position had been filled." He shook his head. "I'm sorry, Kristy. The paperwork had already gone through. There was nothing that could be done."

She tried to catch her breath. Knowing she was at least able to come back to work at the park was the only thing that had gotten her through the past two weeks. "But you said. . ." Her voice trailed off as she willed herself not to panic.

"I know. I said I had a position for you. And I do." He leaned back a little in his chair, visibly relieved to have the bad news off his chest. "You're welcome to stay on as a seasonal ranger."

Seasonal? That was where she'd started nine years earlier, the summer after her freshman year of college. She glanced around, hoping for a paper bag she could breathe into. Of course, what she needed most was a rewind button that would allow her to go back in time and decide not to quit her job. But if she could travel back to the past, knowing what she did now, there wouldn't have been a reason to leave Shiloh in the first place.

"You want me to be a seasonal?" Kristy's voice squeaked. "What about my salary?"

A frown drew his bushy brows together. "There'll be a pay cut. And you'll move to the office shared by the seasonal staff. In fact, Owen has already put your box of office doodads in there."

If she hadn't been so shell-shocked, she probably would've laughed at his word for the contents of the box she'd left in her former office weeks earlier. Instead, all she could think was how she'd planned to stop by and pick up her things once the movers arrived. But the moving van had been permanently rerouted.

"You can still live in park housing. I know you've already packed most of your things, but Owen said he didn't think you'd actually moved anything out yet." He handed her a manila folder. "Your decision, kiddo. We'd love to keep you around. You're a great park ranger. But I understand if you want to go in a different direction now."

She took the file from him and glanced at the paperwork inside. The contents of the folder would effectively help to move her back down the career ladder she'd been climbing.

"What happens in September?" The seasonal positions at Shiloh ran from Memorial Day through Labor Day. And since they were only a few days shy of Memorial Day, she figured she should feel lucky there was even a seasonal position still available. They usually filled pretty quickly.

"Well." He leaned back even farther and pressed his fingertips together. "At that juncture you'll have a few options. Perhaps a permanent position will open here. Or we can look around at other parks and try to get you a transfer."

Or I can leave the park service.

He rose to his feet. "If you want to think about it for a day or two, that's fine."

She knew Hank well enough to know that giving her time to consider the offer was his way of being sympathetic. Despite her trembling legs, she managed to stand. "Thank you," she mumbled and scurried for the stairs, her mind spinning like a recently fired cannonball.

A permanent position opening at Shiloh was pretty much out of the question. Most of the rangers planned to stay until retirement age, some of them even longer. And she wasn't interested in a transfer. This was the park she loved. Kristy had grown up in nearby Savannah, Tennessee, and some of her earliest memories were of the cannons and monuments at Shiloh.

Owen avoided eye contact with her as she descended the stairs.

Thanks a lot, buddy.

He'd obviously known what the meeting was going to be about, but he hadn't had the nerve to give her a warning before she went upstairs. Kristy couldn't blame him though. No one liked to be the bearer of bad news.

And with her newfound knowledge, the mystery of the unfamiliar ranger was solved. The Johnny Depp look-alike was the ranger who now had *her* position. Not to mention *her* office.

She silently gathered her hat and purse from the front desk and took them to the room reserved for seasonal staff. As she passed the office she used to occupy, a fleeting glance told her that Ranger Depp wasn't inside. The seasonal office, if it could even be called an office, was full of old desks and equipment. Kristy turned on the light and took in the sparsely decorated white walls. It was a far cry from the cheerful yellow she'd painted her former office last year. Thankfully, the other members of the seasonal staff wouldn't arrive until Monday. *At least I should have peace until Memorial Day.* She could even move the desks and junk, buy some paint for the walls, and live out the next few days in Pretend Everything's Okay Land.

Except, eventually, she'd have to face reality.

She flipped on the computer and silently tapped her fingers on the desk as she waited forever for it to boot up.

Can I do this? Can I take a step down in pay and status? Seasonals were at the low end of the totem pole. She remembered those days all too well. Getting assigned the tasks no one else wanted to do and being expected to do them without grumbling. Would they do that to her again? Or would she continue to be treated as permanent staff, despite the demotion?

Demotion. Ouch.

Either way, it wouldn't be pleasant.

She glanced down at the box of her things on the floor next to the computer, and tears flooded her eyes. Empty picture frames peeked out from the box flaps. The pictures that had once been in them were nowhere in sight. Someone had wanted to spare her feelings today. Either that, or they didn't want to be stuck with an emotional female to console.

The frames might've been without pictures, but Kristy knew what they'd once held. Her heart pounded as she grabbed all three frames and tossed them in the trash can, taking unexpected pleasure in the sight and sound of shattering glass. A yellow and white wad under a large shard caught her eye. She couldn't resist carefully fishing it out of the can, even though she knew better.

Kristy unwrinkled the ball and smoothed it out on the old beat-up desk, running her hand over the creases in the paper. *Fancy paper*, as Owen called it months ago when he'd first seen it. Her vision blurred with fresh tears, but she didn't need to read the words to know what they said.

For a long moment, she stared down at the engraved invitation.

To her wedding.

CHAPTER 2

The buzzing cell phone put a stop to what could have been a disastrous trip down memory lane. A glance at her phone identified the caller as Vickie Harris, park ranger at the Washington Monument—and one of her best friends in the world. Kristy quickly wiped away the tears and flipped open the phone.

"Hello," she said softly. The old building's thin walls meant phone conversations had to be whispered in order for them to remain private.

"Hey, girl. I had a second and wanted to call and check in on you. How's the first day back?" The concern was evident in Vickie's voice and immediately became the first bright spot in Kristy's morning.

"You're not going to believe this, but I just had a meeting with Hank, and—"

"How is good old Chief Strong?" Vickie cut in. "Still as grumpy as ever?"

Every summer during college, Vickie and Kristy had worked seasonal positions at Shiloh. They quickly learned that beneath Hank's tough exterior was a heart of gold. But after today, Kristy wasn't so sure.

Kristy barely managed to keep her voice down as she filled her friend in on the bombshell that had effectively blown up her morning. Saying it out loud to Vickie only made her predicament all too real.

"No way. What are you going to do?" Anger tinged Vickie's soft Southern drawl. No matter how many years she spent in Washington, Vickie would always be a Southern belle. "You aren't going to take it, are you?"

"I don't see that I have a choice. You know I'm not interested in another park. Besides, I live in park housing. If I don't take it, I'll have to find a new place to live. And I *really* don't want to move right now on top of everything else." The buzzer sounded as the back door opened. Had her replacement entered the building?

"Well, I can understand that, but why can't you just have your old job back?"

"They've already hired someone to fill my position."

"What?" Vickie obviously wasn't expecting this bit of news. "That was fast. Who is it?"

"Captain Jack Sparrow."

"Who?"

Kristy already felt like everyone expected her to have a nervous breakdown. No need to give them any more reason to be suspicious. "Nothing. I haven't met him yet." She looked around at the bare white walls and wrinkled her nose. "Oh well. At least I have one more summer here."

"Oh Kris. I'm so sorry. This has to be tough. Any word from Mark?"

Kristy glanced down again at the wrinkled wedding invitation and rubbed her fingers over the raised letters that spelled out her and Mark's names.

"Nope. None. I don't have anything to say to him anyway." She took a deep breath. Just the mention of Mark and she felt her blood pressure rise.

"Well, I have plenty to say to him." Vickie was almost yelling. "Listen to me. You deserve so much more than he could've ever given you. I know you're hurting. But I promise you this is a good thing."

Kristy could feel the hot tears welling up again. Sometimes being female wasn't all it was cracked up to be.

"I know. I can see that we didn't belong together. And believe me, I've had a lot of time to think about things these past two weeks." She wadded the invitation back into a ball and shoved it into the trash. Where it belonged. "You ever need some alone time? Just go on a honeymoon cruise by yourself. You'll have *plenty* of time to think."

Although, even with all the time she'd had to reflect on her problems, she still wasn't sure which she'd rank as the lowest point of the past two weeks—Mark literally leaving her standing at the altar, or the reality of embarking on their honeymoon alone. She couldn't decide.

"If it's any consolation, I think the worst is over. I'm praying for you."

Kristy was glad someone was praying for her. Ever since the almost wedding, she was having a tough time talking to God. It seemed like her prayer button was stuck on mute.

A rap at the door made her jump. Owen poked his head in and signaled for her to come out front. She held up one finger to let him know she'd be there momentarily, and he disappeared.

"Vick, I need to go help Owen collect visitor fees and get the movie started."

They said their good-byes, and Kristy closed the phone with a snap. As she walked out to the familiar desk, she took a deep breath. It was time to put her troubles aside. After all, rangers were supposed to be tough and ready for anything. She smiled at a visitor who had a question about the driving tour and found her tension lift as she slipped into ranger mode. Whatever the

Annalisa Daughety

circumstances, she was glad to be back.

"The twenty-five-minute movie will begin in five minutes. Please make your way to the theater and be seated." Owen's booming voice was magnified by the loudspeaker. He gave Kristy a wink as she grabbed the remote for the movie. He knew how much she hated making announcements into the microphone. She guessed he must be trying to make up for her lousy morning.

Kristy ushered the last of the visitors into the theater, pressed Play on the remote control panel, and closed the door. Finally. For the first time all morning, things felt almost back to normal. But her resolve faded completely as she came around the corner and saw the job stealer behind the desk with Owen. They were talking and laughing. Like buddies already.

Betrayal stabbed her gut, even though she knew it was ridiculous to expect Owen to ignore someone out of loyalty to her. She forced herself forward. She'd been hoping to put off meeting the new guy until she'd adjusted to the fact that someone had come in and taken over her job. It looked like she was out of time, though.

As Kristy made her way to the spot where the men were standing, she couldn't help but take note of her replacement's appearance. His chiseled jaw gave him the air of someone accustomed to being in charge. Tanned skin and muscled forearms indicated time spent in the great outdoors. As she got closer, she could see the flecks of gold in his dark brown eyes, watching her with interest as she approached. But no matter how nice he was to look at, he had her job. That was a permanent strike against him in her book.

"Kristy, have you met our newest employee?" Owen slipped into his "good ol' boy" routine and gave the new guy a hearty slap on the back.

"No. I haven't had the pleasure." She was determined to be a grown-up about this. But did they have to introduce themselves?

They wore name badges after all. Unfortunately, there didn't seem to be a way around it. At least, not a polite way.

She held out her hand and flashed the brightest smile she could muster. "Hi. I'm Kristy O'Neal. Nice to meet you."

His handshake was firm, just as she'd expected it to be. "Ace Kennedy. And the pleasure is all mine." His lips turned upward in a slow grin as he held on to her hand just a second longer than she would've liked.

You can pour on all the charm you want to, mister. But we're not going to be friends.

"Kristy, will you be up for a bus tour tomorrow?" She could tell Owen was trying to be a nice guy and give her some more time to herself if needed. But she didn't want to be given special treatment just because of what she'd been through. And she especially didn't want Ace to think she was a weak female who let her personal life interfere with her work.

Except that if she hadn't let her personal life interfere with work, she never would've let Mark talk her into quitting her job to marry him and move away. *My dream job. Why did I ever think a life with Mark was worth giving up something I love so much?*

"A bus tour sounds great. Who is it for?"

"It's a group from a senior citizens' center. They want a brief tour. Maybe a couple of hours." Owen made a note on the daily schedule. "There's nothing else going, so I think we can spare you to do it."

Kristy loved to lead bus tours. And once the summer season got going, a ranger-led bus tour would be almost unheard of because things would be too busy in the visitor center. So she was thrilled that Owen would let her lead what was likely to be the last one for several months.

"If it's okay, I'd like to go along on the tour." Ace directed his comment to Owen, but he glanced at Kristy out of the corner of his eye.

Suddenly, the bus tour felt a lot less like a gift and a lot more like a burden.

"That's fine." Owen nodded then turned to her. "You know how it works. Ace here is still learning about the battle."

Unbelievable. Kristy wondered why no one else saw anything wrong with her being demoted and then having to show the ropes to the guy who took her place.

"Sure." She nodded at him. In reality, she would rather have cleaned out a cannon than let Ace tag along on her tour. And cleaning out a cannon was definitely not at the top of her list of fun things to do.

"I will warn you, it's been a long time since I've done a bus tour. Hopefully, I'll give the correct information." She smiled to show that she was joking. Although. . .maybe if she taught Ace all the wrong facts, he'd be out of here.

"Oh, I'm sure you'll do fine." Ace gave her a playful grin. "I've heard you're a great ranger."

Kristy wondered what else he'd heard. He hadn't been present for her public humiliation, but several of their coworkers had. And if she knew anything, it was that the park gossip traveled faster than a speeding bullet.

CHAPTER 3

Ace Kennedy closed the door to his office and collapsed into his desk chair. He hated to admit it, but he was surprised. And it took a lot to surprise him these days.

When he'd accepted the position at Shiloh, he hadn't realized he was walking into something that would open up old wounds. In fact, he'd expected to find a fresh start waiting for him in the small west Tennessee town. Counted on it, even.

Upon his arrival, it had seemed he'd found just that. Green countryside, peaceful river filled with fish, locals who waved when he passed them. It was the picture-perfect place for a man to start over. But his impression had changed two weeks ago, on his first day on the job. Owen had given him a tour of the offices and grounds, finally pausing at the door of his new office.

"Just to warn you, the ranger who worked here before painted the walls. She said the white walls made her feel like she was in a hospital." Owen had opened the door, giving Ace his first look at the cheery yellow that adorned the walls.

"It's certainly bright," he'd remarked.

"You're welcome to paint over it if you want." Owen chuckled.

"Kristy took a lot of flak for her color choice, but she was determined to spruce it up."

Ace had noted the soft tone in Owen's voice when he mentioned Kristy's name. "Nah. No need to paint over the yellow. I'm sure I'll adjust to it."

They'd made their way into the brightly colored office. Aside from the usual computer, printer, and telephone, the room was bare—except for a lone box in the corner stuffed with picture frames and a bunch of artificial flowers. Yellow daisies. Ace's knowledge of flowers was limited, but daisies had been Caroline's favorite flower. And seeing them poking their cheerful yellow heads out of the cardboard box had transported him back to the last time he'd taken daisies to Caroline. He'd quickly pushed the scene away, but that had been the moment he'd known. . . . He might've moved hundreds of miles away, but the old memories had hitched a ride with him.

Owen had followed his gaze and motioned toward the box. "Kristy left some stuff here. She was supposed to drop in and pick it up, but I figure with the wedding this afternoon, she's forgotten."

"She's getting married today?" Ace had asked, trying to seem interested. Better to concentrate on what Owen was saying than dwell on the past.

"Yep. Out at Rhea Springs. Can you believe she's having her wedding at the park? I've been here for nearly thirty years and have never seen a ranger love this park more." Owen had leaned against the door frame and shaken his head. "I'm not sure she'll know what to do with herself now that she's moving away."

Once Owen had left him alone, Ace sat down at the desk and looked around his new office. It was strange, but the yellow did make him feel a little happier. And he'd certainly not been very cheerful lately. Leaving behind everything he'd known in Illinois, he'd headed his truck south. It was only a seven-hour drive, but it was proving to be a tougher transition than he'd expected.

He'd glanced down again at the box of Kristy's things. A photograph sticking out at the corner caught his eye, and he couldn't resist pulling it out. The girl in the picture seemed to leap off the imprint and come to life. Blond, wavy hair and big blue eyes made her a classic beauty. But it was her smile that caught his attention. The camera had captured her in a moment of laughter, the happiness reaching all the way to her eyes. Ace couldn't remember the last time he'd laughed like that. If this was Kristy, then the man she was marrying today was a lucky one.

It hadn't been until the next day that he'd heard the news.

He'd been sitting in his office, reading about the battle, when Owen and Chief Strong came in the back entrance.

"So he just didn't show?" the chief had asked as they'd paused right outside of Ace's office.

"Not a sign of him at all. But you know Kristy. She didn't shed a tear. Just held her head high and walked up to the front in her wedding dress. Said she wanted to thank everyone for coming, but that there wouldn't be a ceremony."

Hank had let out a low whistle. "Whew. Did you hear anyone say why he got cold feet?"

"Nah. I didn't stick around after that. I figured she'd want some space. Hey. . ." Owen had trailed off and cleared his throat. "I know her position has been filled, but do you think there's anything we can do? She hasn't even moved her stuff out of the house yet."

Ace had been shocked at the information. He'd glanced again at the box of her things and wondered how she would bounce back from something like that. He knew firsthand that learning to live again after complete devastation was nearly impossible.

"I do have one position available. But it's seasonal. You think she'd be interested?" the chief had asked.

"It's worth a shot."

A few days later, Owen had moved Kristy's belongings into the seasonal office. Ace had wondered if that meant she'd accepted the temporary position and, again, how she was recovering from the recent blow.

The day before she was supposed to come back, Ace remembered the photographs he'd seen sticking out of the box and went into the seasonal office to look through them. He knew the last thing she would need on her first day back was a reminder, so he removed the pictures of her and her former fiancé from the frames and slipped them facedown in the top drawer. He wadded up the yellow wedding invitation and threw it in the trash. At the time, it had seemed like the least he could do.

The shocker came today. He'd expected Kristy to be fragile and beaten down. But the confident woman he'd just met certainly didn't seem fragile. In fact, she had a fierce look in her eye. He wondered where she found her strength. Of course, whether it was genuine or an act remained to be seen, but for some reason, he wasn't counting her out. And despite her coolness toward him, Ace hoped they could at least be friends.

A knock at the door brought him back to the present.

"Yes?" he called.

Chief Strong poked his head in the door. "Ace, can you come out front? We have a little situation I'd like to discuss with everyone on staff."

Ace jumped up. A situation? "Sure thing." He glanced at his half-eaten sandwich lying on his desk. Lunch could wait. It hadn't been that good anyway.

"This will only take a minute."

He followed the chief out front, where Owen and Kristy were waiting. Noting their puzzled expressions, he guessed impromptu meetings must not be a normal occurrence around here.

"Gang, we've had an incident out on the park," the chief began. "Someone spray-painted the Tennessee Monument."

"You're kidding." The horror in Kristy's voice was a testament to how much the park meant to her.

Owen scratched his chin and frowned. "How bad is it?" he asked.

"Well, it could be worse, I guess. They mainly got the base of the monument, but used a variety of colors. No particular pattern. Tommy Daniels went out there to mow this morning and discovered the damage."

"This morning? Why didn't anyone radio in and let us know?" Owen inquired.

Hank let out a snort. "Some of the maintenance guys tried to clean it off before they let me know. Thankfully, they didn't make the problem worse. It can be fixed, but it's going to be a lot of trouble."

Even though Ace was still learning about the park and all the many monuments, he knew the Tennessee Monument was the newest one on the park. In fact, it was only a few years old. Considering the park was located in Tennessee, he'd thought it strange that the state had only recently commissioned a monument.

Hank held up a bag. "This was beside the monument."

Several bottles of spray paint were visible through the white plastic.

"It looks like the culprit intended to do more but got spooked. I haven't spoken to Steve about it yet, but I'll check to see if he remembers seeing anyone acting odd yesterday while he was on patrol." Shiloh's lone law enforcement ranger, Steve Jackson, patrolled the park nightly.

"Probably just some hoodlum kid, trying to seem cool to his buddies," Owen offered.

Hank nodded. "Could be. But just in case, I want all of you to be on the alert for anything out of the ordinary."

"Of course," Kristy said.

"Not a problem," Owen chimed in.

Then silence. All three looked at Ace.

"Right." He nodded.

So the key to survival here must be to always agree with the chief.

"And since we're coming up on Memorial Day weekend, there's a good possibility that they might strike again. Keep your eyes peeled." And with that, Chief Strong swept past them, carrying the bag of paint up the stairs to his office, still grumbling under his breath.

CHAPTER 4

Kristy frantically ran through her house looking for her ranger hat, her dog, Sam, chasing after her every move. Of all the things to lose. She glanced at her watch. Two minutes until eight. Was there an extra hat somewhere in the storage room at the visitor center? She couldn't be late on her second day back.

"Here you go, Sam!" She threw a couple of dog treats at him and rushed out the door. On days like this she was oh-so-thankful her house was practically next door to the visitor center. She ran as fast as she could up the road toward the center. She cut through the parking lot and skidded to a stop right at the back door, nearly slamming into the person who was just exiting. Arnie Bramblett, park superintendent and her boss's boss, glowered at her.

"Miss O'Neal. Glad you could make it to work this morning."

She lifted up her wrist. "My watch must be a little slow. It won't happen again."

He held the door open for her. "And let's make sure you aren't outside without a hat again, too, shall we?"

The cardinal rule for park rangers: If you're going to be outdoors in uniform, your hat must be on top of your head. Kristy sighed. "I'm sorry. I think there's an extra one in storage. I'll get it before I go outside again." She smiled her brightest smile, hoping the theory about smiles being contagious would hold true. It didn't.

"Fine. And you'll need to speak to Owen. There's a special project I want you on." With that declaration, he turned on his heel, hat firmly on top of his head, and walked toward the administration building.

Kristy slunk into the building, hoping no one else would give her a hard time. Of course, considering it was barely eight in the morning and she'd already had a run-in with the superintendent, she could pretty much bank on her day not getting any worse.

Famous last words.

She threw her purse into the seasonal office and went to the front desk. It looked like everything had already been taken care of. Owen stepped out of the theater and put the remote on the desk.

He raised one eyebrow at her but didn't say anything.

"I know. I'm sorry. Save the lecture, though. I ran into Arnie on my way in. It was brutal."

Owen shook his head. "Don't worry about it. The movie is going. There were only a couple of visitors anyway, and Ace took care of them."

At the mention of Ace, she tensed. She hadn't quite come to grips with the fact that someone else would be doing her job. One of her responsibilities had been running the park's Junior Ranger Program. She'd labored long and hard developing all the activities for kids to do. And now she'd lost it. Just one more thing she'd given up for Mark.

"Did Arnie tell you why he was over here?" Owen asked.

"No. He said you'd fill me in. So what's the big news?"

"Well, before I tell you. . ." He reached under the desk and pulled out a hat. "I believe you left this here yesterday. It was in one of the chairs in the theater." He looked at her questioningly.

Thank goodness. Now she didn't have to put some stinky old replacement hat on her head. "Thanks. I must've laid it down yesterday afternoon when I was shutting down the A/V equipment. Now, what's going on?"

"Well, let's just say that we're all going on a little stakeout tonight."

"What?" Had she heard that correctly?

"Arnie is fit to be tied over the Tennessee Monument. He figures since we're nearing the holiday weekend, it might be a good time for the vandal to strike again."

"So what will we do?"

"Oh, he says he's coming up with a plan." Owen chuckled. "I guess we'll just have to wait and see."

Kristy turned toward the seasonal office. Great. Just what she needed.

"Wait a minute. The stakeout isn't all that you need to know about."

She stopped and turned around. The tone of Owen's voice told her she wasn't going to like what was coming next.

"Arnie and Hank have decided that since you're a seasonal now, you should be considered the 'leader' of the seasonal staff this year."

She furrowed her brow. The leader? There had never been a leader of seasonal staff before. "Meaning?"

"Meaning that training them will be your responsibility."

She made a face.

"You'll like them. Twin boys from Savannah. Matthew and Mason Gerhardt. Both history majors at Union University. Just finishing their freshman year, I think." Owen at least had the decency to look sheepish.

"Great. So basically what you're saying is that I'll be babysitting two teenagers for the summer?"

This day just got better and better.

"At least Arnie and Hank are recognizing your seniority. It could be a lot worse, you know."

She wasn't so sure.

◎◎

It was a good thing Ace didn't have a social life, or he wouldn't be too happy about giving up his night. He looked around at the grumpy faces of the other rangers. It seemed he wasn't the only one less than thrilled about being here at such a late hour.

"Listen up," Superintendent Arnie Bramblett barked like a drill sergeant. "We're going to go out in teams of two. I've handpicked some of the more popular monuments and will assign each team to one."

Ace sighed. It must've been louder than he'd intended, because Kristy shot a quick glance his way. He flashed her a "sorry" with his eyes and turned his attention back to Mr. Bramblett.

"Owen, I'd like for you and Steve to go together. Since Steve is the law enforcement ranger, you'll just be keeping an eye out. Let him handle it if you see anything suspicious."

Owen nodded.

"I'll be going with Hank. Hank has his law enforcement commission, so the same thing will apply to us. I will only be there to be a lookout. I'll be radioing for backup if we run into anything."

"And Kristy, that leaves you to go with Ace. He also has his law enforcement commission. You're only there to radio for help and to keep an eye out for anything suspicious. By no means should you get out of the car if a chase ensues." He gave her a stern look for a moment, and Ace wondered what she'd done to get on the big boss's bad side.

Kristy nodded sheepishly.

Ace cringed when they finally made their way to the parking

lot. On top of assigning them partners and locations, the super-intendent had also issued each team a park service vehicle. And as luck would have it, he and Kristy had gotten the worst one.

They silently walked toward the battered old pickup.

"So do you want to drive, or do you want me to?" Kristy asked.

As far as he knew, those were the only words she'd spoken all night. He got the impression that she'd rather be anywhere but here. On second thought, maybe it wasn't the assignment. Maybe she'd just rather be anywhere than with him.

He didn't care who drove. He just wanted to get along. "It doesn't matter to me. You can drive if you want to."

"Fine."

They climbed into the truck, and Kristy headed toward the Confederate Monument.

"You think we'll see some action?" he asked.

She pressed her lips together, and for a second, he thought she might ignore him. "I have no idea. The Confederate Monument did get damaged by a vandal a few years ago, though. It caused quite a ruckus."

When she didn't offer any more information, Ace wondered if she'd only referenced it to show him how long she'd been around. Owen had warned him that Kristy was pretty attached to her job. She must be having a tough time, considering her current situation.

She expertly pulled the pickup over on the side of the road. The monument was in their line of sight, but they weren't right in front of it.

"This spot okay?" she asked.

"Looks good to me."

She put the truck in park, turned off the key, and slumped down in the seat.

Whoever had said silence was deafening must've been stuck

in a vehicle with someone he didn't know. He looked over at her. Hadn't he resolved that life was too short to live with pretense? Time to put that theory to the test. "So I guess you hate me?"

She sat up straight and stared at him, her blue eyes wide. "What?"

He shrugged. "Why wouldn't you hate me? I moved in and took your job, took your yellow office, and took your pay scale. Does that just about sum it up?"

"You took my Junior Ranger Program, too," she mumbled.

He couldn't hold back a snicker. "Well, by all means, tell me how you really feel."

A small smile teased the corners of her lips. "You asked."

"You know, because of circumstances beyond our control, we may not ever be the best of friends, but if we're going to have to work together, wouldn't it be better if we weren't enemies either?"

The hint of a smile faded. "I guess."

Ace opened the truck door. "I'll go sit on the other side of the monument while you wait here. If you see any trouble, call me on the radio."

She nodded.

He closed the door behind him and began the long journey to the other side of the monument. Had he been out of line with her? He hoped his outburst hadn't made things even worse between them. But he didn't want to have to dread going to work every day.

He crouched down in the clearing just opposite the monument. There was nothing around him but darkness. Mr. Bramblett had insisted that each team stay in their assigned spot for two full hours before returning to the visitor center. He pushed the Indiglo button on his watch. Forty-five minutes had passed. It was going to be a long night.

Suddenly the radio on his hip crackled, breaking the silence.

"Two-ten to two-hundred." It was Owen, calling for Chief Strong.

"Two-hundred, go ahead."

"There's movement near the Bloody Pond."

Ace's heart beat faster. He looked in the direction of the truck. Kristy had the lights on and was pulling onto the road. Was she going to leave him stranded?

He ran to the edge of the pavement, and she pulled up beside him. He barely got the door closed before she took off, tires squealing.

"Is your last name Andretti?" he asked, buckling his seat belt. "The other teams are probably already there. You need to slow down."

She didn't answer.

He felt a twinge of anger. Some people might accuse him of being reckless because he'd done some adventurous things. Bungee jumping and skydiving came to mind. But one thing he didn't tolerate was reckless driving. Ever since Caroline's accident, he'd barely gone over the speed limit. "Kristy. There aren't any lights out here. If you come around a corner and there's someone parked, you'll hit them."

"We're not that far from the Bloody Pond. Besides, there's not going to be anyone parked out here in the middle of the road."

"What about a deer or something? Besides. . ." He glanced over at her, knowing full well that his next sentence would make her hate him even more. But it would also keep her from being in such an all-fired hurry. "You can't get out of the truck when we get there anyway."

Sure enough, she let off the gas.

Kristy pulled the pickup into the parking lot next to the Bloody Pond. The patrol car and SUV were already there. Both vehicles were empty.

Ace pulled his radio off his hip.

"Two-fifty to two-hundred." He called the chief to see what was going on.

No answer.

He locked eyes with Kristy. Her gaze held more worry than anger.

"Try again," she urged, nodding her head toward the radio.

"Two-fifty to two-hundred."

This time the radio crackled to life. "Two-hundred. Go ahead."

"What's your location?"

"We're out at the War Cabin now but are headed back to the vehicles." Now that he knew which direction to look, Ace could just make out their outlines in the distance.

Ace stepped out of the truck and waited for the other teams.

The driver's side door slammed, and Kristy walked over to join him.

"Guess I could get out of the truck after all."

"Sorry about that. It was just that you were going way too fast." He faltered with his explanation, unsure of how much to say. "I lost someone not long ago in a car accident. So I'm a stickler for safety."

"Got it." For a moment, her voice had a soft lilt to it. "And I'm sorry. About your loss, I mean. Really sorry."

"Thank you."

The other rangers finally arrived in the parking lot.

"Was it a wild-goose chase?" Kristy asked.

"Actually, it was a turkey chase." Owen laughed. "Literally."

Mr. Bramblett cut off their laughter. "Thanks for helping out tonight. And I may be calling on you again in the future. We'll catch whoever it is. It might take some time, but we'll do it."

CHAPTER 5

An hour into the tour the following day, Kristy finally felt like she'd gotten her park ranger groove back. The visitors on the bus—a mix of elderly men and women—seemed genuinely interested in what she had to say. After offering her a stiff greeting, Ace had taken a seat at the back of the fifteen-passenger bus. She glanced at him now, frantically taking notes. What were the chances that he was getting it all mixed up?

"On our left is tour stop number three." She directed their attention to a bumpy dirt road and an open field. "Ladies and gentlemen, welcome to the Hornet's Nest." A smile crossed her lips as the passengers, including Ace, sat up straighter and craned their necks to look at the place with the odd name. Visitors loved this spot. "The Civil War soldiers who fought in this area of the battlefield said the bullets whizzing by their heads reminded them of a swarm of hornets."

While many members of the group snapped pictures of the tour stop, Kristy stood at the front and briefly explained what had happened there.

"If you want to get off the bus for a moment to get a better view, we have plenty of time." She didn't expect any of them to take her up on the offer. One look at their shoes—dressy rather than sturdy—told her this was a group who wanted to sit on the bus, look out the window, and enjoy the ride. Over the years, she'd gotten to be an expert at judging a group's energy level by their footwear. "Any questions before we move on?"

"Young lady?" An elderly gentleman with a shock of white hair waved his hand at her. "Do you know if there were any boys from Iowa who fought in this area?"

Before she could answer his question, a voice piped up from the back.

"Yes sir. There were several regiments from Iowa here at Shiloh." Ace stood as he spoke and put his ranger hat on his head.

Kristy could only watch as he confidently strode up the aisle to where she stood. It was his take-charge attitude that gave the truth away.

Her tour had just been hijacked.

She put the microphone in Ace's waiting hand and sank down into a seat.

Fine. Let's see what Ranger Kennedy has up his sleeve. Besides a muscled arm.

"The Eighth Iowa Infantry was especially active in this area of the battlefield." Ace motioned toward the field. "After Captain Hickenlooper's men abandoned their cannons due to heavy Confederate fire, the Eighth Iowa rushed in to try and save them. What followed was a brutal hand-to-hand combat."

Ace was off to a pretty good start, but soon all Kristy could hear was *blah, blah, blah* as he droned on and on about regimental positions and maneuvers. She turned in her seat and checked out the crowd. He'd lost the majority of the visitors already. The women had a glazed-over look, and the men who were still awake were starting to fidget. She knew she had to do something. But what?

Leaning forward in her seat, she nudged the bus driver and

motioned for him to move on. Now all she needed to do was to wrangle the microphone away from Ace and get this tour back under control.

Kristy hopped up and stood next to Ace. Surely he'd wind it down soon. But he was still talking. He gave them a rundown of all the important Northern generals who participated here. Sherman, Grant, Wallace, McClernand. The list was impressive— or it would have been if everyone in the group wasn't in an information-overload coma.

They continued to make their way around the tour route. Suddenly a loud snore came from the middle of the bus. Kristy glanced at Ace.

"And now, Miss O'Neal will tell you what happened here." Ace finally handed over the microphone.

She looked out the bus window to see where they were and froze. She didn't want to tell anyone what happened there. She didn't even want to be there. The last time she'd seen Rhea Springs, she'd been wearing a wedding gown and watching her perfect wedding crumble around her.

Kristy took a breath and tried to formulate something to say. Had he done this on purpose? Was he trying to show her that he might bore visitors to sleep, but he was still higher up on the food chain than she was?

Ace returned to his seat without a backward glance.

The elderly passengers looked at her with worry-lined faces.

She forced a choked chuckle. "This is Rhea Springs, and nothing of much importance happened here. In fact, we've strayed from the regular tour route." She leaned down to the bus driver and directed him to head back. Anything to end this disaster. Normally she'd rather lead tours all day than collect fees, but the visitor center suddenly looked very appealing.

As soon as the bus came to a stop, she bounded down the stairs and positioned herself beside the bus exit. "Thanks for your attention. Please watch your step as you exit the bus." Kristy smiled and shook hands as the visitors began a mass exodus, most of them heading toward the bookstore.

Ace was the final passenger to descend from the bus. Kristy watched as he paused on the bottom step and turned to thank the bus driver then stepped down beside her.

She looked up at his tanned, chiseled face. Had he purposely put her on the spot at Rhea Springs? Or was she overly sensitive and paranoid? Once upon a time, she'd considered herself to be a good judge of character, but that time had passed. Looking at him now, she wasn't sure if he'd intended to humiliate her or not. But since she was through giving people the benefit of the doubt, she would have to believe that he had.

"Great tour. Very good information." He held up his notepad and grinned, his brown eyes sparkling. "I took lots of notes."

"Listen. I don't want to tell you how to do your job." Her job, actually. "But don't you think you were a little too technical with that group? Most tourists would rather hear human interest stories over regimental movements."

His eyebrows drew together. "I was only relaying the facts. I didn't think that was a problem."

"I guess we have different styles." Talk about an understatement. If his tour had been any indication, the manner in which they dispensed information to visitors couldn't have been more different. And even though it made her feel a tiny bit bad, she hoped there would be visitor complaints if he stuck with his way of doing things. If so, it could be helpful to her quest to get her old job back come Labor Day.

Perhaps I should keep my suggestions to myself.

๑๑

Ace had found a new place to sit and think. General William Wallace's headquarters were only a stone's throw from the visitor center's lawn. The monument was set back far enough off the path that he could sit and think and be undetected by anyone. He sat down on the bottom step and looked up at the large monument. One hundred and twenty cannon balls formed a large pyramid, which sat on top of two concrete steps. Ace had just learned yesterday that they were real cannon balls. It seemed he learned something interesting every day here.

And today his lesson had been that Kristy didn't approve of the way he did his job. He hadn't meant to upset her. The snoring man had flustered him, though, and he'd been anxious to turn the tour back over to Kristy. The haunted look in her deep blue eyes as she gazed out the window to check their location had been his first clue that he'd made a grave mistake in timing.

From the frosty glare she'd given him when he exited the bus, he gathered that she would never believe the faux pas had been accidental. He'd thought about telling her that he knew what loss felt like, but she probably wouldn't have listened unless he told her the whole story. And he wasn't ready to share that with anyone. Better just to keep his distance and be careful not to antagonize her again.

CHAPTER 6

Kristy couldn't bring herself to go to worship services at her church yet. She knew it was silly. It was her church home, and everyone there would be completely supportive. But the last time she'd seen most of them, she was explaining that due to lack of a groom, there wasn't going to be a wedding ceremony. And making sure they knew to go to the community center, where a smorgasbord of already-paid-for, already-prepared food was waiting. Suffice to say, she wasn't quite ready to face them yet.

So Sunday morning found her at her mother's congregation in Savannah. The twenty-minute drive and obligatory mother-daughter lunch were worth it if it meant she could hold on to some shred of whatever dignity she still had. And after the "Welcome Back, You've Been Demoted" bomb dropped on her this week, there was very little.

She stepped inside the church building and scanned the lobby for her mother's pouf of reddish hair. Kristy finally spotted her mom, Nancy, chatting with Dorothy Aaron. Nancy and Dorothy had met in a divorce recovery group last year, and they'd become fast friends. Even though it'd been years since Kristy's parents divorced, she was glad her mom had a support system. Especially these past few months. Kristy had been distracted with her engagement, and Sarah, Kristy's younger sister, rarely found the time for a visit.

Kristy gave her mother a hug then smiled at Dorothy. "It's great to see you again."

"You, too. I was just telling your mom how sorry I was to hear about your breakup."

Don't be sorry. I may have dodged a bullet. "Thanks." Kristy managed a smile.

Dorothy's eyes lit up at someone past Kristy's shoulder, and she waved him over. "Kristy, have you ever met my sons?"

It only took a second for Kristy to realize why Dorothy was so eager. The man who was making his way over looked about Kristy's age. Before she'd become engaged, she'd been used to mothers dragging their single sons over for an introduction. If Dorothy's behavior was any indication, it looked like she'd have to get used to it again, now that the ring was off her finger.

The tall guy who ambled over and stood beside Dorothy looked vaguely familiar to Kristy, but she had no idea where she'd seen him. A teenage boy trailed behind him, his handsome features marred by a slightly sour expression on his face. Dorothy beamed at them and then at Kristy.

"This is my oldest son, Robert."

Robert's light brown hair was still damp from the shower, but everything else about him looked well put together. His charcoal gray suit and shiny dress shoes looked expensive. He stepped forward rather formally and offered her a hand.

"Hi, I'm Kristy." She took his hand and gave it a halfhearted shake.

"I think we met a few years ago at a singles' event." Robert's green eyes looked at her appraisingly. He put a hand on Dorothy's shoulder. "I live in Jackson, but Mom promised me a homemade apple pie if I'd come for a visit today. I can't ever turn down her cooking."

Dorothy smiled and patted his hand then turned to her younger son.

"And this is Zach."

Zach barely moved his head in what could have been a nod in Kristy's direction. Or at least she thought he'd acknowledged her.

"Hi, Zach. Nice to meet you."

"Kristy works as a park ranger at Shiloh." Nancy always loved to tell people this fact. Kristy kept hoping the novelty would wear off, but apparently that wouldn't be happening anytime soon. And especially after the week she'd just had, culminating with Ace putting her on the spot at Rhea Springs, the last thing Kristy wanted to do was talk about work. But it looked like she had no choice.

"We live very close to the park. In fact, Zach rides his bike over there sometimes." Dorothy patted the scowling boy on his back.

"Well, if you ever get a flat tire or need some water, I live right beside the visitor center," Kristy said. "You'll know which house is mine because of the barking dog in the window. And we have lots going on tomorrow to celebrate Memorial Day. Y'all should come out if you get the chance."

Zach eyed her suspiciously. "Thanks," he mumbled. "Mom, I'm going to sit with the youth group."

Dorothy nodded as he rushed off. She looked back at Kristy with a hint of red in her face. "Zach's dealing with some things right now."

Kristy smiled. "I remember being his age." She hadn't been so sullen, but she had definitely been too "cool" to sit with her mom during services.

"We'd better get a seat." Robert ushered them toward the sanctuary and held open the door. Kristy followed her mother into a pew, Dorothy trailing behind her.

As soon as they were seated, Dorothy jumped back up. "I think I left my Bible out in the lobby. I'll be right back." She attempted to scoot past Robert.

"I'll go look for it." He started to rise.

"Don't be silly. I'm already up."

Suddenly Dorothy was gone, and Kristy found herself seated next to Robert. She wanted to believe that the maneuver hadn't been planned, especially considering that the deception involved a Bible, of all things. But she'd seen her own mother in action too many times. It was as though once they had single children who were in their late twenties, they lost all sense of subtlety.

Robert glanced over at her and half smiled. Thankfully, the song leader chose that moment to announce the first song. She didn't want to feel compelled to make awkward small talk. After all, there would likely be plenty of that in her future.

Kristy opened her mouth to sing and for the next hour was able to forget her troubles. Her surprisingly good mood got even better when her mother insisted she choose the restaurant after church. Finally, an easy decision. Hagy's Catfish Hotel was one of her all-time favorite places to eat.

"Such a nice young man, that Robert," Nancy declared as the two of them walked though the parking lot.

Kristy stopped in her tracks, high heels digging into the warm asphalt. Surely her mother wasn't serious. Robert's mom she could understand. But her own? It was way too soon to even think like that. "Don't start, Mother." Kristy hit the unlock button. "I just got left at the altar, for crying out loud."

"All I said was he's a nice guy." They climbed into Kristy's white Jeep Liberty and headed toward Hagy's. "He's an accountant, you know. He graduated from UT–Martin." Nancy wasn't going to let it drop without a fight. "And did you notice what a sharp dresser he is?"

Irritated, Kristy turned up the volume on the radio.

Nancy took the hint and pursed her lips.

Bon Jovi could drown out her mother, but he couldn't drown out her thoughts. Kristy clenched the steering wheel and watched the budding trees fly by. It must be painful for the old leaves to die and new ones to take their place. The idea of going on a date with someone new made her feel sick. What she wanted right now was to be left alone. She would probably date again. When she was ready. Which truthfully might be never. But she didn't tell her mother that.

Nancy remained silent as they walked up the wooden stairs to the restaurant. Kristy hoped her silence meant she'd given up on having a conversation about Robert.

Once their plates were heaping with catfish, though, Kristy's hopes were dashed.

"Sweetie, let me give you a little advice." Nancy poured a packet of sweetener into her tea and regarded her daughter as she stirred. "The best thing you can do now is get back out there. You know what they say." She took a sip. "It's like falling off a horse. You have to get right back up there before you lose your nerve."

My mom, the cowgirl.

Kristy resisted the urge to mention the lack of dates her mother had gone on since her divorce.

"Really, Mom. I appreciate your concern. But I'll be fine."

"I only want what's best for you," she said in her familiar I'm-so-offended-you-don't-want-my-motherly-advice voice.

"Let's just drop it, okay?" Kristy spooned some tartar sauce onto her plate.

"Promise you'll at least think about it."

She'd been Nancy O'Neal's daughter for twenty-eight years. She knew how this worked. There was only one response guaranteed to prevent her mother from trying to play matchmaker. "Fine. I'll make you a deal."

Nancy's carefully lined eyebrow rose. "What's that?"

"You can't prompt Dorothy to have Robert ask me out. Don't even mention the idea to her. And if she mentions a setup to you, tell her no. But if he ever decides *on his own* that he wants to go out, I'll accept."

Her mother took another sip of her tea and narrowed her eyes as if mulling over Kristy's offer. "Okay, honey. It's a deal. I won't do any meddling. And if Dorothy mentions it to me, I'll talk her out of it. But if he ever calls, you have to promise you'll go."

Rather than shaking on it, they split a slice of pecan pie. Kristy was pretty confident about the agreement. It should get her mother off her case, at least for a few weeks. And since Robert didn't even live here, by the time she saw him again, he could be married. Especially if Dorothy came across another single Christian girl in his age bracket anytime soon.

CHAPTER 7

This is Kristy. She'll be showing you around the park and training you on all the seasonal responsibilities. Do what she says and you'll be fine." Owen stood in the doorway of the seasonal office, flanked by identical twin teenage boys.

Kristy stood and forced a smile. She took in their freckled faces and strawberry blond hair. Very cute and very young. Had she been that young her first summer here? It seemed like so long ago.

"Hi," they said in unison.

Wow. Good thing name badges were a required part of the uniform, or she'd never tell them apart.

"I'm Matthew." The one on the left stepped forward and stuck out his hand.

She grasped his hand and shook it. "Nice to meet you, Matthew." She turned to his brother. "And you must be Mason."

He blushed and nodded. "Yes, ma'am."

Oh dear. Their mama had obviously raised them to be polite Southern boys, but she hated to be called ma'am. At least wait until she was over thirty for that.

She smiled at them and gestured around the office. "Feel free to put your things in here. Today isn't going to be a normal day since it's a holiday. In fact, I'm usually off on Monday, but since we have a lot going on today, I'm working. How about you two? What are your days off?"

"Tuesday and Wednesday," said Matthew.

"Thursday and Friday," Mason chimed in.

Good. They'd probably do better not having too many working days the same.

"Today you'll both be stationed outside. There'll be several hundred people here for the Memorial Day ceremony in the National Cemetery. I think Owen plans on having one of you stand at the gates and pass out programs. Matthew, why don't you do that?"

He nodded.

"And Mason, you can help park cars. Our lot will be full, so they'll park in the field closest to the cemetery. Owen will be out there as well, and he'll show you what to do."

Kristy put her hat on top of her head. "You guys can just follow me. I'll take you to your stations. Make sure to take your radios in case you need to call for help."

She felt a bit like a mother duck as they followed her out the back door. After stationing Matthew at the gates of the cemetery, she directed Mason to where Owen stood in the nearby field. She would spend the morning at the Memorial Day ceremony handling crowd control, and the afternoon in the visitor center collecting fees. Even though the day was certain to be busy, at least it wouldn't be boring.

"Hi there," a familiar voice called. She turned to see her mother coming up the cemetery path, Dorothy and Zach in tow. "Surprised to see us?"

"There's not much you do that surprises me, Mom." Kristy smiled and greeted her guests.

"We've never been to one of these ceremonies," Dorothy

explained. "Your mom said they were really neat, so we thought we'd check it out."

"Well, you're in time to get a great spot." Kristy pointed toward the podium. "There'll be some patriotic songs, a short speech, and then representatives for all of the wars the United States has participated in will be dressed in replica uniforms and will fire a twenty-one-gun salute. It's pretty cool. Be sure to check out the one representing a Revolutionary War soldier."

Even Zach looked impressed.

"I'll try to catch you after it's over," she told them as she rushed off to help manage the influx of people coming through the gate.

☺☺

Ace looked down at the clicker in his hand. More than seven hundred people had come through the visitor center so far. He and Kristy were working the desk, trying to keep some semblance of order. Because of the heavy number of visitors, they had no choice but to work together as a team. He watched as she greeted a family and collected the five dollars for their entrance fee.

"The movie will start in ten minutes," she said, pointing in the general direction of the movie theater. "Feel free to look around the museum in the meantime. There'll be an announcement before the movie begins." She handed them their orange parking pass, but instead of moving on, they lingered at the counter.

"Can I help you with something else?" she asked, her blond ponytail bobbing as she spoke.

"Actually. . . ," the woman began, "we were wondering if you have a Junior Ranger Program. Kelsey and Jonathan have Junior Ranger badges from all the other parks we've visited." She motioned to the two children standing next to her.

Ace peered over the counter at them. Indeed, they were each wearing Junior Ranger badges from Yellowstone.

46

"We do have a program," Kristy said. "Just a second, and I'll get you the information."

"I can do that," he said—and immediately regretted it. He'd only been trying to help so Kristy could move on to the next family who was waiting to pay. But from the look she shot him, he could see that his helpfulness had been mistaken for something else.

"He'll help you." Kristy's words were clipped as she motioned toward him. Without another word, she turned to the next family. Clearly, he'd messed up again. And just when he thought they were working well together. He turned his attention toward the kids in front of him but couldn't shake the feeling that he'd just made things even worse with his new coworker.

CHAPTER 8

After the exhausting day Kristy had just experienced, nothing would have made her happier than to sink into a hot bubble bath and then climb into bed. A great plan—except that most of her things were still in boxes. It would have been a scavenger hunt to try to find a bottle of bubble bath right now. So, as much as she needed to relax, she knew she couldn't put off unpacking any longer.

What an odd experience to go from planning a future with someone to being all alone. Once Mark's company let him know they were transferring him to Atlanta, he'd taken Kristy house hunting. They'd picked out furniture and wall colors together and even jokingly selected the room that would someday be the nursery. He'd moved into their dream home a month before the wedding date. Kristy looked around at the boxes that now surrounded her. Her heart dropped a little. When she'd packed up her things, she'd expected to unpack them with Mark, in their new house, after they had returned from their honeymoon.

How could so many things change in such a short time?

In hindsight, she could see all the ways they weren't compatible.

Besides the obvious—she showed up for momentous occasions and he didn't.

She'd spent a lot of time on the cruise making a list of reasons a marriage to Mark would've been hard. Following the advice of a self-help book, which guaranteed to have her over him and ready to move on in a month or less, she'd taped the list to the refrigerator door. Usually looking at number one on the list made her feel better. *He wouldn't allow me to ask him how his day was.* But tonight it didn't help. It only made her realize how much time and effort she'd wasted on someone who wasn't worth it. How would she ever be able to trust her own judgment again?

The telephone rang as she was cutting the tape on the second box. Still on her knees and holding the scissors, she crawled toward the phone. Out of habit, she looked at the caller ID before answering. *No way.* She checked one more time to make sure her eyes weren't deceiving her.

Mark.

Her heart pounded in her ears. *Ring.* She didn't want to hear his voice right now. *Ring.* Nothing he could say would change anything. *Ring.* Would it? *Ring.* Definitely not.

"Hi, it's Kristy. Leave a message!"

As her own voice came over the machine, she looked down at her white knuckles wrapped around the scissors. She leaned closer to the phone. A dial tone sounded loudly through the room.

She exhaled the breath she'd been holding and sat back on the carpet. She let the scissors fall from her fingers.

Maybe she should've answered. Really let him have it. Or even better, gone against his rule and asked him how his day had been. For a moment, she considered dialing him back but thought better of it. She'd gone over two weeks without calling. No way she was caving in now.

The phone rang again. This time she lunged for it before the first ring was complete. No use even looking at the caller ID. She was ready to get it over with. See what he had to say for himself.

"Mark." She tried to keep her voice even, but the shakiness won out as she said his name.

"Um. No." An unfamiliar male voice sounded confused.

Kristy held the phone away from her ear to see who it was.

According to the caller ID, Dorothy's son Robert was on the other end.

My mom had better not be behind this. Suddenly, the agreement she'd made with her mother seemed like a very poor decision. But maybe he was calling for something innocent. Like he was inviting her to his mom's birthday or something. *Yeah, right. Because Dorothy and I are BFFs.*

"It's Robert Aaron. We met at church last Sunday." Robert's voice was muffled. Must be a bad connection.

Even though Kristy didn't want to deal with him, she didn't have a choice. Hanging up on him would've been rude. And asking him if he could wait and call back sometime when she wasn't about to have a nervous breakdown might have made her seem a little odd.

"I remember. How are you?" Here was that awkward small talk she had so hoped to avoid.

"I'm fine. Listen, I was wondering if maybe you'd like to go out to dinner with me?" No small talk after all. He cut right to the chase.

If she said no, would he tell his mother, who would in turn tell Nancy, who would call her out on the deal they'd made? Kristy hated to go back on her word. She knew she'd end up feeling guilty. Sometimes she wished she were more like her sister, Sarah, who probably wouldn't have thought twice about backing out of a promise.

"Sure, Robert. When do you have in mind?" *How about a year from now, when I might actually be ready to date?*

"How's Friday? Six thirty? We can try that new seafood place near Pickwick."

Kristy halfheartedly agreed and gave him directions to her house. Maybe he didn't notice the lack of enthusiasm in her voice. Staring at the phone like it was a foreign object, she wondered what she'd just done. If it hadn't been for Mark's out-of-the-blue phone call, she'd have been able to think of some way out of it. But thanks to timing, she had a date. Surely she could get through it.

She hung up the phone and crawled back over to the boxes of her belongings. Friday night was days away. Tonight she'd focus on the hunt for bubble bath.

Sam, her Cavalier King Charles spaniel, was only too eager to help. He sniffed around the fort of boxes excitedly as she tried to unearth the bathroom box. Ten minutes later, she emerged victorious. "Bath Essentials" had been hiding in the corner underneath "Christmas Decor." She spied a bottle of eucalyptus bath soak that promised to soothe away stress and grabbed it. Kristy wasn't big on believing promises, but she'd take a chance on this one.

Bring on the bubbles. Unpacking could wait one more day.

CHAPTER 9

The alarm clock had a major malfunction. The book that came with it said it would allow the sleeper to snooze for nine minutes if the snooze button was pressed. But each day, Kristy's snooze time seemed to be getting shorter and shorter. Or maybe it just seemed that way because of her lack of sleep.

She dragged herself into the kitchen hoping for a coffee jump start and was greeted unenthusiastically by Sam. His head lay between his outstretched front legs. He looked up at her with his big brown eyes, a hurt expression on his face. Beside him was an empty bowl.

"Sammy. I'm so sorry." She scooped some of his special gluten-free dog food out of the canister and filled his bowl.

Her apology was greeted with a haughty sigh. Sam was a tad dramatic. According to some people, he was a lot like his owner.

Once he'd eaten and seemed to have forgiven her for last night's oversight, she tried to make herself look presentable. Hopefully, no one would notice the dark circles underneath her eyes, she thought, as she gave Sam a treat and a belly scratch then began the short walk to the visitor center.

Early June in southwest Tennessee. It didn't get any better than this. Crisp, cool mornings, but by lunchtime it would be nice and warm. Yet not the July kind of warm that made Kristy feel like she lived in a sauna. With each step, the smell of freshly cut grass wafted toward her on the gentle breeze. The sweet aroma, along with the tire tracks running beside the sidewalk, told her the mowing crew had already begun their day.

As she strolled along, drinking in the morning, peace washed over her like a soft spring shower. She tilted her face to the sky and smiled. Mark may have broken her heart, but her spirit was still intact. She still had the ability to enjoy the simple things in life. Nice to know he hadn't been able to take that away.

Just as she stuck her key in the back door of the visitor center, it swung open. Suddenly she thudded back to reality as she came face-to-face with one of the reasons she'd wanted to stay home.

"Morning, Kristy." Ace stood right inside the door, a travel mug of coffee in his hand. It figured that he was an early-morning person. Even though Kristy lived the closest, she was usually the last to arrive. Aside from her first cup of coffee, the only thing that saved her from being a total grump in the mornings was her walk to work. And even that wasn't powerful enough to make her glad to see him.

"Mornin'." She wiggled her key out of the lock and brushed past him without a backward glance. One of her pet peeves was when she had her key in a lock and the door opened from the other side. After she'd gone to the trouble of fishing her keys out of the depths of her bag, she at least wanted to have the satisfaction of turning the lock. But it wasn't meant to be.

Before she headed out front to help get everything ready for the day, she stashed her purse and hat in the seasonal office. She didn't think of it as "her" office and doubted she ever would. To Kristy, the office that belonged to her would always be the one painted daffodil yellow, no matter whose name was on the door.

And no matter who was in there drinking coffee. Besides, Mason's monogrammed L.L.Bean backpack sitting in the middle of the floor let her know that her time of having an office to herself was over.

Thankfully, she was spared from having much interaction with Ace as the morning progressed. The schedule on the wall showed that he was working in the archives all day. Not that she was checking, of course, but she was glad she wouldn't be seeing much of him. It might not be a lot, but she'd take a bright spot wherever she could get it.

"Good morning, Mason." Since today was Matthew's day off, she didn't have to glance at his name badge to know which twin she was speaking to.

"Hi, Miss Kristy." He grinned shyly. From the short time she'd spent with them yesterday, she'd determined that Matthew was the outgoing brother. Mason hung back and let his brother do the talking. Having two days without his brother to rely on would probably be good for him.

"Now don't make me feel like an old lady." She smiled to show she was teasing. "Just Kristy will be fine."

"Sorry." He blushed bright red.

Bless his heart. "Tell you what. Why don't you spend the morning in the office, reading about the battle? There are two great editions of *Blue and Gray* magazine that will tell you everything you need to know."

He nodded and followed her into the office.

She pulled the magazines off the shelf and put them in front of him. "Just be thankful there's not going to be a death march this summer." She grinned.

"A *death march*?" He looked worried. "What's that?"

She leaned against the desk. "Every few summers, our park historian takes the seasonals and any new permanent staff on a two-day outing fondly called 'the death march.' It's awful. Basically, we march the entire battlefield, looking at each position as the soldiers would've done. You learn a lot but will never be so tired or have such blisters on your feet. Over the two days, you march nearly twenty-four hours." She shook her head. "But it does give you new appreciation for what the soldiers went through."

"But we're not going to do that this year?" he asked hopefully.

"You're off the hook this summer. But if I were you, I'd learn as much as I could from those magazines. That way Hank won't change his mind."

When she left, he was totally engrossed in his reading.

She had just greeted the first visitor of the day when Hank burst through the front door. She took one look at his red face and hoped she wasn't going to be on the receiving end of his anger. He swept past her and called for Owen. *Whew.*

"The movie will begin in five minutes," she told the family standing at the desk once they had paid their fees. As soon as they were out of sight, she peeked around the corner to see what was going on outside Owen's office.

"I've already informed Ace of the situation," Hank said.

From their serious expressions, Kristy could tell something big was going on.

Before she could make her way back to the desk, Hank spotted her. "Kristy."

"Yes?" She stepped into the common area outside the offices where they were standing.

"It's happened again." Hank took his hat off and swiped his hand across his forehead.

"Spray paint?"

"Yeah. This time they hit the Missouri Monument." Concern was etched in every line on Hank's face. The fact that the park had been struck again was a bad sign. Vandalism was a big deal at Shiloh. The monuments were very well maintained, but when something happened to one, it was costly to fix.

"When did it happen?"

"Must've been overnight. Ace said he was out there yesterday afternoon and didn't notice anything." Hank put his hat back on his head and took a deep breath. "I'm about to go meet with Mr. Bramblett. I know there were several hundred people through here yesterday, but before I tell him, I thought I'd check to see if anyone noticed any unusual activity." Kristy didn't envy his job. Given Arnie's reaction the last time, he wouldn't take this news very well.

"I didn't see anything unusual. Not that I can think of, anyway." The only strange thing Kristy had seen lately was Ace being in charge of her Junior Ranger Program. And Mark on her caller ID. Come to think of it, maybe it had been a strange week all the way around.

Owen nodded in agreement. "Me neither. And I was out in the park most of the day. How about Steve? Did he notice anything while he was on patrol?"

Hank shook his head. "He didn't see anything. Says he didn't make any traffic stops. He figures whoever did it probably parked off-site and came in by foot." Incidents in the park were few and far between, so Kristy figured Steve was probably disappointed not to have finally seen some action. Especially with the turkey-chasing incident from last week still hanging over him.

The theory made sense. The park was over four thousand acres, so it was impossible for law enforcement to be everywhere at once. If someone wanted to remain unseen, he could have easily walked off the beaten path and not been visible from the paved roads where Steve drove his patrol car. And the week of Memorial Day was such a heavy traffic week, it would've been easy to blend in if someone wanted to be up to no good.

"Well, just keep your eyes peeled for anything out of the ordinary." Hank stepped to the back door. "I'm going to break the news to Arnie. See you later."

Kristy looked at Owen. "Who would keep doing something like this? And why?" She noticed the wall clock and remembered the movie. In the excitement, she'd gotten a couple of minutes off track. She walked out to the desk and grabbed the remote.

Owen dropped into step beside Kristy as she went to start the show. "There's no telling who's behind the mischief. Like I said before, it's probably just some kid who thinks they're being funny."

She ushered a few straggling visitors into the theater and pressed PLAY. What kind of person would think damaging a monument at a national park was funny?

⊙⊙

Ace Kennedy riffled through some files, quickly glancing at each one. If only he could spend all his time in the archives. He knew some people would find this room boring. He grinned. Nothing could be further from the truth. The letters, journals, detailed information about artifacts that had been found on the battlefield. . .every last piece of the past chronicled here came alive when he picked up a document to read it. This place was a history lover's dream.

Not only that, but working in the archives gave him some distance from Kristy. He'd hoped she'd be used to the idea of him occupying her old office by now, but when he saw her this morning, she'd glared at him. Why did he keep doing the wrong thing where she was concerned? First on the bus tour, then with the family wanting Junior Ranger information. He pushed away the thought. He'd long ago resolved to either change something or let it go. He'd tried to follow through with that the night of the stakeout. But even bluntness hadn't changed anything with Kristy. That left letting it go.

He pulled out a pile of photocopied letters. The top one caught his eye and he skimmed the contents. Penned by the wife of a Confederate soldier, the letter had been used in the soldier's defense at his desertion trial. She'd written to her husband and told him their children were starving and if he didn't come home, they would die. *Talk about a guilt trip.* Ace folded the letter and dropped it back into the file. No wonder the poor man had deserted the army. Ace wondered if the man had been charged or if the letter had been enough to set him free. Unfortunately, he'd probably never know.

Knowing the deserting soldier's fate didn't matter—it wasn't important to Ace's mission—but it highlighted for him, again, the only real frustration of history. Sometimes it was impossible to find out how the story ended.

He spent the rest of the afternoon searching through the files. As he locked up, he fought against the feeling of failure. With the busy summer season in full swing now, he might not be able to spend much more time looking through the archives. But he wouldn't give up. *I'll find the information I'm looking for next time.*

CHAPTER 10

When Kristy got home from work, she threw together a sandwich and took it, along with the day's mail, out on her back deck. Delighted to have an audience, Sam played chase the bird, bee, butterfly, and whatever else caught his eye. Kristy laughed at his antics as she kicked off the solid brown, standard-issue shoes and propped her feet up on the deck rail. For a moment, she leaned her head backward and enjoyed the sun on her face. The peace she'd felt on her early morning walk to the visitor center crept back, and she kept her eyes closed, soaking it in.

A bark from Sam jolted her upright. He sat still as a statue, watching a squirrel running along the fence. As the squirrel got close to the spot where he stood, he pounced.

She grinned. "Silly pup. That squirrel is way out of your reach." She picked up her sandwich, and as she ate, she absently flipped through the mail. A white envelope tucked between a Chadwick's catalog and a JCPenney bill caught her eye, and she squealed.

Sam came bounding over, and she waved it at him. "We got a letter from Ainsley, Sammy."

Unimpressed, he barked once as if to scold her for making such a big deal out of something inedible and bounded back over to confront the squirrel.

Kristy tore into the envelope. Her friend Ainsley Davis was the only person she knew who still wrote letters. Even her grandmother e-mailed these days. But Ainsley said letter writing was a lost art she intended to keep alive. She tolerated e-mailing and texting and talked to Kristy on the phone at least once a week, but even so, Kristy could still count on a snail-mail letter or card every few weeks.

The summers Kristy had worked with Ainsley and Vickie at Shiloh as a seasonal held some of her fondest memories from her college years. They'd lived together in park housing, and there hadn't been a dull moment. The three of them were still close, despite the distance that separated them.

Now a park ranger at Grand Canyon National Park, Ainsley had always been interested in biology and science, so her job was perfect for her. She'd been a bit bored with all the history at Shiloh and struggled through the historical programs she'd been required to learn. She and Brad, her firefighter husband, loved living at the Grand Canyon and were always trying to get Kristy to come for a visit.

Dear Kristy,

I hope things are going better for you now. I know you've faced more than your share of challenges these past weeks, but you're going to get through them, and you'll be a stronger person when you do.

God has great things in store for you. You just have to be patient. I know that isn't easy right now, but remember when I met Brad? I wasn't even looking for a friend, much less for love. And I found my soul mate. I have no doubt the same thing will happen to you.

*Now I know you don't want to hear this. . .but I think
I actually agree with your mother. Maybe you should get
back out there. Don't sit home and feel sorry for yourself.
I know there are a couple of churches around there with
some pretty big singles' groups. Get involved. Don't let Mark
steal your happiness. Remember, you deserve the best. And
don't let anyone make you doubt it.*

*Okay, girl, I've gotta go. We're about to go out to dinner.
I'm praying for you every day.*

Let's talk soon! Come see us!

Love,
Ainsley

Kristy spent the next couple of days pondering Ainsley's advice. She wanted to call her and whine, *But I don't want to get back out there. It's scary out there. And I haven't been on a date with anyone but Mark in years.*

Not that dates with Mark were much fun, especially for the past year. Kristy could refer to her handy list for a reminder of that. Number eight on the list of why he wasn't right for her: *He refused to go out to any new places for dinner.* If she hadn't wanted to eat at the Waffle House, El Toro Mexican Restaurant, or Cracker Barrel, she'd been out of luck. So maybe a date with someone who wanted to go to a new place would be nice.

But she was nervous. Not the silly, giddy nervous of a teenager going on a date. But a different kind of nervous. She'd been willing to walk down the aisle with Mark. A man who was so obviously wrong for her that she now had a list a mile long of reasons that made her glad they were no longer together. And in some ways, that bothered her more than being publicly humiliated.

By Friday, Kristy had finally come to terms with her impending dive back into the dating pool. It wouldn't be that bad. Robert was a perfectly nice guy. Besides, it would have been bad manners to call and back out. And as Vickie pointed out, just because they went out to dinner didn't mean they were locked in to anything. But the fact that her heart still felt like it was busted into a million pieces made it hard to get excited about a date with someone new.

CHAPTER 11

No need to panic. Yet. Kristy's bathroom clock showed that she still had an hour left to complete the transformation from park ranger to regular girl. An hour should've been plenty of time.

In a perfect world.

But in "Kristy World," there was always a little glitch. This time, the glitch was Sam. Since he'd been banished to the fenced-in yard while Kristy got ready for her date, she hadn't been surprised by his nonstop barking. But now all she heard was silence.

And that was never a good sign.

She stopped plucking her eyebrows and peeked out the window. Sure enough, he was up to no good. Sam loved his backyard but was a natural-born explorer. And he had apparently decided the grass was greener elsewhere. His little tail end was all she could see as he dug his way out. In a few seconds, he'd be running loose.

Now it was time to panic.

She reached for some pants but remembered the spray tan still glistening on her legs. No pants yet. Not unless she wanted Robert to wonder if she were part zebra. Instead, she grabbed her long, oversized robe and cinched it tight as she hobbled down the hall, toes held apart by separators. She hoped their fresh fire engine red polish only said "first date" and not "desperate." Vickie and Ainsley made her promise to look her best tonight, despite her initial declaration that she was going on the date in her ranger uniform and ponytail.

Kristy dashed out the back door, but Sam had already made his escape. Why did he have a knack for channeling Houdini whenever she had somewhere important to go? On second thought, maybe he was trying to get her back for forgetting to feed him earlier in the week.

"Sam!" She hurried as fast as she could down the driveway, weight on her heels as she did the wet-toenails shuffle. Running barefoot in her fleecy robe wasn't exactly her idea of ladylike behavior. At least she didn't have a full set of rollers in her hair. Just one big Velcro roller at the crown of her head. But that was bad enough.

Even minus the full set of rollers, she had a feeling she looked like a person interviewed on the news after a tornado. *"When I saw Myrtle's lawn mower fly by, I knew we were in trouble. All I got out with was this robe and my autographed picture of Elvis."* Hopefully there wouldn't be any storms or news cameras along her way.

"Sammy, you'd better come back here now!" She hadn't even had a chance to put on deodorant yet and was practically running a marathon. If she ever caught up with him, the dog might not see a bone for a week as punishment.

Kristy finally spotted Sam as she got near the visitor center. With any luck, all the park visitors had gone home for the day. She didn't want anyone to recognize her as "the nice park ranger lady who gave us a map." Living and working at a national park had some perks, but the possibility of running into visitors who expected to have their questions answered long after the park had closed for the day was definitely not one of them.

Sam was sniffing around between a cannon and a plaque

declaring that "one of the decisive battles of the Civil War" had been fought right here. Kristy wondered if this identical plaque was on battlefields all over the South. Every one she'd ever visited seemed to think its particular battle was a decisive one.

She sneaked over to the historic spot and tried to coax Sam to her. "Come here, sweet baby." She bent down and held out a hand. "Let's go get a treat for my boy." Sam regarded her with suspicion. He knew she didn't coo at him unless something he wouldn't like was about to happen. "Does my Sammy want a belly rub?" The instant the words left her mouth, the back door to the visitor center opened. Kristy froze. Maybe they'd think she was a cannon. A very eccentric barefoot cannon in a purple robe.

"Kristy? What are you doing?"

Forget about me being a cannon. Just shoot me out of one. Now.

She stood and brushed a wisp of hair from her eyes, inwardly cringing as she remembered the lone Velcro roller sitting on top of her head. "Hello, Ace."

She pulled the robe tighter and prayed that the yards of material had all her parts covered. And that she seemed casual and confident. "Sam got out of the fence, and I'm just trying to get him to come to me."

Ace's gaze took in the Velcro roller, the robe, and finally her toes. A slow smile spread across his perfectly chiseled face. "Big plans tonight?"

She felt the heat as her face turned red. "Not really. Just going out to dinner." She turned her attention back to the dog and willed him to come to her.

Sam, the traitor, trotted right over to Ace and sat at his feet.

Now it's no bones for two weeks, mister.

"Come on, Sam, let's go home." Kristy made a move toward him. He darted behind Ace's legs and peered up at her. If she hadn't known better, she would've thought it was a mischievous expression that stared back.

We've really got to start obedience school.

"I'm heading down that way." Ace motioned toward the residential area of the park. "Why don't you and Sam hop in my truck, and I'll give you a ride?" He took another peek at her bare feet. "I don't imagine running barefoot is too comfortable."

Kristy decided then and there it was all her mother's fault. She was the one who had always harped on good manners. And it seemed as though ever since Kristy's life had imploded, those manners had been getting her into one situation after another. She should've just hung up when Robert called to ask her out. But no, she had to politely accept. She should've called him later and told him that she couldn't go, but again, she knew how rude it was to cancel a date at the last minute. And now she couldn't think of a way to say no to Ace's offer without being completely boorish. "Thank you," she mumbled.

When Ace opened his truck door, Sam hopped right in. Kristy climbed in behind him, and he jumped onto her lap and pushed his head out the window.

Ace put the truck into gear and snickered softly.

She whipped her head around.

He grinned and motioned toward the dog. "It looks like he's decided he likes you again."

In spite of her embarrassment, her own lips couldn't resist turning upward. In less than a minute, they were in front of her house. She glanced over at Ace and considered apologizing for her appearance. But she was pretty sure it was one of those situations where the less said, the better. "Thanks for the lift. My feet appreciate it."

"Not a problem." With that smile, he could've easily starred in a toothpaste commercial. Or any commercial for that matter. But no matter how he looked, she couldn't forget that he had *her* job. And no matter how immature it was, she planned to hold it against him.

Kristy hoisted Sam from the seat and attempted to walk with dignity up her front path. Not an easy feat, all things considered. Once on the porch, she turned and waved good-bye to Ace.

"Have fun on your date!"

Kristy was pretty sure she saw a wink as he pulled away.

She closed the door behind her and leaned against it. One look at the living room clock and she jerked upright. Only thirty minutes to finish getting ready. Sam scampered to his favorite perch on the back of the couch where he could look out the window.

Just as she walked into the bedroom to find an outfit, the phone rang. She hit the speaker button and made her way over to the closet.

"Hello." Kristy flipped through her overstuffed closet in search of a perfect first date outfit. It had been so long since her last first date, she wasn't sure what to choose. For the millionth time, she wished there were a way out of it.

"Hey girl." Vickie's voice filled the room. "Are you ready for tonight?"

"Actually, no. I had a little mishap, but I'm back on track now." She pulled out her favorite dark denim skirt and wiggled into it.

"A mishap?" Vickie laughed. "That's *so* unlike you."

Kristy was known in her circle of friends for being the one "things happened to." They found it very funny and often told "Kristy stories" to people who didn't even know her. There was nothing worse than meeting a friend of a friend and having her say, "Oh! *Kristy*. Aren't you the one who. . . ?" Fill in the blank.

"What do you think about my dark denim skirt?" She changed the subject. Fashion had always been one of Vickie's strong points, and Kristy desperately missed living with her and getting her stamp of approval before setting foot out of the house.

"Sounds good. And maybe strappy sandals. Try those metallic ones from Ann Taylor Loft that you bought the last time I was there."

Good idea. Kristy pulled the shoes out of the closet and slipped them on. Perfect. Her red toes were a good contrast to the metallic of the shoe, and the spray tan looked pretty natural. And only streaky in a couple of places. Not bad considering the unscheduled marathon.

"I was thinking of short sleeves, but I'll take something to wear over it in case the restaurant is cold. Maybe a cardigan?" Kristy picked up a black cardigan out of her closet and threw it on the bed.

"No, Grandma. Not a cardigan. Take your brown leather jacket. And definitely wear a blue top. It will bring out your eyes."

She grabbed a light blue top with capped sleeves and a square neckline. Perfect. Hopefully no one could tell she didn't have to pick out "real" clothes to wear very often. She spent most of her time in a green and gray polyester uniform and sometimes wondered if her fashion sense was a little skewed as a result.

"Hey. You're off speaker now, and I'm officially dressed. I just have to fix my hair and I'm all set with time to spare." Kristy click-clacked down the hallway to the bathroom, which was still in disarray thanks to her rapid departure earlier. She hoped Robert wouldn't need to use the facilities.

"Okay. I'm sure it will go fine. Don't worry." Vickie hesitated, and Kristy sensed a pep talk coming on. "You're smart, funny, and beautiful. You are moving on with your life. Leaving the past behind. Your future starts today."

Vickie meant well, but she sounded a bit like one of those motivational speakers who speaks to high school assemblies.

Kristy grimaced. "Thanks for that daily affirmation."

Vickie laughed. "Well, all those things are true, and it doesn't hurt for someone to say them out loud to you."

"I appreciate it. And thanks for talking me through the fashion portion of my date. I'll call you later."

Good-byes said, Kristy faced the mirror. Once the Velcro roller was out of her hair, she turned her head upside down for a quick brush. The roller gave the top layer of her blonde hair instant body, and with just a touch of spray, it was done. Her hair looked pretty good, but not like she tried too hard. Just the effect she'd been going for.

"Vickie is right. You will be fine. It's time to move on." Kristy hoped talking to herself in the mirror didn't constitute some kind of crazy. A glance at her watch told her it was almost time. She took a deep breath and tried to calm her nerves.

CHAPTER 12

Kristy had opted not to tell her mother she had accepted Robert's dinner invitation. Sure, she'd be a little mad when she found out, but Kristy didn't need anyone else overanalyzing her social life. She did fine with that all on her own, and Ainsley and Vickie were glad to help when needed. Besides, Robert seemed pleasant enough last Sunday. And he was cute. Even better, he seemed like a good Christian guy, and Kristy knew those weren't easy to come by.

She plopped down on her overstuffed couch and flipped on the television. An episode of *Friends* was on. Maybe it would get rid of her predate jitters. Sam joined her on the couch, resting his head on her leg. "Oh sure, now you're a good dog."

She kept a close watch on the clock. He should arrive in five minutes. She turned the TV off, then back on. There was no need to look like she was just sitting there with nothing better to do than wait for him.

Another episode of *Friends* came on. *Any minute.* It was six thirty on the dot. She smoothed her hair and did a quick lipstick check. She was as ready as she could be. And starving.

At six forty-five, she peeked out the window. No sign of him.

Hmm. It wasn't as if he could get lost. Aside from the large signs proclaiming the park entrance, his mother lived adjacent to the park. So Kristy was certain he knew how to get there.

She started pacing at seven. She could understand being a few minutes late. Thirty minutes was pushing it, though. And she was on her third episode of *Friends*. A marathon maybe.

Now she had a huge knot in her stomach. Partly hunger, partly anxiety. Any excitement she'd been feeling was gone. Where was he? Maybe he'd been held up at work. Maybe his car wouldn't start. Surely he would've had the decency to call and let her know. Maybe his phone battery was dead.

Thirty more minutes later, she was still sitting on the couch going over possible scenarios in her head. Finally, she flipped through her caller ID and found his number. She wasn't sure if it was his home number or cell number, but it was worth a try. When she had everything dialed but the last digit, she chickened out. She didn't want to seem overeager. *Play it cool, Kristy,* she coached herself. *Breezy.*

Finally, she turned the TV off. She'd just seen Ross and Rachel break up, get back together, then break up again, and her date was still a no-show. Maybe there'd been a car accident. A family emergency. Maybe he was carjacked. In this rural Tennessee town? Doubtful.

It had been long enough to justify calling him for real. She picked up the phone and bravely let the call go all the way through. On the third ring, it connected.

"Hi, this is Robert. I'm unable to get to the phone right now. Leave a message at the sound of the tone and. . ." Frustrated, Kristy clicked the phone off.

It was time to face the music. She'd obviously been stood up. Honestly, she'd never actually been stood up before. Unless you counted being left at the altar. But even Mark had the decency to show up on their *first* date.

Did Robert decide I was ugly? Weird? I'll bet it's because I'm a Civil War buff.

Before she could go through a mental checklist of all the reasons Robert probably didn't want to date her, the phone rang. She jumped up to grab it. Surely it was him with an explanation.

"Hey, Kris." Not Robert. It was Ainsley. She settled back down onto the couch.

"Hi." Kristy knew why she was calling and hated to tell her how wrong everyone had been with the whole "get back on the horse" theory.

"So. . .how'd the date go? Oh wait, I just realized what time it is. He's probably still there, isn't he?"

Kristy gazed out the window, wishing she had better news to tell. "No. He didn't show."

"Why not? Is he sick?" Why were all of her friends such optimists when it came to love? She really needed to add another cynic to her group.

"No. He just didn't show." She reached over and smoothed Sam's ear. "As in, he stood me up." There. The proverbial cat was out of the bag.

Silence.

Then. . . "There's got to be a logical explanation. Are you sure you got the date right? Maybe he asked you out for Saturday night instead of Friday." Bless her heart. Kristy knew Ainsley was only trying to make her feel better. Unfortunately, implying that she couldn't even get the day of the week right only made her feel worse.

"I'm pretty sure he just changed his mind. I was a little surprised he called in the first place. He didn't seem too interested in me when we met. And when he finally called, it was like he couldn't wait to hang up." No sense sugarcoating this one. "It's okay. I have to work tomorrow anyway. And besides, you know I wasn't ready for this."

After a lot of work, she finally convinced Ainsley she'd be fine. All she wanted to do was get out of her cute date outfit. Ever since she'd realized Robert wasn't going to show, Kristy felt like her clothing somehow mocked her. She slipped off her sandals and padded down the hallway, Sam at her heels. She carefully hung up her date clothes and threw on a pair of old sweats, a faded T-shirt, and flip-flops. Maybe not her best fashion statement, but she didn't care. As Sam watched with interest, Kristy took off her makeup and brushed her hair back into a ponytail. With her comfy clothes and no-longer-made-up face, the image looking back at her in the mirror hardly resembled the glamour girl Robert would've seen if he'd bothered to show up.

Aside from yet another blow to her self-esteem, the downside to her dinner date standing her up was that now she had to provide her own food. And there were no groceries in the house except for dog food and Pop-Tarts. Neither sounded appetizing. Once again, Kristy wished a restaurant would deliver to her house. Unfortunately, that was one of the drawbacks of living in such an isolated area. So even though she didn't feel like it, she would have to go out.

She took Sam along for company on the short drive to the grocery store. Kristy pulled into a space and rolled the window down a tad so he could get some air. Judging from the nearly empty parking lot, she knew she was one of the few shoppers at the Four Star General Store. And that suited her just fine.

She mindlessly filled her cart with treats to make herself feel better. Chocolate bars, chips, a honey bun; she was Denise Austin's worst nightmare. As she rounded the corner to the frozen food aisle, she saw him. Ace Kennedy.

Just my luck.

She quickly opened the door to the ice cream section and held it open until it started to frost over. There were probably icicles forming on her face, but if she stayed hidden behind the frosted door, maybe he wouldn't be able to see her. *Please don't want ice cream tonight.* She could see his blurry outline as he made his way down the frozen food aisle. If she could've crawled into the freezer, she would have. And if she stood there much longer, she'd be frozen in place.

He came right over and parked his cart beside hers.

Go for the vegetables, Ace. Walk away from the ice cream. She tried to urge him, telepathically, to leave the area, but it didn't seem to be working. Not that she believed in that, but she was desperate.

He reached for the door she was hiding behind, and they had a little tug-of-war.

He won.

"Kristy?"

She didn't know which was worse, the possibility of him figuring out that she'd been stood up, or him seeing her again in a less than attractive state. At least this time she was fully clothed.

"Hello." Her teeth were chattering a little. "I'm just trying to decide which ice cream flavor to buy tonight."

"Right." He looked amused. "Tough decision, but chocolate always gets my vote."

Maybe we do have something in common. She picked up the Breyer's smooth-churned chocolate and put it in her basket. "Sounds good to me, too." Kristy just wanted to get her calorie-filled cart out of there. "I've gotta go." She finally closed the freezer door. It was highly possible that she'd just thawed out the entire section. "Thanks for the input on the ice cream."

"Anytime." He looked like he wanted to say more.

Please don't ask me about my date. She grabbed her cart and forced her lips into a smile. "See you at work tomorrow."

"Actually, tomorrow is my day off," he informed her.

"Oh. So you have 'real' weekends off?" She wondered briefly if he had some kind of inside connection at the park. Since the park was open seven days a week, not many employees had Saturday and Sunday off.

"Sure do. How about you?"

"I'm off Sundays and Mondays."

"I see. Well, hey. That means tomorrow is like your Friday." He looked at her intently.

"Yes." She nodded, suddenly aware of her bare face and ponytail. "I need to go. Sam's in the car."

"Have a good evening."

She could feel his eyes on her as she pushed the cart in the opposite direction. *Don't look back. Just keep going.*

She bypassed the posters of Generals Grant and Lee and headed for the checkout. The Four Star was the only grocery store she knew of where you could buy authentic Civil War souvenirs along with your bread and milk.

Kristy handed her debit card to the cashier. She should've just stayed in bed today. Called in sick of life. First, the dog ran away. Then she got stood up. If anyone had ever needed a do-over, it was her.

Oh well, she'd just have to find her inner Scarlett.

Tomorrow is another day.

CHAPTER 13

Saturday morning dawned bright and clear. Just the opposite of Kristy's mood. But she was trying not to think about the disasters of yesterday. No point in dwelling on what couldn't be changed. So Robert stood her up. Fine. He probably wasn't her type anyway. And so what if she'd made a complete fool of herself in front of Ace? Twice. She hardly knew him. And she certainly didn't like him. So why did it bug her so much? She suddenly remembered that it was his day off and was immediately in better humor.

She threw on her Smokey Bear hat, kissed Sam good-bye, and headed out the door. The walk to the visitor center was much more comfortable than the barefoot run she'd taken the previous day. And Saturdays were always busy at the park, with lots of families and tour groups. No time to think about her problems. Plus, she needed to resume training since both Matthew and Mason would be working today. She hoped to have them take turns tagging along on some of her ranger programs so they could learn how to conduct them.

Since tomorrow was her day off, she only had to get through the day before she would be rewarded with a break. Kristy hadn't

76

mentioned it to Ace last night, but she'd had to fight long and hard to get Sundays off. She couldn't imagine giving up going to Sunday morning services. Now that she was a seasonal, she was a little afraid her days off would change. But so far Hank hadn't mentioned it.

Before she checked the daily schedule, she started a pot of coffee. The drawback of being the only female ranger was that she had to do anything that might be considered "domestic." She watched it brew and savored the smell. Her general rule was "Don't talk to me until you've seen me have at least one cup—loaded with sugar and cream." She knew the caffeine, not to mention the sugar and cream, probably wasn't the healthiest breakfast, but it was the only way she could get her mornings off to a good start.

Her day was loaded with programs, and despite her gloominess, she was thrilled. Lots of programs meant she would spend most of her time outside, talking to visitors. She'd take that any day over being stuck on front-desk duty—having to stand at the desk all day long, taking entrance fees and pointing out the restrooms. No fun. And lots of time to dwell on what was going wrong in her life.

"Good morning." Owen grabbed a Styrofoam cup and waited for the coffee to finish brewing. Upon meeting him, some people thought Owen was quite a force to reckon with. But much like Hank, underneath his gruff exterior, he was a big teddy bear.

"Morning. Thanks for scheduling me outside most of the day." Owen made the daily schedules, and it was always best to stay on his good side.

"No problem." He poured his coffee right to the top of the cup.

Kristy had to fight to keep from flinching as she watched the hot coffee slosh around. He always poured his coffee a little too full, and the old blue carpet that ran between his office and the coffee station featured a trail of little coffee stains.

"You gonna have the twins attend your programs today?" He took a sip of coffee.

"I figured I'd have them switch off. That way one of them can be in here learning how to work the front desk."

He nodded. "Good plan."

"So any more news about the monument vandal?" she asked.

"None. Arnie was pretty mad about getting hit a second time. Said he wanted whoever did it to be found." Owen raked his fingers through his thinning gray hair and splashed a couple of drops of coffee in the process.

"Not much chance of that. Surely they're not stupid enough to do it a third time." Kristy hoped the culprit was long gone.

"Let's hope you're right about that." He took another sip of coffee and ambled back to his office.

Kristy put her hat and purse in the seasonal office, thankful for a few minutes alone before being surrounded by people all day. Despite her desire to forget about the embarrassment of last night, it was still hanging over her like a big black cloud. The coffee helped, but she couldn't completely shake the feeling of discontent.

◎◎

A loud ringing in his ears brought Ace to consciousness. He squinted at the bedside clock. Through bleary eyes, he could barely make out 8:00. And after a night spent poring over thick books, he hadn't gotten to bed until nearly dawn. How had he set the alarm wrong? He squeezed his eyes shut and slammed his hand on the snooze button. But the ringing continued. Even in his tired brain, he knew that left only one other option. Without opening his eyes, he scrabbled around on the bedside table with his fingers until they closed around the phone.

"Hello?"

"Could I speak to Ace, please?" His brain teetered on the brink of recognizing the woman's voice, but he couldn't quite place it.

He sat up and tried to will the grogginess from his voice. "Speaking."

"Um, this is Maggie Hamilton. Caroline's mother."

The name had the effect of cold ice water splashed in his face. "Mrs. Hamilton. What's wrong?"

"Nothing's wrong, dear. I just wanted to let you know. . . . That is, I needed to tell you. . .there are some things of Caroline's I thought you might want." The sadness in her voice as she said the name of her only daughter cut to his heart.

"Oh, well, thanks."

"I know it took us a long time to go through her things. But after the accident, I just couldn't. . ." She trailed off, as if to collect herself. "I couldn't handle it then. It was easier to just put it all in storage."

Ace knew exactly what she meant. He'd done the same with his pain for a long time. Put it in storage. "I understand, Mrs. Hamilton." If he closed his eyes, he could see Caroline, her shiny brown hair glinting in the sun. "I still miss her."

"I know. We all do." Mrs. Hamilton was quiet for a moment. "But, honey, you know, Caroline is in a better place now. Every time I get sad, I think about what she used to say to me when I'd worry about her going somewhere by herself."

"God is with me, so I'm never alone," Ace said, remembering, his eyes suddenly stinging. "She used to say the same thing to me when I'd worry about her taking a cab home alone at night."

Mrs. Hamilton gave a little laugh. "She had a faith that couldn't be shaken. I think we could all learn a lot from the way she lived her life."

"Yes." He certainly had. If her death had taught him anything, it was that he should live his life to the fullest. That there were no guarantees. And especially, that he should let people know how he felt about them.

He gave his address to her and was about to hang up when she spoke. "Oh, Ace?"

"Yes, ma'am?"

"Did you put those beautiful yellow daisies on her grave a few weeks ago?" she asked.

His face grew hot at the realization that his impulsive act had been noticed. "They were always her favorite. And since I was moving. . .well, I wanted to do something special."

"They were perfect. She'd have loved them. Thanks."

After a quick good-bye, he hung up the phone and stared blankly at his bedroom wall. A flood of memories washed over him. The first day they met, as college freshmen. He'd wanted to impress her, but he'd never seen anyone with such dancing brown eyes. And there was the time she'd called him, crying, after her long-term boyfriend had cheated on her during her senior year. Her tears had changed to laughter when he'd offered to go beat the guy up for her. But at least she'd quit crying. And he remembered how hard he'd tried to be serious at the fancy dinner celebration they'd had after they both got "real" jobs. But she'd laughed that night and said she still felt like a kid inside. He'd admitted he did, too.

And then she'd died.

But like her mother said, she wasn't alone. And unless Ace was badly mistaken, wherever she was, she was probably laughing. To his amazement, the memories didn't make him sad anymore. And if Caroline could see that, he knew it made her happy.

CHAPTER 14

Kristy finished explaining the nine steps involved in loading and firing a Civil War musket and was about to demonstrate how to shoot the weapon when she noticed the newest member of her tour group.

Robert Aaron grinned at her from the back row and sheepishly waved his hand in greeting.

Great. He obviously had a major problem with the concept of time. He was only, what? Twenty hours late?

He'd stood her up with no explanation, and now he showed up at work. Right in the middle of a ranger program, with her dressed as a Civil War soldier. In head-to-toe wool, no less. A floppy hat and black boots, both about two sizes too big, completed her look. There was no way to look attractive dressed all in wool, weighted down with lots of equipment, wearing a large hat, and firing a musket. It wasn't feminine. Frankly, it was kind of stinky. And it was definitely not the situation she wanted Robert to see her in. Why confirm his second thoughts?

"Ready." She pulled back the hammer. "Aim." She lifted the gun to her shoulder.

Too bad she didn't get to pick an audience member as a target.

"Fire." She pulled the trigger, and as the shot went off, smoke blew back in her face. She coughed and tried to regain some composure. She had to finish this little talk even if Robert was in the audience.

"This is how the average soldier would've fired a gun during the Civil War," Kristy explained. "Are there any questions?" *Please don't let there be questions.*

"Yeah, I have a question." A big guy leered at her and punched his buddy in the arm. "Would the average soldier have worn red nail polish?" The rest of the audience, including Robert, tittered with laughter. At least Mason, taking notes from the front row, had the decency to shoot Kristy a sympathetic look.

Oops. I knew there was something I forgot to do last night. Her still-polished nails were yet another humiliation to put at Robert's feet.

"No, sir. Red nail polish wasn't standard procedure," she said with as much of a smile as she could muster, wishing it would be appropriate to comment on his mullet and tank top combo. But she had to be nice. Never mind those manners her mother had instilled. In this case, it was her job. Sometimes it stunk to be paid by taxpayers.

"If there are no other questions, this concludes the demonstration. Please have a great day and enjoy your park." Kristy leaned her rifle against the tree and put the bayonet back in the holster on her belt. So glamorous. Robert must be kicking himself for not showing up last night.

He watched as she posed for photos with some of the visitors. These photo ops were as close as she would ever get to being a rock star, and normally she enjoyed them, but not today.

Finally, she was free.

What should someone wearing wool and carrying a firearm say to the guy who had stood her up? A few choice phrases came to her mind. But as a Christian, she'd better not say any of them.

"Hi, Robert." *Jerk.* She took off the floppy brown hat and fanned herself with it.

"Hey." He smiled and motioned toward the musket. "That was some demonstration." Even through her anger, she had to admit he was pretty cute in his green polo and khaki shorts. She'd always been a sucker for the preppy look.

"Thanks." *Where's the apology? Come on, be a man and give me a lame excuse.*

"Is that uniform hot?"

No, Sherlock. What makes you think an all-wool uniform in the summertime is hot?

"It's a little warm." Kristy gripped her musket tightly. All the small talk was making her crazy. "Why, exactly, are you here?"

Robert's eyebrows shot up and his eyes grew wide. "I just thought I'd come see where you work." He brushed his fingers through his thick brown hair. "Ever since you told me you were a ranger, I've been meaning to come out."

Was he for real? Where was the apology? Kristy didn't want to be the one to bring it up, but he wasn't leaving her much of a choice. "So where were you last night?" She tried to sound casual, but even she could hear the words drip with irritation.

Unfortunately, Robert didn't seem to know what she was talking about. *Is he an actor on the side?*

"Last night?" He continued to look puzzled. "What was last night?"

Uh-oh. The conversation wasn't going quite like she thought it would.

"You know. Dinner at the new seafood restaurant. Six thirty." No way was he seriously acting as if he forgot.

"Was there some kind of singles' thing there? I must not have gotten the invitation." He seemed sincere.

What's going on here? "No. Not a singles' thing." Kristy could feel her face getting red. "You called me and asked me out to dinner. And you never showed up." There. She'd made her accusation.

"What?" Robert looked like someone had punched him in the stomach.

A few more minutes and I might.

"Kristy, I'm sorry, but I didn't call you."

She gripped the musket tighter to keep from dropping it. What? Was he seriously trying to act like she was crazy and had made the whole thing up? What did she say now? What if he was suffering from short-term memory loss?

"Um. Yes. You did. You called me Monday night." Kristy remembered it well, because it had been Memorial Day. And the same night Mark had called.

"Monday night I wasn't in town. I was at a conference for work." Robert eyed her suspiciously.

"Well, somebody called me from your number and asked me out. Your name came up on my caller ID." So there.

"Wait a minute." Robert's eyes got wider. "My brother, Zach, was at my house that night. I think he and a couple of his buddies were over there watching movies. He'd been out to Shiloh during the day, but Mom let them hang out at my house that night while she got groceries."

It all began to click in Kristy's head. Zach must've set her up. Was this his idea of a funny prank? And after she'd been nice and offered him water if he was ever riding his bike near her house.

"So you think Zach called me and pretended to be you?" Heat surged into Kristy's face. She'd accepted a fake date. And even worse, Robert knew that if he had asked, she would've said yes. Which meant he mistakenly thought she was interested in him.

"Come to think of it, there was a phone book out when I got back." Robert was clearly horrified. "I hope he didn't call and ask anyone else out."

Kristy hoped not, too. Because that would mean someone else felt as horrible as she did. And she wouldn't wish that on anyone. Except maybe Zach.

CHAPTER 15

Kristy fumbled with her front door as hot tears spilled onto her cheeks. After the embarrassing encounter with Robert, she'd barely been able to keep it together. For some reason, the whole thing with Robert was causing her to relive the demise of her relationship with Mark. Finally, she'd left work early with a headache. The twins were getting pretty good at working the front desk, so she didn't think she'd be missed too much.

Sam greeted her with a bark, and she opened the back door to let him in the fence. She didn't want any witnesses to what she was about to do. Even canine ones. She was perfectly aware that when she was tempted to act on this crazy impulse, she was supposed to call Vickie or Ainsley. She'd given them her word. But she just couldn't help herself.

Kristy opened the closet door and reached into the very back. Her hand made contact with the object she wasn't supposed to look at. The object that everyone who cared about her had offered to set on fire, or at least store at their home.

She carefully hung the pristine white wedding gown on the outside of her closet and unzipped the plastic covering. Her wedding gown. Sleeveless white satin, with just a bit of beading on the bodice. She'd found it about six months ago at a store in Nashville and knew it was the elusive "one" as soon as she'd put it on. Her mother and Vickie both started crying when she stepped out of the dressing room. Kristy had never felt as beautiful as she had while wearing the dress.

Kristy and Mark had known they were getting married almost from their first date. They had the wedding figured out long before there was even a proposal. Music, location, wedding party—planning their day was so easy. If only they'd have paid as much attention to their relationship as they did to their wedding plans.

She pulled her gaze from the gown and opened the bottom dresser drawer. An old Nike box sat inside. She pulled it out and emptied the contents of the box onto her bed, fumbling through old valentines and birthday cards until she found the note she was looking for. Kristy wasn't sure what had possessed Mark to write it on a plain yellow legal pad, the same pad he used to make his packing lists for business trips. Not that it mattered what it was written on. She'd have known that handwriting anywhere.

Dear Kristy,

I've been thinking a lot lately about our relationship. I know we've been together for three years, but I'm starting to think that maybe we aren't meant to be. I wish I would've figured this out sooner, before you helped me pick out the house and put in your notice at work. And especially before our wedding day was upon us. But I don't think I can commit to a lifetime with you. I do still love you, though, and I hope to see you again someday.

Love,
Mark

P.S. If you have any of my things, you can just box them up and mail them to my new house.

The letter had been waiting at her house when she got back from their almost wedding. Not only did Mark leave her at the altar; he didn't have the decency to end the relationship in person. Even after several weeks, the letter still got to her. Although now when she read it, she didn't immediately burst into tears. Now the first emotion she felt was anger. And maybe a little sadness.

Three years. She'd spent three years with a man who promised her the world. They'd had it all planned out. All the way down to the names of the kids they wanted in a couple of years. Unfortunately, Mark's fear of commitment outweighed his love for her.

She looked at the dress for a few more minutes then sat on the bed and read through three years' worth of cards and letters. By the time she got to the pictures of the two of them in happier times, the tears were flowing freely. She told herself this was the last cry she was going to have over him. Although she couldn't help but wonder if she was crying over the loss of Mark—or the loss of the time she'd wasted on Mark.

Looking back over their relationship, Kristy knew he was right. If marrying him had been something she'd really wanted to do, she would've pressed the issue more during the years they'd spent together. Instead, it took him being transferred hundreds of miles away for her to tell him that she thought it was time they did more than just talk about the future.

His response had been great at first. A perfect proposal with a perfect ring. Then they went house hunting and found their dream home, where they would raise a family. Kristy picked out furniture, wall colors, and new flooring. The next logical step was the wedding, and she'd even offered to elope because she knew how nervous weddings made him. But he wanted a real wedding. Except that when it came down to it, he didn't want a wedding at all.

A loud knock on the front door sliced into her pounding

head. The repeated banging propelled her off the bed. She wasn't expecting anyone. And she hated it when people dropped in unannounced. Especially on days like the one she was having. A glance in the mirror revealed that particular brand of red, splotchy face that only came with hours of crying. And she'd never been one to cry pretty, like some girls do.

Kristy glanced out the blinds and groaned. Ace, shifting from one foot to the other, stood on her front porch holding Sam.

Just what she needed.

She could either open the door and let Ace know she'd been crying her eyes out, or do something drastic.

He knocked again.

She chose drastic. She wasn't going to let him see her cry.

"Just a minute," she called to him.

Kristy ran into the bathroom, grabbed some menthol face cream, and slathered it all over her red face. White face-mask face was better than red, crying face any day.

She opened the door and hoped her fake smile looked sincere.

"Thanks for returning my little escape artist." Why was it every time she ended up around him, she was trying to act normal?

He looked at her with worry darkening his eyes. "Here you go." He handed Sam over to her. "Is everything okay?" He leaned toward her a little as they made the exchange, and his gaze seemed to see every tear mark beneath her face cream.

"Oh yeah. I'm fine. Just had a headache and thought this herbal mask might help." *The headache was real at least. But herbal mask? Really? One good sniff and he's gonna know this is Noxzema.*

"I hope you feel better. And if you'd like me to take a look at your fence, I'd be glad to." He patted Sam on the head then brought his gaze back up to meet hers. "It seems like this little guy is determined to get out. I'd hate for anything to happen to him."

Her cheeks ached from smiling. She took a step back and

started to close the door. "Thanks for the offer. Maybe some other time?"

After the door was firmly shut behind her, she stepped to the window and watched him walk down the front path to his truck. She remembered plainly the kindness in his voice the other night at the stakeout when he'd asked her if she hated him. Why was he being so nice to her?

"Maybe he feels sorry for me because he thinks I got left at the altar and lost my mind," she murmured to Sam as she lowered the pup to the floor. "Stay out of trouble while I wash my face." Kristy splashed cool water on her face then stared at the puffy, red eyes in the mirror. Had her mask fooled him at all?

Hopefully she just looked sick. She certainly felt sick.

◎◇◎

"Don't you see? The whole Robert fake date made you own up to your true feelings about Mark." Ainsley was apparently trying to use the psychology class she took in college. "You said yourself that you weren't all that upset when you thought Robert stood you up. You were relieved, which meant you didn't want to go anyway, right?"

"Yeah." Kristy nodded, even though she knew Ainsley couldn't see her.

"So you didn't care until you realized Robert *knew* you would have gone out with him had he *actually* asked. So it's pretty simple to me." Ainsley was really getting into her psychologist role now.

"What's that?" Kristy spooned another scoop of dark chocolate ice cream into her mouth and savored the smooth, rich taste.

"Pride. Your pride is hurt. Again. You don't want to be vulnerable. And you are."

Kristy sighed. "Maybe. Or maybe I was right in the first place and need to be on my own for a little while."

"I think you need to talk to Mark. Get some closure. Didn't you say he called?"

"He called last Monday but didn't leave a message. He always hated leaving messages." Number sixteen on the list of reasons they weren't right for each other.

"Well, answer the phone the next time he calls. Or even better, call him yourself. You know he must be open to talking to you, or he never would've called you in the first place. And I don't think you're going to be able to move on until you've talked to him."

"I don't know. I think that might open up a can of worms."

"Or it might be exactly what you need in order to get over it." She paused. "I think it might be worth a try." At least Ainsley didn't pretend to have all the answers.

Kristy decided a subject change was in order. These past few weeks, it seemed like all their conversations had been about her. "How's everything with you? Any fun news?"

"Actually. . ." Ainsley trailed off and took a deep breath. "Brad and I have decided we're ready to be parents." Her excitement flashed through the phone line and immediately made Kristy feel better. "We've been married now for four years. I think we're finally in a place where we can handle a baby."

"Wow. That's great. You'll be great parents." Of all the couples she knew, Brad and Ainsley were the one she'd always thought would be the best parents.

"We're so excited. Ever since my nephew came to spend a week with us last year, Brad's been talking about how much he wants to be a dad. It's adorable."

"Well, keep me posted."

"Of course. You and Vickie are the only ones who know. If I tell my family, every time they see or talk to me, they'll ask if I'm expecting. And that will get old fast."

Kristy laughed. "You're right. I'll say a little prayer for you, but I promise not to ask. I'll just wait for happy news."

"Great. That's what I was hoping."

They said their good-byes, and Kristy busied herself with a few household chores. An hour later, laundry was done, dishes were done, and Sam was full. She considered calling her mother but thought better of it. They'd already made plans to meet at church tomorrow. Kristy felt sure they could hash out her problems over lunch when she broke the news to her mother about the Robert/Zach incident.

Sinking into a steamy bubble bath, Kristy thought about what Ainsley had confided on the phone. She and Brad were the most "in love" couple she'd ever met, so there was no doubt they'd do great at parenting. In fact, one of the nagging doubts in her own relationship had been that she and Mark had never seemed to be as in sync as Brad and Ainsley. When she'd brought it up to Mark, he'd scoffed and said she shouldn't compare relationships. But she'd always attributed it to the fact that Brad and Ainsley were friends before they dated. Brad was quick to tell people how much he loved being married to his best friend. And Ainsley could spend hours gushing over how blessed she was to have found him.

What must it be like to have a love like that?

CHAPTER 16

It's open," Ace called as he walked down the hallway toward the sound of knocking on his front door.

Owen Branam opened the door part of the way and stuck his head inside. "Are you ready, man?"

"Ready." Ace followed him down the steps and climbed into Owen's old Bronco.

"Steve's meeting us there. Said his wife was glad for him to get out of the house so she can pack." Owen steered the Bronco out of the driveway and toward the park exit.

"Pack? Where's she going?" Ace asked.

"They're taking a trip to Europe. Some kind of second honeymoon. Gonna be gone practically the whole summer." Owen slowed to a stop at the highway and waited for a car to pass.

"Wow. That's quite a vacation."

"Yeah. He had a hard time talking Arnie and Hank into letting him off that long. And after the vandal hit the monuments, they tried to make him stay." Owen flipped the air conditioner a notch higher. "But the tickets he has are nonrefundable, so they went ahead and told him he could have the time off."

"Guess he was relieved."

"More like his wife was. I'm not sure Steve is the world-traveling type, but I guess a man will do a lot for the woman he loves."

Ace chuckled. "I'll say."

He'd been a little hesitant when Owen had asked him if he wanted to have a guys' night out. In his experience, guys' night out usually meant beer and bars, and neither of those things appealed to him. But when Owen mentioned a steak house in Savannah that was supposed to be good, Ace figured it would be a pretty tame night.

They pulled into the crowded parking lot. Despite the cars, the restaurant looked like little more than someone's house. Ace shot a questioning look at Owen.

"Don't let the outside fool you," Owen warned. "The steaks are delicious. And the sweet tea is even better than my grandmother's was, God rest her soul."

Steve was already in a booth, waiting.

"What took y'all so long? I'm a hungry man." He was also a large man. If Ace had to guess, he'd say this wasn't Steve's first time at the steak house.

They ordered steak and baked potatoes all around.

"Could we have some bread, darlin'?" Owen asked the waitress.

"Sure thing, Mr. Owen. It'll be right out."

"Darlin'?" Ace asked once she had left the table.

Owen chuckled. "Welcome to the South."

Ace had definitely noticed a bit of a difference in the sleepy Tennessee town from the city he was used to. It wasn't better or worse, just different. Things seemed a little slower. Cars were slower; people walked slower. But it was kind of nice. There was an abundance of sweet tea and fried food. And it helped that he was a bit taken with the Southern drawl. A grin played across his lips as he remembered Kristy's Southern-flavored spiel to park visitors. He still thought one reason they stayed awake for her and snoozed for him was because of her accent. Of course, when he'd shared that theory with her, she wasn't thrilled.

"So, Ace. What brings you down here?" Steve asked. "Do you have relatives here or something?"

"I'm just here for the job." And access to the archives. But Steve wasn't asking about his personal business. "I worked for the park service in Illinois and decided I was ready to transfer on to a different park."

"And you chose Shiloh?" Steve asked. "Is Civil War history your thing, then?"

"I guess you could say that." Ace knew his ulterior motive for choosing Shiloh would come out eventually, but he was in no hurry to reveal it.

The waitress put heaping mounds of rolls and corn bread in the center of the table.

"Here you go. There's honey, butter, and jelly for the biscuits." She set a bowl full of condiments on the table. "Your steaks will be out soon."

"Thanks," Owen called.

"Darlin'," Ace said with a laugh.

Owen let out a loud guffaw and put a big glob of butter on a steaming biscuit. "So, Ace, are you single? Married? Divorced? Surely a young man like yourself has a lady in his life."

"I'm single. No lady to speak of." He reached for a packet of strawberry jam.

Owen shook his head. "That's a shame."

Steve laughed. "He's smart if you ask me."

"Now, we all know you'd be lost without Amy. So don't you be givin' us that stuff." Owen wiped his mouth with a napkin and took another biscuit from the plate.

Steve grinned, his eyes crinkling at the corners. "You know it."

"Well, what about you, Owen? I know that Steve's married

and getting ready to jet off to Europe, but haven't heard much about your story. Are you married?" Ace asked.

For a moment, a dark cloud came over Owen's normally sunny face.

"Nah." He shook his head. "I was. We were together twenty years. She died nearly five years ago, though. Cancer." He took a sip of tea. "It was the hardest thing I've ever been through."

"I'm sorry, man." Ace knew from losing Caroline how hard it was to lose someone important to you. But to lose someone you'd built a life with must be terrible.

"Thanks. At first, I didn't know how I'd get through. But as they say, time heals."

"Here you go, gentlemen." The waitress set thick steaks and foil-wrapped baked potatoes in front of each of them. "Dig in."

Ace said a silent blessing for the food then bit into the best steak he'd ever had. "Man, Owen, you were sure right about this place."

"Stick with me, boy. I won't steer you wrong."

"Hey, Ace," Steve said in a voice so casual it couldn't have been an accident, "do you and Kristy get along?"

Ace frowned. Unfortunately, the blond still saw him as an enemy. But for his part, they got along. "I guess we do. Why?"

"No reason. Except that I saw you on her porch earlier today while I was out on patrol."

"Oh. Yeah, her dog had gotten out, and I was returning him. Not a big deal."

"I just wondered. You know, the two of you are about the same age." Steve wiggled his bushy gray eyebrows in Ace's direction.

"Now, you know she's in no state to be dating," Owen piped up rather protectively. "Besides, they work together, so that wouldn't be a good idea."

Steve laughed. "Owen thinks he's her daddy," he explained to Ace. "She's been working here so long, we've practically seen her grow up."

"I'm just worried about her is all," Owen said defensively. "Besides, there was some guy out today on one of her programs that had her all riled up. I saw them talking after it was over. And it wasn't long afterward that she went home with a headache." He cut another bite of steak and swished it through the sauce before popping it into his mouth. "She might've fooled Hank, but I saw those tears in her eyes."

Ace remembered the look on her face when she'd stepped onto her porch that afternoon. He'd known then that she'd been crying. That mask hadn't fooled him. But he figured she'd just have to get through it on her own. And as Owen had said, time heals.

"I'm pretty sure you don't need to worry about Kristy and me dating," Ace said. "But if you have any other prospects, send them my way." Deep down, he had to admit that since Caroline's death, no woman had caught his interest like the blue-eyed ranger with the feisty personality. But a man had his pride. And no way he was going to let these guys know he might have an interest in someone who couldn't stand him.

CHAPTER 17

Kristy knew there was one huge drawback in going to church with her mother. It was likely that she'd see Robert's mom. And sure enough, as soon as she entered the building, there were Dorothy and Nancy, engaged in an animated conversation. They spotted Kristy immediately and waved her over.

"I was just telling Nancy how angry I was to hear about what Zach did." Dorothy shook her head. "I'm sorry. I don't know what's gotten into him lately."

Her mom's tight smile told her she was none too happy to have heard the whole sordid story from Dorothy rather than from Kristy's own mouth. Kristy gave her mom a side-armed hug and greeted Dorothy. "Don't worry about it. It was a misunderstanding, I'm sure." The twerp. She hoped he'd gotten his bike taken away. Or whatever it was that would hurt the most.

"He's very sorry," Dorothy said.

A throat cleared behind her and she turned to see Zach, looking anything but sorry. If possible, he was glowering more than last week. "Sorry," he mumbled.

"Apology accepted," Kristy said with more cheer than she felt.

"I'm so relieved that you're not mad," Dorothy said as she put an arm around Zach.

"Don't worry about it." Time for a change of topic. No use rehashing her humiliation with them. "Since y'all live so close to the park, you might want to be on the lookout for a vandal," Kristy said. "Someone spray-painted two of the monuments recently."

"Who would do a thing like that?" Dorothy asked.

"We have no idea. But it makes me so mad." Disgust made her voice vehement.

Her mom chuckled. "Can you tell Kristy loves that park? She can't stand to see anyone even litter in it, much less vandalize the monuments."

"I can imagine. If I see anything strange, I'll let you know." Dorothy squeezed Zach's shoulder. "And so will Zach." She waved at someone who'd just come through the door. "Oh, there's Bonnie. I need to catch her about our ladies' night."

Dorothy and Zach hurried off in opposite directions.

Nancy raised one eyebrow at her daughter. "Why didn't you tell me you had a date with Robert? And don't try changing the subject with me, because it won't work."

Kristy groaned. "Well, as you can see, I actually didn't have a date with him, so I guess it doesn't matter."

"Doesn't matter" was apparently very subjective. Nancy's glare quickly made it apparent that it mattered a great deal to her. "Kristy, we spoke several times last week. You could've mentioned it."

Kristy ducked her head. "I'm sorry. Really. I tried not to make a big deal out of it. I figured I'd give a report after the fact."

Her mom shrugged, and Kristy noticed what might have been a glimmer of sympathy in her eyes. "Since there was no fact to report after, I guess I'll have to assume you'd have at least told me if there had been."

Kristy couldn't keep from smiling a little at her convoluted sentence. Nancy finally broke into a smile, too, and Kristy could tell she was willing to let it slide. "But at least let it be known that I kept my end of the bargain and agreed to go out with him when he called. Well, actually when Zach called."

"True."

They followed the crowd and took a seat in a pew at the back.

Ironically, the sermon was about forgiveness. Something Kristy knew she needed a little extra help with these days. In fact, she felt like there may as well be a spotlight shining directly on her so everyone would know who needed this sermon the most. She promised herself she would study up on forgiveness this week.

After the closing prayer, they made their way to the foyer.

"I need to go to the kitchen to pick up a casserole dish of mine." Nancy held out her purse and Bible. "Will you wait on me here?"

Kristy took her things. "Sure."

As she sat on a bench outside the sanctuary, she heard someone call her name.

Startled, she looked up into Robert's green eyes.

"Mind if I sit here?" He gave her a tentative grin.

She shrugged. "Sure."

He sat down and regarded her intently. "Look, Kristy. I came here today hoping you'd be here. I want to apologize again for my brother. If I'd known you were expecting me, I would've been there with bells on."

"It's fine. Don't worry about it."

"And there's something you should know. When I came out to the park the other day, it was actually with the intention of asking you to dinner. I had no idea my brother had beaten me to it."

It took a few seconds for her to digest the information. "I'm sure Zach didn't mean any harm." She decided it would be best to brush off his other comment.

"I was thinking." Robert looked uncomfortable. "Do you have lunch plans?"

Before she could tell him she'd already made plans to go to lunch with her mother, Nancy breezed over, casserole dish in hand.

"Hello, Robert." She was all smiles as he graciously stood to greet her. "Kristy, I'm not going to be able to have lunch with you after all. I've got to go to the grocery store and make a casserole before tonight. Joy Shupp has been sick with the flu, and I'm supposed to take supper to her family."

Before Kristy could blink, Nancy had grabbed her Bible and purse from the bench, said good-bye, and exited the building. Suddenly, she was very aware that Robert was watching her, waiting for an answer to his lunch invitation.

"Well. I guess I'm free for lunch after all." No way out of it.

"Great." He smiled again.

He ushered her out to his car. A Honda Accord. Practical. Safe. Kind of like her impression of him. There were worse things to be than practical and safe. Number twenty-two on the anti-Mark list: *He wanted a motorcycle even though I was terrified of them.*

"Anywhere in particular you'd like to go?" Robert asked as they left the church parking lot.

"Hagy's is my favorite place around here."

Robert glanced at the clock on the car radio. "We're getting a bit of a late start to go there. It'll be packed on a Sunday. How about we go for pizza? There's a great buffet place right near here."

"That's great with me. Pizza sounds yummy." Truthfully, Kristy hated the thought of eating buffet food. She always thought about all the people who'd breathed on the food she was about to eat. That little plastic germ guard didn't fool her. She was sure the germs would find a way through somehow.

Kristy tried to think of something to talk about. Nothing was worse than an uncomfortable silence. They passed Uptown, a restaurant on Savannah's main drag.

"Have you ever eaten at Uptown?" she asked.

"Only a couple of times. It was good."

"I go there a lot for lunch. It's such a neat atmosphere."

"Maybe we can go there sometime."

"Maybe." *Slow down, buddy. Let's just see how today goes first.*

At the pizza place, she cringed at the crowded parking. They may as well have gone to Hagy's. It looked like they might be in for a wait, which meant more awkward conversation. Sure enough, the hostess said it would be at least ten minutes.

She followed Robert to a vacant bench outside the restaurant.

"So." Robert looked over at her inquisitively. "Do you enjoy being a park ranger?"

"Yeah. I've always loved history, and I grew up here, so I've always had a soft spot for Shiloh as well. Plus, it's a beautiful place to live."

He nodded. "It is. I'm glad Mom and Zach moved to the area. I think it's good for him to live in a rural area. Keeps him out of trouble." He glanced at her and apparently remembered the prank call. His face reddened. "Or, at least, too much trouble."

"I'm over it, Robert."

He looked doubtful.

"I mean it. Chalk my generosity of spirit up to a good sermon about forgiveness, but your brother has a clean slate with me." Kristy didn't dwell on how much easier it was to forgive an adolescent prank than other, more serious matters. She smiled at him. "How about you? My mom said you're an accountant?"

He grinned. "Sounds boring, doesn't it? I've always been a numbers guy. I was an accounting and finance major. Believe it or not, there's a lot of satisfaction when the numbers all come out right."

She'd sensed that about him. He seemed like the kind of guy who liked things balanced.

"How do you feel about motorcycles?" She could see he was taken aback by the question.

"I feel like you'd have to be a little reckless to drive one. And I'd be worried about the insurance."

Good answer, Robert. Score one for you.

"Aaron, party of two." The announcement over the loudspeaker saved her from having to explain her random inquiry.

They followed the hostess to their table, greeting several families from church along the way.

"I guess this is the place to be on a Sunday afternoon." Robert pulled her seat out for her, and she slid into the chair.

"It's one of them at least."

"Do you know what you want, or do you need a minute?" the waitress asked.

Robert looked at her inquisitively, and she nodded.

"I think we're ready," he said. "I believe we both want the buffet." He sent Kristy an inquiring look.

"Um, actually, I think I'll just have a personal pizza." She didn't want to tell him that she hated buffets. "I love the crust on those."

"What topping?" the waitress asked, clearly put off that someone didn't want the buffet.

"Pineapple."

Robert gave her a questioning gaze.

"You can go on to the buffet," the waitress told Robert. "And your personal pineapple will be out in a minute." She turned on her heel and walked into the kitchen.

"I'll wait until your pizza comes," Robert said. "I didn't realize you wouldn't want the buffet, or I wouldn't have suggested this place."

"It's fine. Their personal pizzas are yummy."

The sudden silence at the table was too much for Kristy. "So you live in Jackson?" *Aargh*. She hated first dates. And in spite of her internal protests, this was definitely a date.

Robert didn't seem to mind the predictable question. "I moved to Jackson after college and have been there ever since. It's grown a lot these past couple of years, but I think it still has sort of a small-town feel."

Kristy nodded. "I usually drive over there every week or so, for shopping and groceries." Jackson was about an hour away. "I have several friends who live near there, too."

"It's a good place to be. I'm happy there." He cleared his throat. "I'm house hunting, as a matter of fact."

"That's very exciting."

"It's a little daunting, actually. There are so many options, and it's such a big decision."

"Yeah. I know exactly what you mean." When she and Mark had first started looking at houses together, she'd thought they'd never agree on one.

"Do you plan on putting down roots here?" he asked.

She hated to explain about her recent demotion. And although his mother had probably filled him in on her getting left at the altar, she had no desire to share personal information. "Maybe. We'll see. For now, I'm content with park housing. I'm close to work and it's not too expensive."

The waitress arrived with her pizza and their drinks before she could exercise any more of her rusty social skills.

Robert stood. "I'll be right back." He strode toward the crowded buffet bar and began loading his plate.

He grinned a moment later as he sat down. There were several different types of pizza on his plate. "You know, the only thing about buffets is knowing how many people have breathed on your food." He picked up a slice of pepperoni pizza and bit into it.

At least Kristy could see that they did have a few things

Annalisa Daughety

104

in common. And unlike her, Robert seemed very relaxed. He appeared to be the kind of guy who didn't get wound up too easily. Kind of even-keeled. She was relieved when he kept the conversation going. Not lively chatter, but a steady stream of getting-to-know-you talk. The biggest surprise was that she soon found herself having fun. And although Kristy would never tell her, maybe her mother had been right after all.

CHAPTER 18

Kristy swung by Wal-Mart on her way home for a few items that the Four Star General Store didn't carry. Near the counter, there was a special display of flats of impatiens. She stopped the cart and gently reached out to touch a bloom. Yard work had always relaxed her.

One of the things she'd been most excited about when she and Mark had gone house hunting was looking at the yards and imagining what she would do. She picked up three flats of flowers and slid them into the basket. She didn't need Mark to have a beautiful yard. As she stood in the checkout, she suddenly remembered a poem that had adorned Vickie's wall during college. She couldn't remember the exact words, but it had said something about planting one's own garden and not waiting on anyone else to bring flowers. That was good advice.

When Kristy pulled into her carport, Sam's cute face popped up in the living room window. If she ever forgot to raise the blinds for him when she left, he'd tear them down. He gave her the doggy version of a smile through the windowpane as she passed by. See that? She had someone waiting for her every time she came home.

Who needed a husband?

Loud yapping was punctuated by the ringing phone, and she struggled with the keys trying to get inside to answer it.

Despite Sam's determination to get right in her path, she somehow managed to make it across the living room without tripping over him in her heels. "Hello?" She slipped the high heels off of her aching feet and sank down into the recliner.

"Kristy. I'm so glad I caught you." Sarah's words were clipped. Her sister didn't sound glad, but Kristy opted to give her the benefit of the doubt.

"I wanted to make sure you knew that we'll be coming to Savannah for the Fourth of July. We're celebrating Emma's second birthday at the same time we celebrate Mom's." Sarah and her husband, Andrew, lived in Little Rock, Arkansas, near his parents. They made the four-hour drive to Sarah's Tennessee hometown a few times a year. But only when it didn't interfere with their schedule.

"I'll put it on my calendar. How are the kids?"

"Oh, you know. Emma is a chatterbox, and Walker just learned to crawl. He's growing so fast."

"I'd love to see pictures if you get a chance."

"Sure. I'll try and e-mail some recent ones next week. I've been horribly busy lately with Emma in Mother's Day Out and Walker getting into everything. Plus, we're redoing the kitchen, so that's just taken up tons of time."

"That's fine. Just whenever you have a spare moment."

Sarah laughed. "Those are few and far between. Maybe you'll understand someday."

Well, that didn't take very long. Ever since Sarah got married, she'd made it a point to remind Kristy of how different their lives had turned out. When she began having children, it got even worse. To hear Sarah tell it, because Kristy was single, she couldn't fathom the responsibilities that came with her life. In fact, when Kristy had announced her engagement, Sarah didn't offer congratulations and excitement. Instead, she'd commented that she was glad Kristy's "real" life was finally starting and cautioned her about a ticking biological clock. And people wondered why the two of them weren't close. "Right. Someday." Kristy was in no mood for an argument, but she also wasn't going to listen to her sister anymore. "Thanks for calling, Sarah. I'll see you next month." By the time she hung up, she was seething. Sarah knew just how to push her buttons.

CHAPTER 19

Kristy took out her frustration on the dirt. There was no need to borrow a tiller. Once an angst-filled park ranger was let loose in the flower bed, even the toughest weeds didn't have a chance. Sam watched with interest through the window, barking every now and then to make sure his presence was remembered. By the time she pulled up the last weed, she felt a little calmer. She wiped the sweat from her forehead and sat back to admire the freshly worked dirt ready to plant. The possibilities were endless.

She began digging holes in the dirt and setting the impatiens into place and couldn't stop her mind from wandering back to the trouble with her sister. Sarah thought she had the perfect life. If she wanted to, she could probably have a team of gardeners on standby to make sure her blooms were color-coordinated with her latest kitchen remodel.

"Don't let her get to you," Kristy muttered to herself as she worked to get back a happy attitude. "It's not worth it. And at least you aren't too busy to know the enjoyment of planting your own flowers."

It wasn't until the third plant was in the ground that she

started to feel better. Sarah was just being herself. Her *new* self. The past few years, every time Kristy reached her boiling point with Sarah, their mother had been there to remind her of the past. *Just be thankful she's turned out the way she has,* her mother had said more than once.

Sarah was barely a year younger, but at times, especially during their teens and early twenties, it had seemed they were from different planets. Where Kristy was conservative, whether it be in dress or action, Sarah was outlandish. Wild.

Looking back, Kristy couldn't even remember all of the scrapes Sarah had been in. And if there'd been a bad boy within a mile radius, he'd somehow found his way into her life. Church didn't help; college made it worse. Even now, Kristy was amazed that their mother had been able to keep her composure. Even sending Sarah to live with their dad for a summer didn't help straighten her out.

During Kristy's senior year of college, she'd brought a group of friends home for a weekend. In that group was Andrew Parker. A humble Bible major from Arkansas, Andrew was in school to be a youth minister. Sarah, despite Kristy's loud protests, came home that weekend, too. Kristy had been horrified. She'd been afraid Sarah would embarrass her in front of her friends, a rather tame group who preferred playing board games and renting movies to going out to clubs or bars. She'd just known Sarah would get in front of them and dress outrageously or say something off-color.

So it was no wonder that she'd been completely shocked when she went into the kitchen for a refill of tea and found Sarah and Andrew deep in conversation at the kitchen table. From that point on, Sarah had straightened up. She'd apologized to their mother and rededicated herself at church. Sarah and Andrew married a few years later, and ever since, Sarah had been leading a normal life.

At first, Kristy had been thrilled. She thought she finally had her sister again, and they'd be close like when they were kids.

But instead, Sarah took every opportunity to rub her happiness in Kristy's face. It was almost as if Sarah was a different person toward Kristy than she was to everyone else. And Kristy wasn't quite sure which version was real.

At least she lives far away and we don't have to see each other much.

A loud knocking sound brought her back to reality, and she looked up. Sam was practically throwing himself against the window and barking his head off, his eyes trained on the driveway. Kristy looked behind her to see what had his attention.

Someone was standing at the edge of her yard, watching her work.

⊙⊙

Ace wished he'd just walked on by without stopping. He probably would have, except that Sam had spotted him and alerted Kristy. "Is this a bad time?" he asked, walking over to the freshly dug flower bed where she was kneeling.

"No. I'm just planting flowers." She sat back on her heels and dusted the dirt off her hands.

"They look nice." He smiled down at her and shielded his eyes from the sun.

"Is something wrong? Did the vandal hit again?" She stood up and brushed the dirt from her knees. With her T-shirt, shorts, and blond ponytail sticking out of a baseball cap, she looked sporty. Like the kind of girl who could run a marathon or beat him in tennis. And despite the smudge of dirt on her cheek, Ace was mesmerized.

"No. Nothing's wrong. I dropped Owen off at the visitor center and ended up hanging out there for a while. Then I thought I'd walk down here and see if you wanted me to take a look at your fence." He walked up to the window and pecked on it where Sam looked out at him, still excited to have a visitor.

111

"Why was Owen with you today? It's not his day off." She gathered the empty flower containers and placed them inside one of the trash cans sitting at the side of the house.

"He took his lunch break early and went with me to church." Ace tapped again at Sam.

She looked at him with wide eyes. "Oh?"

"Yeah." He shrugged. "We went out for steaks last night, and I asked him if he attended services anywhere. He said he hadn't in a long time, so I invited him to go with me." He wished he knew what she was thinking.

"Wow. That's great. He stopped going after his wife died." She put the lid on the trash can. "It's odd, isn't it? How, for some people, the death of a loved one brings them closer to God, but for others, it seems to take them further away."

Ace had been one of the latter at first, so he could at least empathize with Owen. Blaming God had been the easy way out. Except that once he turned his back on his faith, his entire life seemed devoid of meaning. Thankfully, he'd gotten back on the right track. And now maybe he could help Owen find the way.

"Yes. But I guess sometimes people don't always cope with things in the right way. Owen seemed happy to be there this morning, though. I'm pretty sure he'll go again sometime." He glanced over at her. "And you're welcome to come with us if you ever want to. Since I moved here, I've been going to church in Jacks Creek. It's a small church, but the people are wonderful. They're all really friendly and made me feel right at home." Jacks Creek was a small community about twenty minutes away. He'd stumbled upon the church one afternoon as he was driving around trying to adjust to his new surroundings.

"I go to church in Savannah. I used to attend the church here until. . ." She trailed off, and a touch of sadness flashed across her face. "Until recently, when I started going with my mother. But thanks for the invite."

He figured he knew why she was attending a different church. "No problem. So, anyway, do you want me to take a look at your fence?" he asked, suddenly uncomfortable. He didn't want to force his friendship on her. Was it just because she didn't like him that he was so drawn to her? He almost wished he could be sure that was it. Less chance of getting his heart broken that way.

She hesitated long enough to make him nervous. Maybe this wasn't his best idea. So much for spontaneity. He opened his mouth to retract the offer.

Before he could speak, she looked up at him. "I'd actually be glad for you to look at it if you're sure you don't mind."

"Great. Just let me run home and change into work clothes first." He motioned toward his crisp khakis and navy-and-red-striped polo shirt. "These are my good clothes, and I'd better not mess them up. I'm not used to the concept of having to drive quite a ways to get to a store. And since most of my wardrobe is gray and green, I don't have an abundance of dressy clothes." Inwardly, he groaned. Could he be any more of a geek? Like she cared about his wardrobe.

She smiled, and Ace was pretty sure it was the first genuine smile she'd ever given him.

"I understand completely. It's the plight of the park ranger. Why have a lot of clothes when you wear the same uniform every day?" She treated him to another grin.

"Exactly. See you in a bit, then." He watched as she went inside and heard her call to Sam as she closed the door.

Finally. He felt a small victory as he walked back to the visitor center. Maybe he could show her that even though he'd taken her job, her office, her paycheck, oh, and lest he forget, her Junior Ranger Program, he wasn't such a bad guy after all.

CHAPTER 20

Kristy grabbed a bottle of water from the fridge and held it against her forehead. Why had she agreed to let him look at her fence? She could probably fix it herself. But during this morning's sermon about forgiveness, Ace's face had been one of the many that had flashed through her mind. So even though she wasn't happy he had her job, she knew she should at least try to get along with him. After all, it wasn't his fault.

Sam's wild barking announced Ace's return.

She peeked through the blinds and saw him, still sitting in the cab of his truck. Hoisting Sam in her arms, she stepped outside and sat on the porch swing. Ace unloaded various tools and equipment out of his truck. This was a man ready for anything. He'd probably been a Boy Scout as a kid.

"Wow. I didn't know you were such a handyman kind of guy," she called.

"There's a lot you don't know about me." He looked up from his toolbox and met her gaze. "Maybe we can change that."

Kristy felt a blush rise up her face. Did he just flirt with her, or was it her imagination? Since her flirting skills were a little rusty, she decided to chalk it up to imagination. But even so, she walked through the house and out onto the back deck. Just in case he needed any help.

In the backyard, Ace immediately found the spot where Sam could shimmy underneath. He dropped his tools down and started working.

Kristy watered every plant on her deck, the hardy ones more than once. Then she snagged a broom from the small plastic closet against the wall and started sweeping. Slowly. Occasionally, she couldn't help it if Ace came into her line of vision. Seeing the backyard was an occupational hazard of sweeping the back deck.

Sam had no inhibitions, and he scampered around Ace, running over his tools and even his legs. Kristy couldn't help but notice how patient Ace was with the hyperactive pup.

"Can I get you something to drink? All I have is sweet tea and bottled water." Martha Stewart she might not be, but she could at least get him a drink.

"Tea would be great. I'm starting to get used to perpetually sweet tea." He grinned at her and brushed the sweat off his tanned forehead. "And I think this little guy might need a drink, too."

They both looked at Sam, who happily ran in circles around Ace's toolbox, his pink tongue hanging out and his stubby tail wagging. He loved nothing more than having an audience.

The front doorbell rang just as she got the pitcher of tea out. She set it carefully on the counter. She went months with no company; then suddenly today her house was the place to be. She put her eye up to the peephole and bit back a gasp.

Mark was standing on her front porch, holding an envelope in his hand.

⊙⊙

The second doorbell ring shook Kristy back to reality. She took a deep breath and steadied herself against the door. Her heart was pounding so hard, she was sure Mark could hear it even through the heavy wooden door. This day certainly wasn't turning out the way she'd planned. But then again, lately they rarely did.

Ace stepped through the back door just as the doorbell sounded a third time. He looked at her frozen form inquisitively and opened his mouth to speak.

Before a sound could escape his lips, Kristy rushed to where he was standing and clasped her hand over his mouth. Her eyes locked with his as she shook her head and silently tried to convey her desperation. Once she was sure he'd gotten the point, she removed her hand. She stood on her tiptoes and whispered in his ear, "Please don't make a sound. I don't want him to know I'm here."

Ace gazed down at her, close enough that she could feel his breath against her face. He bent down and put his lips near her ear. "Don't worry." He reached out and took hold of her trembling arms. "Just breathe. He'll leave soon." Barely a whisper, but she took comfort in the words.

Kristy nodded. She closed her eyes and let Ace hold her steady. Finally, the doorbell ringing stopped. She heard a rustling sound at the door, then the motor of Mark's vehicle.

Ace let go of her arms, and Kristy sank onto the couch. Why today? Why while he was here? Ace set a glass of tea in front of her. "You should probably drink this. You're really pale."

She took a sip and looked up apologetically. "Sorry about that. I'm just not ready to talk to him yet." She looked over at him. "I guess you know who that was, right?"

He nodded. "I've heard about what happened. I'm sorry." He sat on the overstuffed chair across from her. "Do you want to talk about it?"

"I just wish you hadn't seen me react like that. I'm not usually so weak." She took another sip of tea and set her glass down on the mahogany coffee table. "It was a surprise for him to show up here, and if there's one thing I'm not a fan of anymore, it's surprises."

"I guess I can't blame you."

"So anyway. . ." Kristy trailed off, her cheeks flushed with embarrassment at the scene Ace had just witnessed. "He sent me an e-mail a couple of days ago, saying he'd be in the area visiting family. I didn't respond, though. I never thought he might stop by. He probably only wanted to see if I still had any of his stuff. Or something like that."

Ace nodded. "But you know, I think I heard him leave something out there. Do you want me to see what it is?"

"No. I'll do it. Thanks, though." No need for him to get any more involved.

Sam's bark let them know he was ready to be let in.

Kristy opened the patio door, and the dog bolted inside, headed for the water bowl.

"I finished the fence." Ace motioned toward the backyard. "The little guy shouldn't be making any quick escapes now."

"Thank you. I really appreciate your helping out. And again, I'm sorry about. . .before. . .with Mark."

"It's not a problem. I'd be glad to help you any way I can. And don't give it a second thought. We've all been in situations like that before. Well, maybe not exactly like that, but you know what I mean." This time, his grin showed a tiny dimple Kristy hadn't noticed before. "Let me just get my tools, and I'll be out of your way." He strode through the patio door and into the yard, Sam at his heels.

Kristy watched from the patio as he collected his things. She wished she didn't care what he thought about her. But for some reason, the fact that he'd seen her fall apart at the thought of facing Mark made her feel sick. Throughout the whole ordeal with Mark, no one had seen how shaken up she was. Even her mother had assumed she was dealing fine with the breakup because of her stoic exterior. But to Kristy, it was just the best way to keep it together. It would've been easy to break down and cry to her family or friends. But she couldn't stand the thought of them pitying her more than they probably already did. So she'd held the tears inside, put on a brave face, and waited until she was alone to let her emotions go. And although today there were no tears in front of Ace, she was sure she'd worn her feelings on her sleeve.

"I'll just go out through the gate," he called. "Enjoy your day off tomorrow. See you at work on Tuesday."

"Thanks again."

As soon as Ace's truck pulled out of the driveway, Kristy flung open her front door to see what Mark had left behind. An envelope with her name on it lay halfway underneath the welcome mat. She reached down and grabbed it, wondering what else Mark had to say to her. In her opinion, his actions had already said it all.

Curiosity overtook her, and she tore into the envelope, shaking the contents onto the couch. Three savings bonds in her name were paper-clipped together, her name on a sticky note on the top one. She looked inside the envelope. No note or anything. Her grandparents had given her the savings bonds several Christmases ago, and Mark had insisted on putting them in his safe-deposit box because he said she'd lose them. Number eighteen on the list. *He always said I was scatterbrained and made fun of me for losing my keys and other items.*

Kristy's irritation bubbled to the surface. He could've easily just mailed them to her. But no. He'd probably come today expecting to see her still beaten down and broken. Maybe he thought she would beg him back or something. Now she was even more certain of her earlier decision not to open the door.

CHAPTER 21

Ace hadn't slept well the night before. His dreams were laden with images of a casket sprinkled with yellow daisies and a blond figure running from Rhea Springs. He didn't need a shrink to tell him who'd been on his mind last night. Caroline as usual, but Kristy was a new character in his dream world.

Pulling his truck into the visitor center parking lot, he glanced through the trees toward her house. After yesterday's near run-in with Mark, he wondered how she was doing. And what it was that Mark had left for her on the porch.

"Mornin', man." Owen greeted him as he came through the door.

"Good morning." Ace put his hat up on the stand and joined in the necessary activities to open the center.

Matthew came around the corner, holding the movie remote. "The theater is ready," he announced.

"Great." Ace glanced in the seasonal office. "Hey, Mason," he called.

Mason looked up from the binder he was reading and waved in greeting.

Ace stepped through the swinging doors to the front desk. It looked like they were nearly ready to open.

Owen whistled a few bars of "Rocky Top" as he closed the cash register drawer.

"You're in a chipper mood." Ace slid his master key into the front door and unlocked the bolt. They were ready for business.

"It might be your Monday, but it's my Friday." Owen chuckled.

"Right." In order to stay open seven days a week, the rangers' days off were staggered. "Big plans?"

"Heading to Knoxville to visit my mama. I'm hitting the road as soon as I'm off work."

"Sounds fun."

Monday was typically a slow day at Shiloh, as the small number of visitors attested. Ace was relieved to get out of the building to lead a walking tour.

"Welcome to the Shiloh National Cemetery." This was only the second cemetery walking tour he'd led, and he felt a familiar nervous twinge, especially since Matthew was standing in the back taking notes. Ace had tagged along on a few of Kristy's ranger programs. She was so at ease. He wondered if he'd ever feel like he knew the material the way she did.

"The poem you see on the plaques along the cemetery path is entitled "Bivouac of the Dead" by Theodore O'Hara. It is the only poem of sorts allowed in any national cemetery. The interesting part is that Mr. O'Hara was a Confederate. So while his poem may lie between the hallowed walls of the cemetery gates, he himself cannot." Ace had incorporated some of the tidbits he'd heard Kristy relay to the visitors into his own program. He knew she would only see that as unfair copying, but he hoped maybe at some point she could see it as flattery.

The visitors followed him dutifully along the cemetery path, asking questions and stopping to take photos. Before he knew it, it was time to wrap it up and head back to the visitor center. His next program wasn't scheduled until late in the afternoon, and he was looking forward to spending some time in the library. He'd spent the weekend reading about the battle and the formation of the park, but there were other details he was interested in learning more about.

"Learning about the generals here, huh?" Owen asked later as Ace emerged from the library, book in hand.

"Yep. I know the basics of who was here but am hoping this will tell me more about them."

"Good idea. As you learn more, we'll increase your program load. And have you given any thought to the Junior Ranger Program?"

The Junior Ranger Program was the thorn in his side. He wanted nothing to do with it, considering it was Kristy's pet project. But he'd never been one to shirk duty. "I've been looking over it. I think there are a couple of changes I'd like to make, but it looks pretty good to me." He knew she was going to have a fit, but he felt like some of the activities required of kids trying to earn a Junior Ranger badge were too hard.

"Good luck with that." Owen snickered and walked back into his office.

Guess Owen knows a touchy subject when he sees one. Ace looked down at the book he'd just checked out of the park library. Would this one have the information he needed?

Kristy frowned at the notice posted on the bulletin board. Big red letters told her there was to be another stakeout. It seemed the monument bandit had struck again. What luck she had.

"What's the deal?" she asked Hank as he came through the back door.

"This time they hit the Kentucky Monument. Arnie is fit to be tied. We're short-staffed right now, too. With Steve out of the country and Owen in Knoxville, we'll all have to be extra diligent."

"What's the plan?" she asked.

"He wants you and Ace to cover the Bloody Pond tonight. Arnie and I will be out at Fraley Field. It seems like the vandal is striking pretty late. We'll be out from ten until midnight."

She groaned.

"Sorry, kid. Just focus on all that overtime pay." Hank guffawed as though he'd made a funny joke while he made his way to the staircase leading to his office.

"Bad news?"

She turned to face Ace, who was leaning against the door frame of her former office. "I guess we'll be staking out again tonight."

He nodded. "It looks that way. I can come pick you up if you'd like."

Kristy shrugged. "Don't worry about it. I'll meet you in the parking lot. Fifteen till ten?"

"Sounds good. If you change your mind, though, I'd be glad to swing by."

She smiled despite herself. "Thanks for the offer, but I'll just walk down."

The phone was ringing as she unlocked her door after work. After a back-and-forth dance with Sam, she finally reached the phone.

"Hello."

"Kristy?"

"Yes." Sam jumped into her lap and got a good lick in on her face before she could move from his reach.

"It's Robert. How are you?"

"I'm doing great. How about you? Any luck with the house hunt?"

"I'm still looking. I've at least narrowed down neighborhoods."

She grabbed Sam's favorite toy from a wicker basket next to the couch and threw it across the room. He leaped from her lap to fetch it. "That's great."

"I wanted to tell you what a good time I had at lunch the other day. And I thought maybe if you're free one night this week, we could go to dinner. If you want to, that is." Despite the even tone of his voice, uncertainty came through the line.

Kristy thought for a moment. Robert was a nice, dependable guy. Maybe her heart didn't pound when she was near him, but she had enjoyed their time together on Sunday. "Dinner sounds nice. I actually have to work some nights this week, but not until later. So if you don't mind an early dinner, any night would be fine with me." Hopefully tonight would be the night they caught the vandal, and she would be spared of many more hours alone with Ace.

"How about Friday? Say, seven?"

"Sounds great. See you then." *And you'd better show up this time.*

CHAPTER 22

Ace paced beside the pickup truck. They were supposed to be in place in five minutes or Mr. Bramblett would be grumbling. Where was she? He checked his watch one more time and shook his head.

Jumping in the truck and driving to her house tempted him, but he had a feeling there was no better way to get their night off on the wrong foot. Finally, he spotted a figure coming up the path. *It's about time.*

"Did you forget? I know you aren't looking forward to this, but both of us will be at fault if we're late."

"Sorry." She rushed over to the truck and climbed in the passenger seat.

No arguments over who'll drive? What's going on here? Ace had been fully prepared to insist on driving this time, especially after her lead foot last week.

"I had some trouble at home."

He glanced over at her as he headed the truck toward the Bloody Pond. She was definitely upset about something; he could see it on her face. "What happened?"

"I'm not sure. You know those flowers I planted the other day?"

"Yeah. They looked nice."

"Well, something dug them up. Every last flower, root and all, is gone. Do you know of any animal that eats impatiens?"

"Maybe a raccoon?" He had no idea but hated to admit it. Wildlife wasn't his area of expertise.

"I don't know. They were there when I got home from work, because I remember looking at them and thinking they were pretty. But when I let Sam out, I happened to see the empty space in the flower bed. I took a flashlight and looked all around the house." She sighed. "But I didn't see a trace of the flowers, or of a critter. It just makes me so mad."

"I think there are some traps in Steve's office. You can set one out and see what kind of animal you come up with. I'll help you release it if you end up catching something." He parked the truck along the side of the road, the pond visible in the distance.

"Thanks. I may do that tomorrow." She drummed her fingers on the truck door and gazed out the window.

Ace rolled the windows down. "I brought some mosquito repellent." He handed her the orange bottle.

"Thanks. I always know summer is finally here when the mosquitoes come out." Kristy hopped out of the truck and sprayed her arms and legs. "Here you go." She threw the bottle across the pickup bed to the driver's side, where he stood waiting to catch it.

Once they were back inside the truck, a long silence ensued. Ace felt like each minute dragged on for an hour. He looked over at Kristy. Did she think the silence was awkward? She probably hated being stuck out here with him. He'd been happier than normal all day and had known the reason behind his happiness. It was the prospect of spending time alone with her. Ever since the day he'd fixed her fence, he couldn't get her off his mind. He wished she'd at least give friendship with him a fair chance.

"Look, Kristy. About the other day. . ." He trailed off.

"I really don't want to talk about it. Mark had some of my things he needed to drop off, that's all. I'm just sorry I acted like such a baby." She didn't look at him as she spoke. Instead, she focused on the radio that lay in her hand, ready for use in case they saw anything out of the ordinary.

"Not a problem." He shifted in his seat. "I've got an idea. I know this isn't exactly a fun way to spend an evening, trapped in a truck with the guy who has your job and all." He looked over at her and was pleased to see her lips turn upward a tiny bit. Finally. "Who knows how many nights Mr. Bramblett is going to have us out here, though. So I was thinking. We need a way to pass the time."

She looked at him with interest. "And what exactly do you propose?"

"I used to hang out in coffee shops a lot, believe it or not. There is nothing better than a good cup of coffee and long conversation. Anyway, some friends and I used to play a game every time we met at the coffee shop. I was thinking maybe you and I could play."

"If you suggest we play Truth or Dare, I'm getting out of this truck right now and walking home."

He laughed. "Not Truth or Dare. It's actually a game we made up. We called it the one-question game."

"Go on." She turned toward him and propped her elbow on the back of the seat.

"The theory is this: In every relationship, no matter what the circumstance, whether you've known the person for a day or for a decade, there is always one question you want to ask them. Nothing is off limits. The only rule is that you have to answer honestly. You can go into as much or as little detail as you want. And the person who does the asking has to answer the same question." He raised one eyebrow at her. "Are you in?"

She gave a loud sigh. "I guess. It's better than just sitting here."

"Great. Do you want to ask first, or do you want me to?"

"Since you're the inventor of the game, I'll let you do the honor. But be gentle. Don't ask anything too hard at first." She smiled at him.

Ace leaned his head back against the seat and thought for a moment. There were a million questions he wanted to ask this girl. But the limited knowledge he had of her told him not to start out with anything too personal. Hopefully they'd build to that later. He sat up and looked over at her. "Okay. I've got it. What scares you? And I don't mean like spiders or snakes. Or animals who eat flowers." He grinned.

She bit her bottom lip and was silent for a moment. "What scares me?" She glanced at him. "That's kind of hard. A lot scares me." She took a deep breath. "I guess waking up one day and completely regretting the choices I've made. Losing my mom. That scares me a lot." She looked thoughtful. "Being separated from God. You know. Sometimes I go through times when my relationship with Him is stronger than other times. It's scary to think about what it would be like if I fell away completely."

He nodded.

"I could probably go on." She smiled. "But I think that's enough for now. And how about you, Mr. Kennedy? What scares you?"

"My, aren't we formal? Well, Miss O'Neal, I also have a long list of scary things. Don't let my macho exterior fool you."

She laughed. "Don't worry, I won't."

"Okay, here goes. Being a disappointment to my family. That's scary. The brevity of life scares me a lot. We take it for granted that we'll be here forever, that we'll have all the chances in the world to do the things we want to do. And life can be wiped out so fast—a speeding car, a crashing plane, a heart attack. And *poof*, it's gone." He shrugged, wondering if she thought he was crazy and surprised that he cared. "And I actually agree with you about fearing being separated from God. I went through a time in my life when I did fall away. I lived every second in fear. I knew I wasn't living right.

And I knew the consequences. Thankfully, I realized my life meant nothing without Him in it." He met her gaze and gave her a slow smile. The tense expression had finally faded from her face. Maybe she was enjoying spending time with him.

Kristy reached up and turned the dome light on. She held her wrist up and checked the time on her watch. "Not too much longer."

Or maybe not. "Do you want to check in with the boss men? See if we get the all-clear to leave our post for the night?"

"Good idea." She reached for her radio.

CHAPTER 23

Kristy cradled the phone to her ear as she loaded the dishwasher. How did one person use so many dishes?

"So what exactly happens on these stakeouts?" Vickie asked. "You just look out the window and wait on something to happen?"

"Pretty much. They don't make us do it every night, but since tonight is Friday, we'll be out there again later. They haven't been all that bad, actually. Ace has this crazy game for us to play while we sit in the truck."

"Game, huh? That sounds fun. . ." She trailed off. "So are you guys friends now, or what?"

"Friends might be pushing it. I've accepted the fact that he has my job. I'm just trying to make the best of an unpleasant situation." Kristy watched Sam out her kitchen window. He was running in little circles, chasing a fly. Silly dog.

"That's very grown-up of you." Vickie laughed. "So what about the church guy? Any news there?"

"Actually, he's taking me to dinner tonight. It'll be an early evening, though." Kristy opened the patio door, and Sam bolted inside.

"Right. Because of the covert undercover operation. With the handsome ranger. Boy, your life is tough."

"Stop it. You make it sound much more exciting than it is. Anyway, I should go. I'm not close to being ready, and Robert should be here soon."

After all the effort she'd put into what she thought was going to be their first date, she couldn't bring herself to get too fixed up for this one. Dark jeans, a red sleeveless sweater, and her favorite black heels would have to do. She raked a brush through her hair and swiped some rose-colored lip gloss on her lips. When the doorbell rang, she was ready.

Outside, Robert walked her around to the passenger side of the Honda and opened the door.

He climbed into the driver's seat and carefully fastened his seat belt. "How does Chinese food sound? There's a pretty good place in Savannah," Robert said once they were out of the driveway.

"That sounds perfect."

Kristy racked her brain trying to think of something to say. Savannah suddenly seemed very far away, and she wished they'd just gone to Hagy's. "Have you had a nice week?" she finally asked.

"It was uneventful." Robert adjusted his rearview mirror. "How about you? Has it been an exciting week at the park?"

"Actually, we're still trying to find out who is vandalizing some of the monuments. Even though the vandal hasn't struck since Memorial Day, the park superintendent is afraid it might happen again soon. So I'll be putting in a lot of extra hours these next few days, on top of my regular schedule. It's not bad, really. And of course, the overtime pay is nice."

Kristy kept a steady stream of small talk going until they reached the restaurant. Finding something to say to him was a lot of work. Or maybe she was just out of practice. She had been out of the dating game for a long time, after all.

Robert finally found a parking spot in front of the China

Garden. Based on the number of cars in the lot, everyone in Savannah must've had a craving for kung pao chicken. The tangy aroma of Chinese food greeted them as they stepped into the packed restaurant. After a twenty-minute wait, they were seated at a table near the kitchen.

"So have you had any more luck with the house hunting?" Kristy asked once their plates were piled high from the buffet.

"I'm actually getting ready to make an offer on one." Robert wiped his mouth with a napkin. "It's a fixer-upper, but I think it has a lot of potential."

"That's great." Kristy concentrated on her food. The conversation wasn't quite as easy as during their impromptu lunch. Maybe the fact that it was a real date made Robert nervous or something. "This food is really good."

Robert shrugged. "I've had better, but for a small town I guess it's okay. My mom is the one who told me about it."

Another long silence passed, and Kristy heard uproarious laughter from an adjacent table. *Too bad we aren't sitting with them.* Time to take a page out of Ace's playbook. "So, Robert, how about we play a game?"

Robert didn't seem too enthused about the one-question game, but he was a good enough sport to go along with it.

Kristy finished explaining the rules. "I'll go first. What scares you?" she asked.

"Tax season. And a stock market crash." Robert chuckled. "How about you?"

Kristy bit her lip and tried not to compare Robert's face-value answer to Ace's articulate and thoughtful one. After all, Robert didn't invent the game. "Oh, you know. Spiders and snakes. Stuff like that."

Robert took a sip of his soda. "Right. A typical girl, huh?" He smiled.

She shrugged. "That's me. Typical." She looked at her watch.

"You know, we're really going to be pushing it to get me back to the park. We're supposed to start our stakeout at nine. Since it's the weekend, Arnie wants us out there earlier than last night." She dabbed at her mouth with her napkin. "So I guess we should go."

"We can't leave until we open our fortune cookies." He passed her the tiny tray. "You first."

She gave him a small smile. Insisting they open their fortune cookies surprised her. And the fact that Robert had done something unexpected was even more astounding. She kept her eyes on him as she tore the plastic wrapper off of the cookie and pulled out the little slip of paper. She looked down at it and grinned. "Your luck is about to change." She brought her gaze back up to meet his. "That's good news. What does yours say?"

He unfolded his own piece of paper. "You will soon find what you are seeking." He snorted. "Sounds like a bunch of hooey to me." He wadded his paper up and threw it on the table. "Let's go."

◎◎

Once again, Ace found himself pacing. And waiting on his blond stakeout partner. Where was she *this* time? Had the neighborhood raccoon eaten some more of her plants? Although he wasn't convinced a raccoon was the culprit.

Headlights in the distance caught his attention. Since it was after dark, no one should be on park grounds now unless they lived here. Or were visiting someone who lived here. A maroon Honda Accord pulled up beside him. Probably someone needing directions. Ace waited for the driver to roll down the window, but instead a well-dressed man emerged from the car. He nodded at Ace and walked over to the passenger side to open the door.

Kristy climbed out, looking embarrassed. "Thanks," she said to the man who stood awkwardly beside the car. She glanced at Ace waiting on the sidewalk. "Sorry," she said sheepishly. "Our dinner ran long."

"Not a problem," he said, stepping toward them. He stuck his hand out. "Ace Kennedy."

The tall guy clasped his hand and shook it firmly. "Robert Aaron. Nice to meet you."

Ace nodded then turned to Kristy. "You ready? We're late."

She looked at Robert. "Thanks for dinner," she said. "I'll see you later."

"Sounds good," Robert said stiffly. He stood there for another second, as if unsure whether it was okay to leave Kristy with Ace or not.

Don't worry, buddy. I'll take care of her.

With another backward glance, Robert finally climbed back into the Honda and drove off.

"Hot date?" Ace asked once they were in the truck. He tried to keep the jealousy out of his voice.

She grimaced. "Dinner. Sorry I was late. I guess everyone was in the mood for Chinese tonight."

"Don't worry about it. You look nice, by the way." He started the ignition and backed out of the parking space. Nice was an understatement. She was beautiful in the green and gray uniform. In her sporty flower-planting clothes, she'd been adorable. But now, all fixed up, she was a knockout. He tried to push the thought out of his head.

"Thanks. I thought I'd have time to run home and change."

"What? You don't enjoy staking out in heels?" He laughed.

"To tell you the truth, I don't especially like *wearing* heels. Much less staking out in them."

Ace slammed on the brakes as they went by the road leading to the residential area. He put the truck in reverse. Maybe there was still time for him to get on her good side.

"You don't have to do that. Really. It's my own fault for being late."

"I don't want you to be uncomfortable. Tonight might be the

night we have to chase on foot. I wouldn't want you getting your heels all stuck in the mud and not being able to get any traction." He pulled up in front of her house. "According to my watch, you've got two minutes before we need to be in place."

She hopped out. "I'll hurry," she called over her shoulder as she ran up to the door.

What was the deal with the Honda guy? Robert, was it? Based on her reaction to Mark showing up on her doorstep, he was pretty sure she hadn't dealt with the breakup yet. So what was she doing on a date with some preppy guy? And how could he get over the jealous feeling growing inside him?

CHAPTER 24

Kristy threw on an old pair of Levis and a Buford Pusser 5K T-shirt. She glanced in the full-length mirror. It wasn't going to put her in the fashion hall of fame, but it would certainly be more comfortable than her date clothes. She slid on her tennis shoes without even untying them and grabbed a ponytail holder from the counter. "Bye, Sam. You're in charge." She patted his head and closed the door behind her.

"So you're a quick-change artist, huh?" Ace asked as she climbed into the truck. "Less than two minutes. Impressive."

She glanced over at him. "You can accuse me of being many things, but high maintenance isn't one of them." She pulled her hair back and quickly wound it into a bun, securing it with the ponytail holder that was around her wrist.

"Yeah, I'm not high maintenance either."

She laughed. "Good to know."

As they backed out, the headlights shone across her yard.

"Wait. Can you stop for a second?" she asked.

He mashed on the brakes. "Did you forget something?"

"No. Look over there." She pointed at the side of her house.

"Did you just see someone standing there?"

Ace maneuvered the truck around so the side of her yard was lit up. No sign of anything strange. "I didn't. Do you think you saw a person?"

She peered out the window, scanning the side yard. "I guess not. It was just for a second, I thought I saw something running. Could've been an animal."

"Doesn't Chief Strong have a cat?" he asked.

"Yes. General Grant." She laughed. "And he does like to explore, so it very well could've been him."

"General Grant the cat? Wow."

She grinned. That cat had been the bane of Sam's existence ever since they'd moved in. It wasn't unusual for her to come home and find General Grant on her porch, locked in a staring contest with Sam through the window. And people say animals don't have personalities.

Ace turned the truck onto the tour route. "So tonight we're supposed to be stationed at Albert Sidney Johnston's death site?"

"Right. And here's a bit of Shiloh trivia for you. A few years ago, the park service had to remove the tree that General Johnston was supposedly propped up against when he died. You'd have thought we'd changed the name of the park. People were outraged."

"It was that big of a deal?" Ace slowed down as they passed the Bloody Pond.

"Seriously. After many, many complaints, we put a little marker up where the tree used to be. But in our defense, the tree was completely rotten and there was nothing else that could be done. It had to be removed."

"Plus, anyone who knows their history knows General Johnston was actually taken down into the nearby ravine by his comrades." Ace pulled the truck as far off the beaten path as possible and cut the engine. They had a clear view of the Johnston Mortuary Monument.

"Well, well. Someone's been studying his history. And what's the lesson we can all learn from the death of the highest-ranked American general in history ever to be killed in battle?"

"Well, first of all, if you have your own personal physician, keep him with you at all times rather than sending him to other areas of the battlefield. And second, if you have a lifesaving tourniquet in your pocket. . .remember to use it!"

"Poor Albert Sidney." Kristy shook her head and unbuckled her seat belt. "But in his defense, he didn't know he'd been hit until it was too late."

"Indeed." Ace turned toward her in the seat. "So, not to be nosy or anything, but how was your date?"

Kristy tensed. "Fine." She shrugged. "We had Chinese food. It was nice." Nice enough anyway. At least Robert would never break her heart. That was one thing she knew for certain.

"Good. Glad you're moving on."

"It was time."

Whip-poor-wills sounded in the distance. Kristy cracked the window, and the truck filled with the faintest scent of honeysuckle. She took a deep breath and leaned her head against the seat. This would've been a perfect evening to sit out on her back porch swing with a glass of tea. *Stupid vandals.*

"You ready for round two of our game?" Ace finally asked.

She sat upright and looked over at him. In the darkness, she could barely make out the shape of his face. "Round two. Sure thing."

He nodded in her direction. "Your turn to ask this time. But remember the rule."

"Okay." She bit her lip. What did she want to know about him? That she didn't mind him also knowing about her? Tricky game. "I've got one. What's your biggest regret?"

He regarded her seriously for a long moment.

"Too tough? I can think of another one if you'd like." She

paused, giving him another minute to think. "What's wrong? Is your life filled with so many regrets you can't narrow it down?"

Ace raked his fingers through his thick brown hair. "Not too tough. And if you must know, I do have a lot of regrets. But I'm learning to get over them."

"Fair enough." She kept an eye on the mortuary monument for a second. Nothing. This stakeout stuff was such a waste of time.

"Remember when I told you I'd lost someone close to me in an accident?"

She nodded. "Yes. And I'm really sorry about driving crazy that night. I didn't know."

"Of course you didn't. How could you? It's not something I talk about much." He shifted in his seat. "Anyway, it was my best friend. Her name was Caroline. We met our freshman year of college and just clicked. You know?"

Kristy nodded that she did, in fact, know.

"Every time some guy would break her heart, she'd cry on my shoulder. She'd give me pointers on how to be a good boyfriend, and we'd even double-date sometimes just so we could check up on the other's significant others." He laughed. "My roommate thought I was crazy for not dating her myself, but I was always afraid of ruining the friendship. After college, we both lived in the same city. We had standing plans every Thursday where we'd talk about our week, celebrate the highs and lows. Looking back, I know now why I never had a successful relationship. How could anyone compete with how close Caroline and I were?"

"That makes sense," Kristy said. "Sometimes there's a fine line between friendship and more."

He nodded. "Anyway, one night over dinner, Caroline was acting weird. She'd just broken up with her boyfriend, so I assumed that was what was bothering her. But I was wrong. At the end of the evening, she grabbed my hand and told me there was something she needed to tell me. She ended up saying that she was in love with me and had been for years, but she'd been waiting on me to make the first move. I was floored. I had no idea she felt that way. I mean, sure, we flirted and all, but I guess I never saw any of the signs. Looking back, they were definitely there. I felt like such an idiot. The problem was that I was afraid of losing my best friend. So I tried just brushing her off. I told her she was probably just feeling down because she was alone and it was nearly Christmas. I could see immediately that I wasn't handling it right. She left, furious with me, and I was just such a stupid guy. The truth was, I didn't know how to handle it. I knew that if she and I got together, it would be the real deal. And at that point in my life, I wasn't ready for that."

Ace shifted in his seat. "I just sat there at the restaurant, trying to figure out what to do. But before I could do anything, the waiter came rushing to my table. Caroline had left the restaurant, and I guess she was so upset, she didn't see the car coming around the corner until it was too late. The guy was speeding, and even though he swerved, he still hit her."

Kristy let out a gasp. "I'm so sorry. I can't imagine how horrible that must've been for you."

Ace nodded. "I went with her to the hospital, but it was too late. At least I was able to talk to her in the ambulance. I told her I loved her, too, which was the absolute truth. I did love her." He met Kristy's gaze. "I did. I just wasn't ready for that kind of love right then. Long story short, she died a few hours later at the hospital. She was a registered organ donor, though, and because of it, she saved the lives of seven people." He smiled. "That was the only bright spot. Caroline would've loved that." He cleared his throat. "So there you have it. One of my many regrets, but definitely the biggest one. I wish I would've known what to say in that moment. That I'd have gone after her immediately. Or that I'd been able to say what she wanted to hear. Anything that would've prevented her from rushing out like that."

"Wow." Kristy fought the urge to reach out and grab his hand. "Ace, that's awful. I don't even know what to say."

He shrugged. "Not a lot anyone can say. But that's my answer. Now your turn."

She could see he was ready to change the subject. Not that she blamed him. It must be tough to shoulder the blame for something like that. Even though she knew Caroline's death wasn't his fault, she could see that he hadn't been able to forgive himself for it. Would he ever be able to let that guilt go? At least her regret didn't involve a loss of life.

"I, too, have a lot of regrets. But I can easily narrow it down to one." She took a deep breath. "I had just turned twenty-five," she began.

CHAPTER 25

Ace hadn't meant to tell her about Caroline. He was always afraid it made him sound like a real jerk. The guy who couldn't say the words the girl needed to hear and ultimately caused her death by his stupidity. But the question had thrown him for a loop. Of course, his biggest regret was not knowing the right words to say on that fateful night. And he figured he might as well tell Kristy the truth. After all, Caroline's death was part of who he was now. He glanced over at Kristy's profile. She had paused her story, as if trying to figure out the right words.

"Having trouble forming sentences?" he asked.

She smiled. "Something like that. Actually, I'm trying to think of how to explain my biggest regret without boring you with too much information. No need to load you down with my life drama."

He laughed. "As you've already heard, my life has some drama of its own. So load away. I can take it." Nothing she could say could be worse than what he'd just told her. She'd have to convince him she was a terrorist or a mobster to put her on the same level as him. And he knew enough about her to know that neither of those things was the case.

"Right. Well, you've probably already guessed that my biggest regret has to do with Mark. But I'll bet it's not in the way you think."

"I thought he probably played into it somehow." He shot an encouraging grin at her. He had figured Mark would be her regret. Probably regret that she'd ever met him or something along those lines.

"Yes. But it actually isn't that I wish I hadn't dated him. I refuse to let myself regret three whole years of my life. That would just be too sad." She sighed. "So all I can do is look at those years as time that was preparing me to be a better, stronger person. I did learn a lot about myself, especially in the aftermath of our relationship."

He nodded. "I'm sure. I think we all find out what we're made of when we face a deep personal crisis. Some of us crash and burn, and some rise from the ashes." He patted the seat between them. "You were definitely in the latter group."

"I don't know about that. I crashed for a while. In fact, I'm still not quite whole. But the regret I feel actually has nothing to do with Mark and everything to do with me. See, the whole time we were together, I took my focus off of everything but him. I let him be first. Over my friends, my family, even my relationship with the Lord." She shook her head. "That's just not the way it's supposed to be."

"True. But sometimes when you're actually in something, you can't see the bad parts of it. A little time and distance provide all kinds of insights that maybe you couldn't see because you were too close to the situation. Kind of a forest-and-trees thing, you know?"

She smiled at him. "I couldn't have said it better myself."

"Well, like I said before, I have lots of regrets. I've learned that I can either let them eat me up, or I can move forward and try not to make the same mistakes." And it was true. If he'd learned anything from Caroline, it was that he was going to let people know how he felt. Even if they didn't want to know. Because you never knew when your window of opportunity would be closed forever.

"So that's my main regret. That I let Mark become the focus of my life. And that I allowed him to use me as his own personal doormat."

He saw her tiny smile in the darkness and was struck by how vulnerable she looked. Normally she exuded a toughness, but tonight he glimpsed the tenderness beneath her surface. What kind of man in his right mind would've treated a girl like her with such disrespect?

CHAPTER 26

"A truce? Call it that if it makes you feel better, but I'd call it something else." Ainsley laughed.

"Stop it. I get what you're implying. And you are way off base. It's that dumb game. Or the darkness. Or the fact that otherwise I have to sit in uncomfortable silence with a man I barely know." Kristy leaned her head back on the porch swing cushion and felt the sun warm her face. "And don't really want to know, for that matter."

"Well, regardless, it certainly sounds like you're getting to know him pretty fast."

"It isn't like that. We're just talking as a way to pass the time. I'm still not a fan of him. You won't believe what Owen told me yesterday." The disgust crept into her voice.

"Enlighten me," Ainsley said.

"Ace is totally screwing up the Junior Ranger Program. He's not following the guidelines and is just giving out badges without even checking up on their paperwork. There are rules to the program for a reason."

"The horror." Ainsley laughed. "Sorry. I can't help it. I know you are a stickler for rules and all, but there are worse things the guy could be doing."

"You don't understand. The program worked perfectly. And I designed it that way. Now he's totally lax about the guidelines. And I can't do anything about it."

"It seems to me that maybe you could just talk to him. Explain your concerns and see what he says. He sounds like a reasonable guy."

And that is just how Ainsley would've handled it. Matter-of-factly. No nonsense. But not Kristy. She'd always admired her friend for being able to face things head-on.

"Right. I'm sure you're right. But the thing is, it isn't my program anymore. I have a little pride, you know."

A loud chuckle came from the other end of the phone. "You do have a little pride. Some might say a little too much."

Kristy rolled her eyes. Even miles away, her friend knew her all too well. "But if I say anything to him about it, he'll just think I'm bitter about everything."

"And?"

"And I'm trying hard not to be. Or at least not to let it show. So I think I'll just try not to think about it."

"Sure. Because that always works so well for you."

Ouch. Kristy still clutched the phone to her ear, but she couldn't speak.

As if she realized she'd gone one step too far, Ainsley gave a sweet self-deprecating chuckle. "Oh, Kristy. You know I'm kidding. If it makes you feel better to try not to think about it, then do that. But you know as well as I do that it's going to bother you until you confront him about it. And you deserve to tell him what you think. You built that program. Before you came along, it didn't exist. And you never know—he might be happy for the input."

Kristy was pretty sure that was doubtful but hated to keep on.

She knew Ainsley was only trying to help. "Thanks for the advice. So, moving along, anything new with you?"

"Nothing much." Ainsley laughed. "I don't have near the escapades you do. I'm just a boring old married lady."

"And you love it."

They said their good-byes, and Kristy busied herself around the house. It was one of those perfect days off. In fact, she was still in the shorts and T-shirt she'd slept in. No makeup on her face and hair in a bun. Once the house was clean, she returned to the deck, this time sitting on the lowest step, watching as Sam happily ran the perimeter of the yard.

If Mark could see her now, she knew what he would say. Number thirty-two on the list: *He hated it when I had lazy days off.* In fact, he accused her of being an unproductive member of society if she hadn't showered and put on makeup by 10:00 a.m. If he could only see her now. She leaned back against the steps, propping herself up on her elbows, and stretched her legs out in front of her. The sun lulled her into a drowsy state, and she began to think back on the past weeks.

Images of her recent life flashed in front of her. Mark down on one knee at his apartment. The sea of guests staring back at her in horror as she announced there wouldn't be a wedding. The honeymoon cruise she'd forced herself to go on, even though it sent the knife deeper into her heart. She'd been sure at that point that she'd never recover from the blow.

She sat up. She was recovering. Maybe not recovered. Yet. But at least she was no longer weepy. And she'd caught herself laughing a few days ago. Really laughing. Not just going through the motions. Owen and Ace had been quite the comedy team as they told her about the night Ace had convinced Owen and several of the maintenance guys to go with him for sushi. "Bait," Ace had laughed. "Henry took one bite, spit it out, and told the waiter in no uncertain terms that he just couldn't eat bait and could he please have a hamburger instead. And to make it well done." Kristy smiled at the memory. Ace had certainly shaken up the park with that little outing.

Several memories of the last few weeks flitted through her mind. She was afraid to admit it, but deep down she knew the handsome ranger had shaken her up a bit, too.

CHAPTER 27

Ace knew he must be out of his mind. It didn't take a rocket scientist to know that Kristy was still reeling from her broken engagement. Plus, it looked like she was seeing that Robert guy on a regular basis now. He'd overhead her telling Owen about a movie they'd gone to see. At least he'd stopped himself from making a wisecrack about Robert. That certainly wouldn't have won him any points with her.

But he couldn't seem to get her off his mind. The way she cheerfully greeted the visitors, so that even the gruffest Civil War buffs left the desk smiling. Or the way even the drab gray and green uniform made her skin glow like that of a cover model. But it was more than all that. She had a quality that drew him to her.

As his grandpa used to say, he was smitten. Not that it mattered. Most days, she ran hot and cold with him. Her demeanor was chilly toward him in the visitor center. He could see it on her face—obvious disapproval of how he handled certain things. But the time they spent alone together in the old pickup was different. She was warm and open. The way she listened to him and asked insightful questions showed that she was interested in what he had to say. Those moments lingered in his mind and made it hard for him to keep his mind on business.

He hadn't been at all sure it was smart to open their stakeouts to personal questions, but given the alternative—silence—it had seemed to be a good idea. And he had nothing to hide. Well, maybe some things, but the odds of her actually asking him the true reason behind his move to Shiloh were slim. He'd chance it if it meant he could get to know her on such a personal level.

He wondered what she'd say if she knew he'd been praying for her every night. Praying that God would heal her of her pain and give her the strength to move on and find His path for her life. He'd found a great verse in Psalm 147. "He heals the brokenhearted and bandages their wounds." Ace thought seriously about sharing that with her but was pretty sure she would deny being brokenhearted.

So it seemed all he could do was wait it out. Slowly get to know her. Become her friend. But if his feelings got any stronger, he was going to have to let her know. If he'd learned anything from Caroline, it was that time was fleeting. And Ace wanted to make sure he didn't leave anything unsaid.

Even if what he had to say might not be anything she wanted to hear.

◎◡◎

Kristy was on time for once. She chalked it up to insomnia. Last night she'd tossed and turned and never felt as if she completely fell asleep. When she glanced at the clock this morning and saw that there were only fifteen minutes left before her alarm went off, she gave up and started her day. Who needs sleep anyway? But she was jealous when she left the house and Sam was still curled up tightly on his plush doggy bed. He at least opened one eye when she said good-bye, but she knew he was likely still lost in dreamland, chasing squirrels and cats.

"Good morning," she called as she entered the visitor center.

A grunt came from Owen's office.

She popped her head inside and raised an eyebrow. "Are we grumpy today?"

He turned toward her, his eyes bloodshot and his hair disheveled. "I fell asleep on the couch last night in front of a Braves game. Hate it when I do that," he grumbled. "Now I have a crick in my neck and a headache."

"I have some aspirin in my purse. And I'll start a pot of coffee."

He grunted again and turned back to his computer.

She threw her things in the seasonal office and noticed that Matthew's backpack was in the middle of the floor. Guess he'd gotten here early, too. Hopefully that meant he'd also begun opening up the center. She'd get to see how well she'd trained him.

Kristy grabbed the carafe from the coffeemaker and took it to the bathroom sink to fill it up. Her mind drifted back to Owen's bloodshot eyes, and she wondered if accidentally falling asleep on the couch was all that was wrong with him. She worried sometimes about him all alone. She remembered when his wife lost her battle with cancer. That was nearly five years ago. And as far as she knew, other than a few dates here and there, he was usually a loner. Hmm.

"Hey, K." Matthew unlocked the visitor center door and nodded in her direction.

She shook her head and smiled. She supposed "K" was better than "Miss Kristy," which was what he'd started out calling her, much to her chagrin. Made her feel like a kindergarten teacher.

"Morning, Matthew. Thanks for getting everything opened."

"Not a problem. We're all set. And guess what?" He followed her to the coffeepot and watched as she poured the water into the coffeemaker.

"What?" She pressed the button and heard the sweet sound of the machine brewing.

"Owen put me on the schedule to do a rifle demonstration today! I get to fire the gun." Matthew beamed, his blue eyes dancing.

"Congratulations. I remember the first time I got to do one by myself. That must mean you've passed the test, huh?" she teased. Owen drilled all the seasonals nonstop about the nine steps it took to load and fire the musket. She was pretty sure that her first summer at Shiloh, she dreamed about those steps.

"Yeah. We did a demo together yesterday, and afterwards, he told me I was ready to go solo. I'm a little nervous, though," he admitted.

"You'll be fine. Just remember to take your time. And if anyone asks a question you can't answer, what do you say?"

"Follow me to the visitor center, and we'll find out together." He grinned.

"I've taught you well, grasshopper."

"Huh?" Confusion washed over his face.

She shook her head. "Never mind. I'm an old lady." She smiled. "But you'll do great. Really."

"Thanks. I hope so."

The bell rang on the front door.

"I'll go take care of them." Matthew hurried off to greet the first visitors of the day.

Kristy poured a cup of coffee and carried it into Owen's office. She set it on the desk in front of him. "Here you go. Maybe this will help."

Owen looked at her through puffy eyes. "Thanks." His voice was gravelly. He shook his head. "I probably should've just called in sick today."

Kristy stepped inside the office and pulled the door closed. Matthew could handle things for a few minutes. She'd seen the look in Owen's eyes, and she recognized it as one she saw sometimes in her own mirror. Something was wrong.

"You okay?"

He shrugged. "Nothing for you to worry about. I'm just having one of those days."

"I see." She waited to see if he wanted to tell her about it. They'd worked together enough years for her to know that sometimes he needed her to be a sounding board.

"It's been five years to the day since I lost Helen. I thought by now maybe I wouldn't hurt so bad over it. But I sure do miss her." He looked up at Kristy. "There's nothing worse than loneliness."

Kristy put her hand on his shoulder. "I'm so sorry. Is there anything I can do?"

He sighed deeply and leaned his head back against his office chair. "Maybe. But it might sound crazy."

She smiled. "Try me."

"Well, I have these tickets to a concert next week in Memphis. My sister was supposed to go with me, but she backed out."

Did he want her to go with him? Where was he going with this?

"Anyway, it hit me yesterday that I don't have anyone else to invite. I guess I could take one of the guys. Ace, maybe. But I was thinking. . ." He trailed off.

Suddenly she understood. He was trying to find out if she knew anyone who might like to go with him. She grinned. "Tell you what. Let me make a phone call. We'll see if we can't find someone to go with you." She started to leave the office then stopped. "Wait. What's the concert?" she asked.

"Brad Paisley. Should be a good one." He smiled sheepishly. "I'll spring for dinner, too, if that will help you convince someone to go with me."

Kristy closed the door behind her and peeked at the front desk. Matthew was entertaining a group of college girls with a "ranger" story. She glanced at her watch. The movie should've started three minutes ago. "Could you hand me the remote, Ranger?" she said with a grin.

His face turned beet red. He grabbed the remote and passed it to Kristy then hurriedly took the girls' money and ushered them toward the movie.

Kristy pressed the PLAY button and dashed off to her office to make a call. It was time to play matchmaker.

CHAPTER 28

As Kristy made her way to the visitor center on the morning of the Fourth of July, it was already blazing hot. She'd had to carry Sam outside to get him to do his business. He'd let her know in no uncertain terms that there wasn't a dog in his right mind who'd want to go outside during a heat wave, even if his owner spoke sweetly of treats and shaved ice. But he'd finally relented like the good dog he seldom was.

By the time she reached the employee entrance, she could feel the sweat beading on her forehead underneath her hat. From the looks of the cars already beginning to fill the parking lot, she knew it was going to be one of those days. No one on staff was off today; it was all hands on deck.

She quickly set the coffee to brewing. By the time she finally stepped out to the front desk, Owen, Ace, Matthew, and Mason were congregating near the cash register.

"What's going on?" she asked.

"The vandal struck again last night." Owen's face was grim. "Arnie is fit to be tied. Says if Steve doesn't get back from vacation soon, he's going to personally get on a Europe-bound plane and drag him home."

Figured Arnie would find a way to pass the blame along to someone who wasn't even on this continent. "Which monument did they get this time?"

"Texas." Ace shook his head. "This was the worst one so far. Two different colors of spray paint."

"The bottom line is that we need to be on full alert today. There'll be a ton of traffic in and out of here, and our programs will likely be loaded with people. If you see anything suspicious, let me know," Owen said. "Obviously whoever is doing this is someone familiar with the park, so we're looking for someone who's been here before."

The front door chimed as the day's first visitor opened it. Mason greeted the family, and Matthew reached for the microphone to announce the start time of the movie.

Kristy followed Ace and Owen through the swinging doors that led to the ranger offices. It sounded like it was going to be one of those days. "So does this mean another stakeout is in our near future?" she asked.

Owen groaned. "You know it. I hope you didn't have anything exciting planned to celebrate tonight. Hank's in with Arnie right now, so I'm sure we'll get our orders soon." He poured some coffee into his UT mug and went to his office.

"Guess you'll be spending the holiday with me." Ace grinned at her.

She stared at him over her coffee. "It's my favorite holiday, you know. I always go watch the fireworks at Pickwick."

Pickwick Dam was a favorite spot for locals during the summer. The Tennessee River flowed right through the area, making it a mecca for fishing, boating, or just relaxing near the water. Every year, there was a spectacular fireworks display on the Fourth of July. Kristy was actually supposed to watch this year's festivities with Robert. She made a mental note to call him as soon as she had a free moment and let him know that she had to work. He probably wouldn't be too happy, but maybe he could still come. She was certain his little brother would love to go see the show with him.

"Maybe we'll still be able to see some of the fireworks, depending on where Mr. Bramblett has us stationed." Ace leaned against the doorway of his office and grinned as she made her way into the seasonal office.

Kristy turned the computer on and pulled her cell phone out of her purse. May as well get it over with.

"Hello." Robert's deep voice sounded on the other end.

"Hi. It's Kristy."

"I thought you were working today. Did you end up with the day off?" he asked.

"No. I mean, I am at work. I just needed to tell you something." She cleared her throat.

"Oh? What's up?"

"Well, actually, I can't make it tonight. We had more vandalism last night, and since it's a holiday, we're going to be staking out again. So I won't be able to go to Pickwick for the fireworks. I'm sorry." She did feel awful. He'd seemed so excited and said they'd stop and get stuff for a picnic and watch the fireworks over the river.

"That's too bad. I can't believe you have to work tonight after working all day today. And on a holiday, too."

"I know. But that's the price I pay to work at America's favorite national park."

Her little joke fell flat, and he was silent.

"Maybe you can still catch the fireworks. I'm sure Zach would love to go with you."

He sighed. "Probably so. And I was planning on heading over that way soon anyway. Mom bought him one of those aboveground pools for the backyard, and I promised her I'd help set it up."

"That's nice. I'm truly sorry, Robert. I hate to cancel. But Arnie is pretty adamant about our catching this vandal. I know it keeps cutting into our time together, though. I hope you understand."

"I do. Don't worry about it. Really. Not another thought. Maybe we can get together Friday? Put our little plan into action?"

She laughed. "Sounds perfect. I'll make sure Owen is available. You talk to your mom today."

"I'll do it. I'll call you tomorrow. And, Kristy?"

"Yes?"

"Happy Fourth of July."

"Thanks. You, too."

They said their good-byes and Kristy snapped her phone closed. She wondered what Owen would say about a get-to-know-you double date. As soon as he'd let on that he might be interested in a fix-up, Robert's mother, Dorothy, had popped into her mind. She and Owen were about the same age, and Robert had mentioned that she'd recently confided in him of her desire to start dating again. He was all for it, and when Kristy had called him last week about the possibility of a fix-up, he'd been totally on board. Now she just had to make sure Owen was available for dinner on Friday. She was enjoying her little stint as matchmaker so much, she wondered if she was turning into her mother. Pushing that thought away, she went to find Owen. Time to put the plan into action, as Robert had so aptly put it.

CHAPTER 29

So maybe if we told the boss that the Fourth of July is your favorite holiday. . ." Ace let his words drift off when Kristy gave him a blank look.

"What?" Her brows drew together.

"I could—" Ace shrugged. "You said—"

A distracted smile lifted her lips as she looked past him. "Hey, Ace. There's Owen, and I need to talk to him."

As opposed to me. The person you obviously don't *need to talk to.* Ace watched her follow the older ranger into his office. When he'd realized that Kristy was going to have to spend her favorite holiday cooped up in an old truck with him instead of on a blanket somewhere watching fireworks with friends, he'd decided to be noble and help her get out of the stakeout. But she was too preoccupied to even talk to him.

He stared at the closed door. Oh well. At least he'd tried. He couldn't keep a smile from his face. Sitting out there alone would've been pretty awful. It would be better to have company. Especially if the company was Kristy. A niggling thought rose to the surface. Any time they spent staking out was time she wasn't spending with Robert. He was ashamed of how satisfied that made him feel.

"Ace, can you come here for a second?" Mason called from the front desk just as Ace was starting to wonder what Kristy needed to talk to Owen about privately.

Grateful for the distraction, he swung open the doors that separated the offices from the front desk area. They always reminded him of saloon doors straight out of a John Wayne movie. He had to fight the urge to swagger a little bit and call Mason "Pilgrim."

"What's up?" he asked. Being around the twins made him feel so out of touch, what with their slang terms and constant texting. He'd had to threaten to confiscate their BlackBerrys early on. He didn't tell them, but he'd never even sent a text message.

"I accidentally rang this lady up as a family because she has her little girl with her, but it turns out her daughter is under three, so she's free. So I need to change it to an individual fee instead of family." Mason's face was red to the roots of his blond hair, his trademark dimple nowhere to be seen.

"It's okay. We can just void it and start over. Don't worry about it." Ace pointed out the correct button on the cash register. "Now take the original receipt and write on the back of it that it is void because of cashier error."

Mason ducked his head and did as instructed.

"Excuse me." The woman tapped her hand on the counter, and Ace looked into blue eyes that seemed strangely familiar. Did he know her?

"I don't have much time to spend here." Her snippy tone made it sound like she couldn't imagine a worse place to be. "And I don't see why I need to pay the entrance fee anyway. I'm not here for a tour. I just need to speak to one of the rangers that works here." She shifted the toddler to her other hip.

"I'm s–s–sorry, ma'am." Mason's stammering was so soft Ace could barely hear him, but he stood his ground. "All visitors have to pay the fee, regardless of if they take the tour or not."

The woman's nostrils flared, and she glanced toward the ceiling then narrowed her eyes at Mason. "Let me speak to the manager, please."

Okay, enough. This wasn't a restaurant. "Mason, you've been out here for a long time. Why don't you take a break." Turning to the woman, Ace smiled. "I'm as close to a manager as you're going to get, and Mason was telling the truth. The entrance fee is for everyone who *enters* the park. The upside is that your fees are good for a week, so if you don't have time to take the tour today, you can always come back later on in the week."

The woman's blue eyes blazed at him. "No, thank you," she said disdainfully. "I just need to speak to one of your staff members. Can you please see if Kristy O'Neal is available?"

"Sure. Hang on a second and I'll see if she's in her office."

He stepped away from the desk. Who was this woman? What did she want with Kristy? He retreated through the swinging doors and tapped on the seasonal office door.

Kristy was seated at the computer, engrossed in whatever was on the screen. She didn't even look up.

He tapped again, and this time it was enough to shake her out of the computer-induced trance.

"Sorry. Just reading an e-mail." She looked sheepish, as though he'd caught her doing something she wasn't supposed to. Was it a message from Robert that had her so enthralled?

He nodded toward the front desk. "Someone here to see you. A very angry blond woman."

She groaned. "I didn't think she'd come here to see me."

He raised an eyebrow. "So you know her? She's not just some disgruntled visitor who didn't enjoy your cemetery tour?"

She clicked out of the e-mail she'd been reading. "She's my sister."

"That explains the eyes." He smiled at her. "But to be honest, the similarity stops there."

She smiled, and it almost reached those blue eyes. "She's really a lovely person—although, come to think of it, she probably would hate my tour-guide skills."

He watched as she smoothed her hair and rose slowly from the desk. It was as if she were preparing for battle. And given the countenance of the woman at the front desk, maybe she was.

"Are you gonna introduce me?"

"Of course."

He followed her to the front desk. Normally, he'd always believed you could tell a lot about someone by their relatives. But not this time.

"Sarah. It's so nice to see you." Kristy's forced cheerfulness was evident. There was no love lost between these two.

Sarah nodded coolly. "I needed to speak to you about Mom's gift." She bent down and scooped up the toddler who'd been pulling at her crisp khakis. "You remember Emma."

Kristy's face brightened. "How could I not remember my only niece? Hey, Emma-girl. Say hi to Aunt Kristy." She reached out and tickled the child's tummy, and Emma let out a squeal of laughter. "Oh. Sarah, this is Ace Kennedy. He's a new employee here." Kristy motioned toward Ace.

Sarah regarded him over the counter. "Yes, we've spoken." She begrudgingly thrust her hand forward, and he shook it.

"Nice to meet you, Sarah," he drawled.

Sarah and Emma followed Kristy into the seasonal office without another word to him.

ॐ

Kristy couldn't believe Sarah was actually at the park. All these years she'd been working there, and Sarah had only stepped foot a couple of times on park grounds. And one of those times was as a guest at her almost wedding.

"So. This is your office, huh?" Sarah scanned the crowded, plain room, one perfectly arched eyebrow raised. "Very festive."

"My other office—" Kristy stopped. The yellow office wasn't hers anymore, and bringing it up would just give Sarah a chance to rub salt in her wounds.

But Sarah picked up on the inference. Her mouth twisted as if she'd eaten a lemon. "That's right. Mom said you'd been demoted." She spit the last word out as if it were dirty. Then she shifted to a tight smile. "Too bad. I know you liked your job, though for the life of me, I don't know why."

Kristy stifled a sigh. *And Happy Fourth of July to me.* What had she done to deserve this visit?

"Why are you here, exactly?" Kristy asked, her eyes on Emma's chubby cheeks. Oh, how she wished she knew her niece and nephew better.

"Andrew and I got Mom that grandfather clock she's always wanted. It was pretty expensive. I just thought you might want to go in on it. No big deal if you don't. Your part would be a hundred bucks, though." She set Emma down in Kristy's chair. "But that might be more than you wanted to spend."

Kristy had already gotten her mother a gift. A twenty-five-dollar Barnes & Noble gift card. But Sarah had never asked her to go in on a gift before. At least not since they were both out of high school. She hated to be rude about it. "Sure. Let me just write you a check."

Sarah plopped down in the blue plastic chair in the corner of the office. "Great."

Kristy dug through her purse for her checkbook and finally came up victorious. "So how long are you here?" she asked as she wrote the check.

"We're leaving tomorrow. We're having company the rest of the week."

"Oh?" Kristy said absentmindedly as she tore the check from the book.

"Yeah. Dad's coming to stay with us for a few days."

With the check still in her hand, Kristy froze as if she'd been immersed into very cold water. Sarah and their father were in contact? That didn't come as a complete shock. But that they were close enough for him to spend a few days as a guest in her home? That piece of news took her breath away. She looked up at Sarah's smug face. The reason for her sisterly visit was suddenly obvious. She was only there to drop a bombshell.

CHAPTER 30

Ace didn't mean to eavesdrop. But his office shared a paper-thin wall with the seasonal office, and he couldn't help but hear every word exchanged between Kristy and Sarah. And even if he hadn't been able to hear their words, he was pretty sure the feeling of tension would've carried over into his office anyway. There had been complete silence since Sarah had announced their dad was coming to visit her. He vaguely remembered Owen and Steve talking about Kristy's estrangement from her father. Steve had even joked that Owen considered himself a surrogate father for her at times.

"Dad is coming to stay with you?" Kristy's voice rose with each word.

"He wants to get to know his grandkids. Says he might not have any others for a while, since his son is still in high school and you. . ." She trailed off. "Well, let's just say that he's not expecting you to make him a grandfather anytime soon." Sarah laughed.

That was below the belt, even for someone who seemed oblivious to common courtesy. He waited for Kristy's response, surprised to find that he was actually holding his breath in anticipation. He wanted her to let her sister really have it.

"I see." Kristy's voice was so quiet now that he could barely hear it. "Is that really what he said, or are you just filling in the words for him?"

"That was nearly an exact quote, actually. He also had some choice words about your farce of a wedding. He thought, as did I, that Mark was quite a catch. Too bad you found a way to mess it up." Ace didn't have to see the sneer on Sarah's face to know it was there. "Dad says you're just too much like Mom."

"And I consider that a compliment. Here's the money for the clock. I have to go now. I have a rifle demonstration in twenty minutes."

Ace was rooted to his chair, his fists balled up in anger. *That's it? She's just going to let her sister treat her that way?* He shoved to his feet, struggling against the urge to storm into the room and tell Sarah what he thought of her. But he doubted Kristy would appreciate his involvement in what was obviously a sensitive situation.

"Bye, Emma." Kristy's voice softened, her affection for her niece evident.

"Bye, Kwisty."

Ace blew out his breath. *Sweet child. Hope she doesn't turn out like her mother. Here's hoping she grows up to be more like her aunt.*

He stepped to the door in time to see Sarah and Emma exit the office area. He glanced in the direction of the seasonal office and was struck by the haunted expression on Kristy's face.

He considered walking on by, but he couldn't. He met her gaze. "You okay?"

"I guess you heard all that, huh?" The dullness in her eyes hadn't been there an hour earlier.

"Sorry. She's a real piece of work." He leaned against the door frame. "I wouldn't put much stock in anything she says, though. Most of it was probably just to get a rise out of you."

Kristy shuffled some papers on her desk and brought her fist softly down on the pages. "It worked."

He nodded. "I can only imagine. Do you actually have a rifle demo in a minute, or was that just an excuse?"

"I do. In fact, I should've already changed. The chance to wear head-to-toe wool during a July heat wave just makes my day even better."

He raised an eyebrow. "And just think, I'm the guy who gets to spend hours with you closed up in a truck tonight. . .after you've spent time outside in head-to-toe wool. Guess we know who the lucky one is, right?" He retreated into the hall, his gaze still on her face.

Her mouth turned upward a tiny bit. "I promise to shower before the stakeout."

Getting that small smile from her felt like winning the Ranger of the Year award. "Thank you kindly, ma'am," he drawled in his best John Wayne imitation before he sauntered through the swinging doors. He heard her laughter as the doors swung closed behind him. He hated to admit it, but hearing someone cause pain to Kristy had made him want to rush in and rescue her.

A hollow feeling settled in his gut as memories flooded him. He was no one's superhero, especially not Kristy's.

☉☉

Kristy blinked rapidly as she buttoned the Civil War uniform jacket. *Soldiers don't cry.* Even if her life did seem like her own version of a Civil War sometimes. She draped a haversack over her right shoulder and an ammunition bag over her left shoulder, securing them to her body with a wide belt, and blinked some more.

She knew better than to listen to Sarah. But the thought of Sarah and their father having a conversation about her messed-up life made her sick. She faltered a little in the Battle of the Tears as a lone tear trickled down her face. She angrily wiped it away. She grabbed a bayonet from the locker and stuck it into the holder on her belt. She was about to go face a crowd of people. Besides, she'd cried enough tears over her sister and dad. Hadn't she used them all up already?

Straightening up, she took in her reflection in the full-length mirror. *Soldiers don't cry,* she reminded herself again. But even soldiers had errant thoughts sometimes, and her own flooded in on her.

If her dad and sister thought she had in some way "messed things up" with Mark, they were wrong. She hadn't messed things up. If they really knew her, or knew anything about her, they would know that the breakup had been inevitable. She and Mark were wrong for each other. Sadly, that knowledge didn't lessen her pain. Heartbreak was heartbreak, even if ending the relationship made sense.

Couldn't they be supportive for once in her life? Her dad had only met Mark twice. He was certainly in no position to judge whether Mark was the one for her. She remembered the way he'd insisted that Mark ask him for her hand, even though the engagement ring was already on her finger. It had infuriated her, but she'd played along. The thought that this man, who'd abandoned his family, still thought he should get a say-so in her life was absurd. But she hadn't wanted to hurt his feelings, so she'd begged Mark to abide by her dad's wishes and ask his permission.

And, of course, her dad had also insisted on being there to walk her down the aisle and had wanted to make sure his name was listed on the wedding invitations. Like she was his property. She'd wanted to scream, "I'm not yours to give." But again, she couldn't bear the thought of hurting him. Because she knew that somewhere, deep down, he was sorry for leaving. He just hid it well, under barbs and sarcasm. Sarah was so much like him. And she was so much like their mother. Complete opposites. No wonder they were unable to live happily ever after.

She stared at her reflection for another second. The tears were finally under control. She was ready to face the world, her true identity hidden under the costume. For the next half hour, she wouldn't be Kristy O'Neal, girl who didn't know who she was anymore. She'd just be a common Civil War soldier, explaining the hardships of war.

Her brogan boots clacked against the hard tile floor as she stepped through the swinging doors. Ace gave her a wink as she trooped by.

"Look, Mommy, a soldier!" a little boy squealed as she passed by.

She tossed him a smile as she began the journey to the split-rail fence where the program would take place. She was looking forward to it. Any amount of time she got to spend pretending to be someone else was precious. Would she ever enjoy just being herself again?

CHAPTER 31

Finally. The last visitor had exited the building. The clicking sound the lock made as he turned his key had never sounded so sweet. Ace glanced at the desk. Kristy and Matthew were furiously counting the money, and he knew both were hoping it would come out balanced with the register tape. Otherwise, they'd have to recount again, and if it still came out wrong, they'd have to fill out tedious paperwork.

"It's even," Matthew said gleefully and raised his hand for a high five from Kristy.

"The theater is finished," Mason announced, walking into view.

"Big plans tonight, guys?" Ace asked.

"Meeting some friends at Pickwick for the fireworks."

He glanced at Kristy's glum face. He wondered if she was still upset by her sister's visit, or if she was just sad that she'd be spending her favorite holiday staking out with him.

"Sounds nice. Why don't you guys get out of here? We'll finish up."

The twins didn't waste another second. Before he could wave good-bye, they'd grabbed their backpacks from the seasonal office and were headed out the door.

He felt Kristy's eyes on him. "Come on," he said, walking over to where she was leaning against the desk. "You remember what it was like to be nineteen and have fun plans. Surely you would've wanted the cool guy at work to let you scoot out a little early."

"Cool guy, huh? If it makes you feel better about being over thirty, then keep on calling yourself that." Her blue eyes danced as she looked playfully at him. "But I'm pretty sure I heard Matthew call you 'Gramps' the other day when you were complaining about your backache."

He winced. "Ha-ha." She could kid him all she wanted if it meant she hadn't let Sarah completely ruin her favorite holiday.

"So have you heard where we're supposed to be tonight?" Kristy picked up a stray receipt from the floor and dropped it in the trash can underneath the desk.

"Owen's gone over to Mr. Bramblett's office right now. Should be back any second to let us know what the game plan is." He flipped the loudspeaker switch to Off. "If you'll check the ladies' room, we'll be through here."

He held his breath. Would she think he was bossing her around? Just a few weeks ago, his statement would've set her off. But she didn't say a word as she went to check the restrooms for straggling visitors.

The back door burst open as Owen blew in like a hurricane. His naturally ruddy face was even redder than normal, and Ace couldn't tell if it was from the heat or from his obvious anger.

"This thing is out of control," Owen ranted, erasing any doubt about the reason for his red face. "He's talking about having us install cameras at all of the major monuments. Cameras. Like we're some kind of convenience store or something." Owen put his hat on the table beside the door and brushed his sticky hair off his forehead. "And it's so blasted hot out there. Tonight's gonna be miserable."

Ace nodded.

Kristy came through the swinging doors. "Well, what's the plan?" she asked, coming over to where they stood.

Owen snorted. "Plan. The plan is that we'd better catch this idiot before the park goes broke paying all of us overtime. Arnie actually asked me what the rangers would think about just donating their time to catching the vandal."

Ace exchanged a glance with Kristy. He was pretty sure the overtime pay was the only upside for her. For him, the extra money was nice, but he was getting a lot closer to admitting that he enjoyed using the time to get to know Kristy without distractions.

"Anyway, the two of you are supposed to park near the Tennessee Monument," Owen said.

"But that was the first one vandalized," Kristy pointed out.

"Exactly. Arnie figures the vandal won't strike there twice, so you can park near it and be undetected. But he actually wants you to keep an eye on the Illinois Monument."

She nodded. "That makes sense. The Illinois is a popular monument, and we'll have a clear view of it from the Tennessee." She laughed. "And if it gets too hot, we can always take a dip in Water Oaks Pond."

Owen laughed gruffly. "Maybe you should stay out of the pond. Your luck, that'd be when the vandal would strike. Arnie's head would explode for sure if that happened."

"Okay, we'll stay on alert," she agreed. "But we might have to run the truck's AC some. I think it's still supposed to be in the nineties most of the night."

"Can't say I blame you there. I'm gonna be at the Wisconsin. I'm mostly just worried about staying awake. Since Steve's still on his European vacation, I'll be sittin' out there alone. Talk about a long night."

Ace felt for the guy, having to sit out there by himself with no one to talk to. The time he spent with Kristy always passed so quickly. Each time the radio crackled with someone letting them know they could call it a night, he was amazed at how the time had flown. And amazed at all of the things he'd hoped to tell her and to find out about her. It had been a long time since he'd met anyone as interesting as Kristy. And it was as if she didn't even know it. She was so unassuming. He only wished he could make her see him as someone other than just the guy who'd taken over her yellow office.

CHAPTER 32

Kristy was happy to have a couple of hours of peace before she had to go back to work. What with Sarah's ugly visit and another e-mail from Mark, imploring her to contact him, she felt like she was at her wit's end.

She wished she were able to go and enjoy the holiday tonight instead of working. And it wasn't that she dreaded spending time with Ace. It was just that it was so confusing. Because of his stupid game, she'd started to open up to him. Telling him all that stuff about her fears and regrets. Those were things she'd never shared with anyone. It was just weird.

She showered and changed into denim capris and a sleeveless red top. Somewhere in the depths of her closet were some white flip-flops. Her best attempt at a patriotic outfit, despite the fact that she wouldn't be doing anything festive tonight. No point in getting too fixed up, though. She decided to let her hair air dry, even though it meant there'd be waves to contend with. It was just too hot to use the blow dryer. A bit of makeup and she was ready with an hour to spare.

The ringing doorbell startled her. She wasn't expecting anyone.

173

Sam at her heels, she went to peek out the window to see who it was. Robert and Zach stood on her front porch, each holding something covered with aluminum foil.

Kristy opened the door. "Hi. What are you guys doing here?" she asked.

Robert smiled broadly and held up his platter. "We grilled burgers at Mom's and brought some for you."

Zach was less cheerful with his greeting. "Mom sent you some banana pudding, too," he said with a frown.

"Thanks. Come on in." She directed them to the kitchen table.

Robert removed the foil with gusto, exposing a platter of burgers and buns. "Ta-da. Marinated in Dale's Sauce. Your choice of American, cheddar, or Swiss cheese." He grinned.

"You didn't have to do this. But I'm certainly glad you did. I'm starving. This sure beats the Lean Cuisine I was planning."

Robert laughed. "Well, I hated to think of you spending the whole day working. So I thought we'd bring a little taste of the Fourth to you."

Zach knelt down to scratch Sam's belly. "Good boy," he crooned.

So it was possible for Zach to have a good time. She was glad to see it. "Do you have a dog, Zach?"

He looked up, his hand still stroking Sam's soft fur. "Not since we moved. Our house doesn't have a fenced yard, so Dad got to keep our dog." He frowned. "But Mom says maybe we can get a cat sometime."

She met Robert's gaze. Poor kid. It was no wonder he was so miserable. Parents split, moved to a new town, had to leave his friends and his dog behind. She was beginning to understand Zach's sullenness.

"I'm going to try to work on that fence soon," Robert said. "And then we'll be able to bring Gingerbread to her new home."

Kristy grinned. "Gingerbread? That's a cute name."

A small smile from Zach. "I got her at Christmastime. The very first thing she did was jump in my lap and eat a cookie off the plate in front of me."

"A gingerbread cookie?"

"Yep."

She fought the urge to reach out and hug Zach. Underneath his preteen angst, he was probably a really sweet kid.

"Dig in." Robert motioned toward the burgers.

Ace paced the length of his living room, his tennis shoes squeaking against the newly varnished wood floors. He glanced over at his open laptop, mocking him from across the room. Why was this so hard?

Words normally came easily to him, but not today. Maybe it was because it was a holiday and his subconsciousness thought he deserved the day off. But at the rate he was going, he'd never finish his current project.

He thumbed through *This Great Battlefield of Shiloh* as if it would inspire him, but to no avail. He glanced at his watch. It was time to leave to go meet Kristy. He shut his computer down and grabbed his keys.

In an odd turn of events, she was waiting for him in the parking lot. And he'd expected to have to wait for her as usual. Maybe she was eager to see him. Yeah, right. More likely, she was eager to get the night started so it could end.

He pulled his truck into the space closest to where she stood and turned off the ignition. Grabbing his keys and radio, he hopped out of the Chevy.

"Aren't you proud? I beat you here for once." She grinned at him, her blue eyes dancing.

"Impressive. I figured I'd have time to walk down to maintenance and get the truck before you got here."

"I didn't even think about that, or I would've already gone to get it."

"Not a problem. I wore my running shoes, so I'll go." He motioned at her flip-flops. "You can just wait here."

She grinned. "Hey. Don't make fun of my footwear. I can move quite well in flip-flops, thank you very much. I'll just walk down with you."

They set off down the hill, and Ace couldn't help but admire her red toenails. She always surprised him. Such a neat mixture of tomboy and girlie girl. "Your hair's different tonight."

She raked a hand through her blond hair. "Yeah. I let it air dry, so it's wavy tonight. And of course, thanks to the humidity, I'm sure it will look like a lion's mane before the night is over." She held up a wrist with a band around it. "But never fear. I can contain it if it gets too big and threatens to force us out of the truck cab."

He laughed. "Well, I like it. I think it looks pretty like that."

She looked startled.

Why had he opened his mouth?

"Thanks."

They silently climbed in the truck, Ace at the wheel. It seemed that their earlier arguments about who would drive were a thing of the past. Kristy seemed content just to be a passenger. She was quieter than normal tonight.

"So. You think this'll be the night we catch the guy?" he asked.

"What makes you so sure it's a guy? It could be a woman, you know."

"Fine. You think this'll be the night we catch the person?" he asked again, emphasizing *person* for her benefit.

She laughed. "It probably is a guy. Just giving you a hard time."

He was glad to see she was in a good mood. He parked the truck near Water Oaks Pond. The Illinois Monument was in clear view. It had a very large gray stone base, with a regal woman seated on a throne. Mother Illinois watching out for her sons. Since Illinois was Ace's home state, the monument was one of his favorites.

He turned the air on full blast. "Soak it up before I cut it off."

Kristy unbuckled her seat belt and leaned forward in the seat, nearly pressing her face to the vent. She closed her eyes, the picture of peace.

He watched as the blast of air blew her bangs off her forehead. He wondered what it would feel like to reach out and run his hand along the side of her face. Her skin looked so soft.

"Are you watching me?" she asked, her eyes still closed.

"Yes."

"Well, stop it."

He sighed and turned off the ignition. The blast of cool air stopped and the truck seemed to fill immediately with warmth.

Kristy sat back and looked over at him. "I suppose we'll be playing round three tonight?"

"I thought you might be tired of our game." He smiled. "But I've got one doozy of a question for you, though. I spent all day deciding what it was going to be."

"All day, huh? I'm intrigued."

"Good. Okay, here goes." He paused dramatically.

"Well?" she said, her eyes widening in anticipation.

"Do you think there is only one true love for everyone? And if so, do you think you've already met yours?"

He could see that his question had surprised her. He supposed it was a little personal, but he figured he'd take a shot.

She was suddenly engrossed in the walkie-talkie lying on the seat beside her. She turned it over and over, as if searching its exterior for the answer to his question. Finally, she stopped and laid the device down in her lap.

Her gaze met his in the near darkness. "I don't believe true love exists," she said matter-of-factly.

CHAPTER 33

A tiny part of her hated him right then for choosing that particular question. Saying the words out loud was painful. But she was tired of running from the truth. And the truth was that at that moment in time, she didn't believe. She couldn't.

"Wait a minute. Let me get this straight." He shook his head. "You were engaged to be married. You are now dating some guy you met at church. Presumably a nice guy. But yet you don't believe true love exists?"

She sighed. She should've just made up an answer. Told him what he wanted to hear. But she was tired. Tired of trying so hard to please everyone. It was time to let the ugly truth out. "Yes, I was engaged. And yes, I did love Mark. To some extent. But I never thought he was some great love of my life."

"Then why did you agree to marry him? How could you almost spend your life with someone you didn't even consider your true love?"

She cleared her throat. "You sound like some kind of fairy tale. Life is not a fairy tale. Real love is hard and messy, and people get hurt." She shrugged her shoulders. "I guess with Mark I just thought we were pretty compatible. We got along most of the time. We liked the same pizza toppings. So I figured we'd make it work."

He stared at her as if she had horns growing out of the hair that she could feel getting bigger by the second. "Wait a minute. You were going to commit your life to someone based on the fact that you both liked pepperoni?"

"Pineapple, actually. And no. It wasn't based on the pizza topping. I was just using that as an example. Obviously a bad one." She rubbed her forehead. "Don't you get it? Because I don't think that fairy tale love exists, the best I can hope for is compatibility. You know?" She looked over at him. Even in the darkness, she could see that he did not understand where she was coming from.

"I don't mean to sound like some hopeless romantic, but it makes me a little sad to hear you say this." He bit his lip. "Have you always felt this way?"

She thought back. "Maybe not always. I mean, as a little girl I was all about the fairy tales. Happily ever after and all that jazz. But somewhere along the way, I wised up. My dad left us when I was twelve. Pretty soon after that, my aunt and uncle split up. By the time we were in high school, most of my friends' parents were at least separated." She shook her head. "Not a lot of happily-ever-after examples, you know?"

She leaned her head back against the seat. "I shouldn't have told you, I guess. Now you'll think I'm crazy." She gazed at the drooping material on the truck ceiling and ran her fingers along the design of thumbtacks someone had used to keep the material from coming off. "Haven't you ever just thought that maybe it's all too much trouble? It shouldn't always be so hard."

"I disagree. Anything worth having is worth fighting for. Worth the tough times. Love isn't always easy. It's not supposed to be. But true love is worth it." He had a faraway look in his eye.

She expected him to burst out in song any minute. She had him pegged as an '80s ballad kind of guy. In fact, it was likely that in the back of his closet, there was a box of mix tapes and love letters.

"Okay. I'll concede to you that true love, *if* it existed, would be worth the hard times. But I stand by my initial answer. And I can give you all the examples you'd like. My parents. Mark and me. Brad and Jennifer. Charles and Diana. Scarlett and Rhett. Romeo and Juliet." She ticked each couple, both real and fictional, off on her hand. "See? All couples who thought they were perfect matches. And we know how they all turned out."

"But, Kristy. Those are just a few specific examples. I can give you plenty for the other side. And being a student of history, I'm a little ashamed of you. There are examples of great loves throughout history. They spanned wars and famines and holocausts."

How could she argue with that?

"And I'm surprised at you, Shiloh ranger extraordinaire. One of my favorite love stories comes straight from this battlefield."

Somehow, she knew instantly which story he was going to reference. But she didn't let on because he seemed so excited.

"General William Wallace was stationed here at Shiloh in early spring of 1862. His wife, Ann, was back home in Illinois. Throughout the months, Will and Ann wrote letters back and forth, some of them quite romantic. By the time Will was in camp at Shiloh, Ann had a strange feeling. She just knew she needed to go to her husband. She sent a letter, pleading with him to allow her to make the trip to Tennessee, even though it would be dangerous. Will, ever the gentleman, was too worried for her safety. He implored her to stay put, saying he'd be home on leave soon and they'd be together."

Kristy took in the soft expression on his face. He really was a hopeless romantic.

"But Ann was adamant. She had to see her husband and was

unable to shake the feeling. She set out on the journey alone, which was nearly unheard of in that day and time. She arrived in Savannah the evening after the first day of the battle and managed to find a boat that would take her to the riverboat stationed at Shiloh, which was serving as a makeshift hospital. Once on board, she ran into her brother, who was serving in the army alongside her husband. One look into his eyes and she knew—her husband was dead. Ann was devastated. She spent the night on the boat, serving as a nurse to the wounded and dying men."

Kristy never tired of this story. She'd read the letters over and over again and had even done a ranger program one summer based on the story. But still, she let Ace tell it. Somehow, hearing the story told from his perspective brought it to life even more.

"The next morning, before the battle began again, Will's men went back to the field to collect his body. They brought it back to the riverboat where Ann waited. She immediately ran to her husband's side once they brought his body on board, but miracle of miracles, he was still alive. Another boat came and took Ann and Will to Savannah to the Cherry Mansion. Although Will was severely wounded, he regained consciousness and was able to talk to his wife, and they were able to say their good-byes. His final words stayed with her forever and were passed down in their family through the letters Ann wrote. He grasped her hand and said, 'We'll meet again in heaven.'"

He looked over at Kristy and smiled. "Now if that isn't a story of true love, I don't know what is."

"Fine. It is a beautiful story, I admit. But it doesn't change things for me."

"So you mean to tell me that you can't give me a single example of true love?"

She rolled her eyes. "Elizabeth Bennett and Mr. Darcy."

"A nonfictional example? As in a modern-day, someone-you-actually-know example."

"I'll think about it and get back to you."

"Fine. And for the record, while I think there are probably a small handful of people in the world who could be my true love, I believe that God has one in particular in store for me."

CHAPTER 34

Ace was horrified. He'd never met anyone who was so jaded about love. It was odd. She wasn't bitter. It wasn't as if she gave off an anti-man vibe. In fact, she seemed pro-relationship. Just anti-true love. All that talk about just settling for someone she was compatible with. He thought all women believed in romance. It seemed that he thought wrong.

The radio on the seat between them crackled, and Owen's voice filled the silence. "Two-ten to two-fifty."

Ace grabbed the radio and mashed the button. "Two-fifty, go ahead."

"We can call it a night. There's been no activity anywhere that we know of."

"Copy." Ace laid the radio back down on the seat.

As the truck roared to life, they heard the crackling of fireworks. The big display had begun. He glanced at Kristy. "I'll try to get us out of the trees so we can at least see some of the fireworks."

"Thanks. I've watched the fireworks over the river every year since I was a little kid. I'd hate to not see any fireworks at all tonight."

But as it turned out, time wasn't on their side. By the time Ace pulled the truck into the parking lot, the last embers of fireworks were scattering over the river.

"I'm sorry you missed them," he told her.

She sighed. "Oh well. Maybe next year."

"You want me to give you a ride to your house?"

"Nah. I'll just walk."

They got out of the truck and started off in separate directions, she toward the residential circle, and he toward the main parking lot where his Chevy waited.

"Hey," he called.

She stopped and turned toward him. "Yeah?"

"Don't forget. You're supposed to be thinking of a modern-day example of true love." He grinned. "I know you can do it."

"We'll see."

⊙∽⊙

Kristy slipped on a pair of old running shorts and a Chi Beta Chi T-shirt from college. She ran a brush through her thick hair and twisted it into a bun. What a night.

"Come here, Sam." She stepped onto the deck and held the door open for Sam.

He ran through, happy she was home. As he began his nightly ritual of circling the yard, sniffing for evidence of General Grant, the cat, or a wayward squirrel, Kristy sank into the plush cushion of the porch swing.

Ace and his questions. She was impressed that he'd known Will and Ann's story so well, though. She'd tried a million times to tell that story to Mark, and he'd always been uninterested. Even when she showed him copies of their love letters, he turned his nose up. History is history, he'd said.

And she knew she must've sounded like a major cynic to Ace. But after all she'd been through, first with her dad leaving, and then

184

with Mark leaving her at the altar. . .wasn't she just being a realist? She leaned her head back and looked at the stars. She knew they were so far away, yet there in the darkness of her backyard, they seemed so close she felt like she could reach out and grab one.

Sam barked his alert bark, and Kristy stood up.

She peeked through the slats of her fence and saw Ace's truck in her driveway. Had she left something in the truck tonight? She scooped Sam up in her arms so he wouldn't run away as she opened the gate.

"I'm back here," she called.

She watched as he made his way to where she stood, one arm behind his back.

Ace came through the gate and closed it behind him. "Sorry to bother you. I know it's late. But it's still the Fourth of July, and there's something I think you need."

She let Sam wriggle out of her arms. "What's that?"

He pulled something from behind his back.

For a second, she wasn't sure what it was. A bunch of little sticks, fanned out and tied together with a big red bow. She looked at him with wonder.

"It's a bouquet of sparklers." He laughed. "Since you missed the fireworks and all."

Before she could think of what she was doing, she grabbed him and hugged him tightly.

"Thank you," she said, pulling back from the embrace, a little embarrassed. She wasn't usually so impulsive. "This is the best surprise I've had in a long time." And it was.

He pulled a lighter out of his pocket and nodded his head toward the bouquet. "Pick one."

She pulled one out and held it out to him.

He clicked the lighter, and suddenly the sparkler lit up the backyard like a shooting star.

"I haven't held a sparkler in years." She made little zigzag motions with her hand and watched as the sparkler fizzed out.

"Aren't you supposed to write your name with it or something?" he asked.

She laughed. "Yes, I guess you are. Here, let me do two at a time. I'll write your name, too." She plucked two more sparklers out of the bouquet and held them out for him to light.

☙

It had definitely been a gamble, bringing her a bouquet of sparklers. But he wasn't afraid of looking stupid if it meant gleaning a smile like the one Kristy had given him when she'd seen it. The light coming from the sparklers was dim by comparison.

He watched as she twirled barefoot in the yard, writing their names in the air. Hard to believe this girl didn't think true love existed. But if he had anything to do with it, someday soon she would.

CHAPTER 35

"Hold on. So you're telling me that not only did Robert bring you grilled burgers, but then Ace brought a bouquet of sparklers? On the same day?" Vickie asked incredulously.

Kristy sighed. "Yes. But you're making a much bigger deal out of it than it was."

"Man. There's never a shortage of drama for you, is there?"

"There's no drama. Robert was being sweet. I'd be willing to bet it was his mom's idea anyway. And Ace. Well. . ." She trailed off. "He was just trying to make up for me missing the fireworks. I told him it was my favorite holiday and all."

"If these were olden days, we'd say you have two suitors." Vickie laughed. "I think it's time you faced that fact. They're obviously both crazy about you."

"You're wrong." Kristy took a sip of her morning coffee and glanced at the clock. She had another minute to talk before she had to leave for work. But she'd have to be careful. When she talked to Vickie or Ainsley, time slipped away from her. "Robert is a little interested. I'll give you that one. We don't have that much to say to each other, though. And Ace is just friendly. He doesn't know anyone around here. We've just spent a lot of time together lately, and as much as I like to complain about his ability to do my job, at least I can acknowledge that he's a good guy."

"Whatever. You can tell yourself that all you want to, but I'm convinced that he sees you as more than just a coworker."

"You're right. He also sees me as his friend."

"If you say so." But Vickie's tone said she thought differently.

"Anyway. . ." Kristy was eager to change the subject. "Have you talked to Ainsley lately?"

"Yesterday. She and Brad are going to some kind of spa this weekend. Must be nice, right?"

"A spa? And he agreed to go? She really does have the perfect man, doesn't she?" Kristy asked.

"She has the perfect husband, you have two men fighting for your attention, and me? Well, I'm working late again tonight and then looking forward to the latest delivery from Netflix."

Despite her friend's joking tone, Kristy picked up on a little sadness. Vickie was painfully shy and never dated except for the rare times she agreed to a fix-up.

"Hang in there, Vick. The right guy is probably just around the corner."

Kristy wanted to remind Vickie that if she didn't get involved with anyone, she wouldn't end up with a broken heart. But she thought it best to spare her friend from the cynicism she'd shared with Ace the previous night.

They said their good-byes and Kristy rushed out the door.

Late again.

⟡

"If you look into this thick underbrush, you can imagine how hard it would've been to maneuver on foot. Much less on a horse. Or even worse, with an artillery piece." Ace directed the crowd's attention to the center of the Hornet's Nest. "But that's just what went on in this area. Thousands of men were concentrated here. Some of the worst fighting took place on this very spot."

The crowd stared back at him, blank expressions on their faces. A couple standing in the back turned quietly and began walking back toward the parking area. He remembered Kristy's advice about sharing human interest stories. Worth a try.

"Of course, the thing to remember is that these were people, just like you and me. They had families waiting on them at home. They had hopes and dreams. And many of them gave their lives right here on the battlefield. The Civil War was full of stories of sacrifice." He paused to take a breath. He hadn't lost any more visitors, so maybe he was onto something. "In this area of the battlefield, there were a couple of Union soldiers retreating from their position. One of them was hit, and he fell against his buddy. Before he died, he said one last word. The word was 'Mama.' He was thinking about home, hundreds of miles away, as he died." Ace noticed an older lady wiping a tear from the corner of her eye. "So, ladies and gentleman, as you explore the park today, each time you see a marker, I want you to realize that they are more than just pretty monuments. They are reminders of the men who fought and died on the very spots where we stand." He nodded at the crowd. "Thank you, and enjoy your park."

An older couple fell in step beside him as he made his way to where the park pickup truck sat. "Thank you, young man. That was a lovely tour," the man said, wiping his forehead with a handkerchief.

"You sure brought the history alive," said the lady. "I taught high school history years ago and brought my students to Shiloh every spring. But we never heard such a good talk." She beamed at him.

He thanked them profusely and climbed into the truck. Kristy had been right on the mark about what the crowds liked to hear. Somehow, a little piece of her had begun to seep into every tour he gave.

CHAPTER 36

Why had she ever thought playing matchmaker was a good idea? Kristy poured some food in Sam's bowl and looked at her watch one more time. Owen should have been here ten minutes ago. She was sure Robert and Dorothy were probably already waiting at the restaurant. And according to the phone call from her mother earlier in the day, Dorothy had told her twenty times in the past twenty-four hours that she hadn't been on a first date in over thirty years and she was a nervous wreck. Kristy was sure their tardiness would only add to Dorothy's stress.

A honk sounded in the driveway. She peeked out the blinds at Owen's truck. "Finally." She grabbed her purse and rushed out the door, calling good-bye to Sam over her shoulder.

"Sorry I'm late," Owen said as soon as she got inside the Bronco. "I didn't know what to wear." He smoothed his green polo shirt. "Is this okay?"

She glanced over at him. Crisply ironed khakis and brown dress shoes completed his look. "You clean up nicely." She grinned. "Seriously, who helped dress you?"

He looked sheepish. "My sister. I made the mistake of telling her you were introducing me to someone, and she showed up on my doorstep today with a JC Penney's bag." He turned left onto Highway 22 and headed toward Pickwick. "I hated to turn down free clothes. She said this was my birthday gift."

"Well, I think you look great. And don't be nervous. It's just dinner."

"Right. Dinner."

There was no mistaking the apprehension on his face.

"Tell me again where we're meeting them?" he asked, concentrating on the road.

"That new barbeque place that just opened." Barbeque had been Robert's idea. She'd thought for sure he'd have chosen Hagy's, knowing it was her favorite place, but he'd suggested barbeque instead.

"Every time I drive by there, the parking lot's full."

"I'm sure it will be good. And I think Robert made reservations, so we won't have to wait."

"Reservations?" Owen glanced at her. "For real?"

She nodded. "I don't think it's something they normally do, but I'm sure Robert insisted."

Owen guided the truck into the crowded parking lot. "See? What'd I tell you? Packed."

She looked out the window at the vehicles. She hadn't even known there were this many people in the county. "I guess I'm not surprised. A new restaurant opening is big news."

"Me goin' out on a date is big news. I must be crazy," Owen muttered as he opened his door and jumped out.

Before she could climb out, he was at her side opening her door. "Look at you. You're such a gentleman." She glanced at him as they walked up to the entrance. "I bet Dorothy flips over you."

Owen just sighed and held the heavy wooden door open for her.

The hostess looked at her expectantly. "We're meeting a couple of people here. The reservation was under the name Aaron."

The hostess scanned her list. "Yes. They're already here. Just follow me."

Kristy turned to Owen and noticed his worried expression.

"You'll be fine," she whispered. "Just be yourself."

"Myself is the kind of guy who spills barbeque down the front of his new shirt," he whispered back.

She smiled. "Just eat carefully."

Robert stood as they reached the table. "Hello."

"Robert, Dorothy, this is Owen," Kristy said.

Owen shook Robert's hand first then turned to Dorothy.

A hint of a blush touched Dorothy's round cheeks as she reached out to shake Owen's hand. "Nice to meet you, Owen." She smiled sweetly, her blue eyes dancing.

"You, too." Owen nodded at her as he took the seat across from her.

"Sorry we're a little late." Kristy sat down across from Robert. "Have you been here long?"

"Just a few minutes."

Kristy shot an encouraging smile in Dorothy's direction, taking in her short-sleeved sweater and black pants. If she were guessing, she'd say Owen wasn't the only one with a new outfit on tonight.

"So," Owen said to Dorothy after they ordered. "Where do you work?"

"At the bank." She patted Robert on the arm. "I guess working with numbers runs in our family."

"Mother, being a teller isn't the same as being an account—"

Owen laughed like she'd made a great joke and acted like Robert hadn't spoken. "So I guess you know Larry Tidwell?"

"Sure do." She fluffed up her short blond hair and leaned in a little closer to Owen.

"Larry and I go way back. We went to high school together." He grinned mischievously. "I could tell you some stories."

Dorothy giggled.

Kristy watched the exchange. It seemed like right before her eyes they'd transformed from two people pushing sixty to teenagers on a first date. It was sweet.

By the time their food arrived, Owen and Dorothy were still finding people they knew in common.

"It must just be a small world." Dorothy beamed at him.

"So are you still having trouble with vandalism?" asked Robert, taking a sip of sweet tea.

Kristy and Owen both nodded.

"We still haven't caught the guy." Owen carefully raised a forkful of barbequed pork to his mouth.

Kristy watched in amusement. She'd been surprised he hadn't ordered ribs, since they were supposed to be the specialty. He was taking great pains to impress Dorothy.

"You've got a little sauce there." Robert pointed at Kristy's chin.

She quickly put a napkin to her face. Honestly. No one should ever go out on a date to eat barbeque unless they were completely comfortable with one another. Although, as the evening progressed, she sensed that Owen and Dorothy were pretty comfortable. Maybe it was because they were older or something.

When the waitress brought the bill, Owen insisted on paying for everyone's dinner, even though Robert put up a fuss.

"My treat. As a thanks for introducing me to Dorothy." He grinned at her.

Dorothy's cheeks turned a little pink, but she looked pleased.

Kristy fell in step beside Robert as they quietly made their way to the parking lot. She heard Owen and Dorothy behind them speaking animatedly about something. *Hmm.*

Once in the parking lot, Dorothy turned to Robert. "Son, why don't you take Kristy home?" she said. "Owen offered to give me a ride."

Kristy and Robert exchanged glances.

"Sure," Kristy said. "That'd be great."

She followed Robert to his Honda. He opened the passenger door for her. Just as she was climbing in, she heard Dorothy's and Owen's laughter from across the parking lot. They certainly seemed to be enjoying themselves.

She wished she could say the same for herself.

CHAPTER 37

"That seemed to go well," Kristy said as Robert turned toward the park.

He nodded. "I'm glad. It's about time my mom had a little fun." He looked over at her. "It's been ages since I've heard her laugh like that."

"Same goes for Owen. I'm not sure I've seen him look that happy. At least not in a long time." She could barely make out the shape of the cannons as they got nearer to the park entrance. "And he's such a nice guy, too."

"I can tell. Besides, I know you wouldn't set my mom up with some loser." He brought the Honda to a stop in her driveway.

Kristy unfastened her seat belt and grabbed her purse. "Even if they only end up as friends, we've at least helped to bring two lonely people together."

He silently got out of the car and came around to open her door.

She tried to rise gracefully from the Honda. It sat so low to the ground, she always hated how awkward it felt to get out of it.

"Do you want to come in?" she asked. She couldn't think of

a polite way around inviting him inside, especially since he was already out of the car.

"Sure. But just for a few minutes. I know you have to work tomorrow."

He held the storm door open for her while she unlocked the dead bolt on the wood door and then followed her inside.

She motioned toward the couch. "Have a seat."

He strode across the living room and sat stiffly on the plush sofa.

Sam immediately jumped in his lap, licking a greeting.

"Sorry. Just move him if he annoys you."

Robert promptly lifted Sam from his lap and set the dog on the floor.

Well, that was straightforward. And she'd never wanted to be one of those people who lived by a "Love me, love my dog" motto. Still, it stung. She forced a smile.

"Can I get you something to drink? I have sweet tea, water, and Coke."

"Sweet tea would be great, thanks."

Kristy hurried into the kitchen and filled two glasses. Sam scampered around at her feet, rolling a ball that was almost as big as he was. Every time the ball would move, he would pounce on it and growl. "You're such a tough guy," she said as she stepped over him and his toy.

"Here you go." She handed Robert a glass and sat down beside him.

He took a sip. "Yum. This is almost as good as my mom's."

"Thanks." At least she supposed she'd take that as a compliment. Either way, she sensed it was time for a distraction. She flipped on the television, and soon the living room was filled with the muted sounds of the Cosbys. Thank goodness for TV Land.

"So, Kristy. . . ," Robert began. "Why don't you tell me a little bit more about yourself?"

She didn't know where to start. "Like what? You already know a lot about me."

"Where do you see yourself in five years?"

She suddenly felt like she was in the middle of an awful job interview. "Hopefully still here, working as a ranger. Although my job security runs out Labor Day." She had filled him in already about her job status, so he was aware that she might be out of a job come September. "Other than that, I don't know. It'd be nice if I owned a home by then." She shrugged.

"What about a husband? Kids?"

"I'm not sure."

"But you do want a husband and kids someday, right?"

She got the feeling he was fishing for information. And wasn't sure she liked it. "I guess. Maybe. With the right guy."

He nodded. Her answer seemed to satisfy him.

"How about you?" she asked.

"Oh. In five years, I definitely want to be settled down. I'm closing on the house next week, so barring something unforeseen, I should definitely be a homeowner. And ideally, I'd like to be married and at least have already had one child by then."

It was all so planned out. "Do you already have their names picked out?" she teased.

Without cracking a smile, he nodded. "Rose if it's a girl, after my grandmother. And if it's a boy, James Robert. After my grandfather and myself."

Wow. She had totally been kidding. "That's nice," she murmured. *Especially if your future wife has no desire to have any input in naming her children.*

"I guess I should hit the road. It's nearly an hour back to Jackson." He stood. "And I know you have to get up early for work tomorrow."

She followed him to the door. Uh-oh. Thus far, she had avoided much physical contact with him. But her luck might've just run out. He definitely had that look in his eye, as if he thought it was time in the schedule to try for a kiss. And it wasn't that she was repulsed by him. It was just that she wasn't sure she was ready to take their relationship to the next level. At this point, they were just friends. But one kiss and she had the feeling Robert would think it meant they were headed for a future with little Rose and James Robert soon to follow.

"Thanks for dinner. It was fun." She hung back a little to keep some distance between them.

He lingered at the door. "Why don't you walk me out?"

She desperately willed the phone to ring so she'd have an excuse to stay inside, but it didn't. She followed him out to the car.

"We'll have to do this again soon." He grinned at her.

The next thing she knew, he'd pulled her in for a hug. "I had a nice time," he said softly next to her ear.

The second he released her, she took a large step back and gave him a smile. "Talk to you soon."

His brows drew together and he looked like he was about to say something, but he gave her a little wave and got in the car.

Whew. She'd dodged the kiss she was pretty sure he'd planned to attempt. She watched as he backed out of the driveway then turned to walk back to the porch.

Kristy froze. The trash cans at the side of her house had been knocked over. She stepped off the concrete to where the cans lay. All of her trash bags had been opened, and several days' worth of trash was strewn about. A frown settled on her face. She knew she'd closed the lids tightly as she always did. Something bigger than a cat must've knocked them over and pulled the lids off. A raccoon, maybe? She hated to blame General Grant for anything else. She'd already complained about him being the likely culprit who pulled up her flowers.

Kristy dragged the trash cans back to their normal spot and put them back upright. She glanced around at the mounds of garbage she could see strewn across her yard in the darkness. Had an animal wreaked this much havoc? Or had the vandal decided to branch out a little? Maybe pull up a few flowers and spread some trash around as kind of a vandalism appetizer? An uneasy feeling settled in her stomach. Whoever did this, it didn't feel like an animal.

It felt personal.

CHAPTER 38

The next week, Kristy found herself wondering if she'd stepped into some kind of alternate universe. Not only had her trash cans been turned upside down again, making her late for work, but she came in to find Owen, starry-eyed, telling Ace and Matthew about his latest date.

It seemed like her matchmaking plan had worked a little too well. Owen and Dorothy had had a wonderful time at the concert and had even gotten together once since then. "And it's all thanks to Kristy," Owen said as she slunk to the front desk, hoping they were all so engrossed in Owen's story they wouldn't notice that she was nearly fifteen minutes late. At least she hadn't run into Arnie or Hank on her way in.

Ace stepped into her office later, a gorgeous grin dancing across his face. "Interesting that someone who doesn't believe in love would play Cupid."

She looked up from her computer and rolled her eyes. "Companionship. That's what I was going for. Just someone for Owen to hang out with sometimes. No one said anything about love."

"Try telling him that. He's in his office right now ordering flowers to be sent to her office." He leaned against the file cabinet. "And the woman is who? Your boyfriend's mother?"

"He's not my boyfriend."

Ace let out a disbelieving snort.

Kristy busied herself at the computer, hoping her silence would prompt Ace to leave her alone. But no such luck. He walked over and stood behind her, staring at the computer screen.

"Flowers pulled up. Trash cans knocked over. Trash cans knocked over *again*," he read over her shoulder.

She pushed the power button on her monitor and stared at the gray screen.

"What is this?" he asked quietly.

She shrugged. "Just a list of things."

"Things? Things that have happened at your house lately?"

The caring in his voice brought her gaze up to his face.

His brown eyes were full of concern. "I thought your flowers disappearing was an isolated event." He put his hand on her shoulder. "Why didn't you tell me?"

She shivered then quickly converted the shiver into another shrug. "I don't know. I wasn't sure it was anything." *Get a handle on this, Ranger O'Neal, she warned herself. Shivering when he touches your shoulder falls dangerously near Cupid territory.* "Besides, what are we going to have to do now? Stake out my place?" She forced a chuckle.

He patted her shoulder and dropped his hand. "That might not be a bad idea."

"Ace, I was kidding! You are not spending your off time at my house."

He took a step back.

If she didn't know better, she'd have thought that was hurt that flashed across his face. Still, she hadn't meant to sound so blunt. "You know what I mean."

He nodded. "I'll drop it for now if you promise to keep me posted on anything else that happens."

"Scout's honor," she said and crossed her heart with her finger.

He narrowed his eyes in mock suspicion. "You weren't a Girl Scout, were you?"

"Nope. But I'm a ranger." She grinned at him. "So ranger's honor. Is that better?"

He grinned. "I trust you." He stepped out then stuck his head back in. "Completely."

She sat there for several minutes thinking about that assurance. She believed he did completely trust her.

And to her surprise, the feeling was mutual.

CHAPTER 39

"W ere we featured on the Travel Channel and no one bothered to tell us?" Kristy asked Owen as she emerged from starting the movie for a full theater.

"You know how it is. Last-chance family vacations before the kids start having band, football, and cheerleading practices." He wiped his brow. "But it has been a madhouse."

Visitors had been lined up at the door that morning before they even opened—a sure sign of a busy day. Kristy supposed Owen was right. There weren't too many Saturdays left before summer would be over. In fact, Matthew and Mason didn't have much time left until they headed back to college. Seasonals who were in college rarely stayed on until Labor Day due to the start of classes. So before long, Kristy would have the seasonal office all to herself again. But only for a short time, because come Labor Day, she'd be out of a job.

She knew she should start making plans for whatever would come next but was putting it off. Tomorrow she'd make herself get a Sunday paper and begin the tedious task of searching for a job. The problem was, the only thing she'd ever wanted to be was a park ranger. She sighed loudly.

"You sound like the weight of the world is on your shoulders." Owen's tone was jovial, but his eyes let her know he was concerned.

She shrugged. "Just trying to figure out what to do next."

He looked at his watch. "My advice would be. . .lunch." He grinned.

"You know what I mean. Next in life." She cut her eyes at him. "Not in the next fifteen minutes."

He chuckled. "We're all trying to figure out what to do next in life. My advice is just to keep your focus on the moment you're currently living. We aren't promised anything more than that."

"In that case, perhaps I will go to lunch. Is that okay?"

"Yep. Me and the twins can hold down the fort. Why don't you take the full hour today? I know you've been cutting them short lately. We'll get along okay until you get back."

She had been cutting her lunches short but didn't know anyone had noticed. Things had been so hectic lately, and Matthew and Mason sometimes got overloaded with visitors. She knew it was time to let them sink or swim on their own, but she couldn't help feeling responsible for them still.

On the way out the door, she mentally went over the contents of her refrigerator. It didn't take long. Saying she was overdue for a trip to the grocery store would be an understatement. She was so engrossed in her thoughts, she didn't see the blue truck pull up beside her until it honked. She looked up.

Ace smiled at her from the driver's seat. "Hey," he called. "You headed to lunch?"

She nodded.

"Why don't you hop in and go eat with me?"

She thought for a moment. Sam would be fine. She could always go let him out when she got back. "Sure."

She climbed up in the truck. "What are you doing at the visitor center on your day off?"

"Actually, I was coming to find you." He stopped to let a family cross in front of the truck on their way to the park bookstore. "Thought I'd see if you wanted to have lunch with me today."

"That was nice. I was just thinking that I don't have many groceries in my house."

"How's Hagy's?" he asked.

"That sounds good." Okay, it sounded better than good, but she'd contain her excitement. She took her hat off and placed it on the floorboard. "But we've had a ton of visitors today, so it might be really crowded."

"Let's take our chances," he said as he turned onto Highway 22, headed toward the restaurant. "They're pretty quick, so even if we have to wait, it shouldn't be long."

At Hagy's, she cringed at the crowded parking. Ace put their name on the list and guided her to a seat outside on the large deck overlooking the Tennessee River.

They sank into wooden chairs shaped like fish.

She sighed contentedly.

Ace looked over at her inquisitively. "Was that good or bad?"

"Definitely good. I love sitting out here looking at the river roll by." She gazed out at the river. "Isn't it beautiful?"

"It sure is."

"Kennedy, party of two."

They followed the hostess to their table. Several families that had visited the park earlier in the day called out greetings to Kristy along the way.

"Does that make you feel like a celebrity?" Ace pulled her seat out for her, and she slid into the chair.

"Very funny. If I didn't have on my uniform, they wouldn't even know I was the same person."

"Do you know what you want, or do you need a minute?" the waitress asked, each word punctuated by the chomp of her gum.

Ace looked at Kristy, and she shook her head.

205

"I think we're ready," he said. "You first." He nodded his head at Kristy.

"I'll have the catfish platter with a baked potato, coleslaw, and sweet tea." She didn't have to think twice about her order. Some might say she was in a rut, always ordering the same thing. But to Kristy, there was no need to risk ordering something new when she knew she'd be happy with the same thing she always ordered.

"I'll have the same, please." Ace passed his menu to the waitress.

"So it's been a crazy day?" he asked once they had their drinks.

"Nonstop. It seems that today is a popular day for family reunions and Boy Scout campouts."

"I see." He took a sip of his tea. "Anything else going on?"

"Not really."

"Anything else happen at your house?" His eyes were filled with concern.

She shook her head. "No. And the more I think about it, the more I'm convinced it was probably just an animal. Possum, raccoon, General Grant, or maybe even a dog or a coyote." She ticked the potential suspects off on her fingers.

He shook his head. "I'm just not sure an animal could get the lids off your trash cans. I definitely think that would take opposable thumbs."

She sat back in her seat. "So you're convinced a person did it?"

"I'm convinced you need to be careful. And be aware of your surroundings."

"I'll be fine."

"And I'll be worried."

They eyed each other.

The waitress set two steaming plates of fried catfish in front of them.

"Do you mind if I say a prayer before we eat?" he asked.

"Sure."

Ace bowed his head. "Heavenly Father, thank You for the meal we are about to eat. We are humbled by the many blessings You give us every day. Please help us to be Your hands and feet as we go about our daily lives." He cleared his throat. "Lord, please be with Kristy. Keep her safe and show her the path You have for her life. In Jesus' name. Amen."

"Amen," Kristy said. She was touched, actually. It was rare that she heard anyone pray specifically for her. In fact, she couldn't remember the last time.

"How's your food?" he asked.

"Delicious. This is my favorite place."

"I know. Why do you think I suggested it?" He smiled. "Haven't you figured out that I try to make you happy?"

For a second her stomach felt fluttery. More and more often lately, a smile from him affected her that way.

"So did you do anything fun last night? On one of your few nights to not be stuck in the truck with me?" he asked, dipping a piece of fish into his tartar sauce.

"I went to a movie with Robert."

She saw a look flash across his face. Just for a moment. Almost as if she'd slapped him.

"That sounds fun. Did you see anything good?" Ace asked, grabbing a hush puppy from the basket between them.

"Some action movie." She shrugged. "It was okay. If you like movies about futuristic robots taking over the world."

Which she didn't. Somehow, each date she went on with Robert seemed more awkward than the last. She couldn't put her finger on it. He was always pleasant and polite. But at the end of the night, she always felt like he still had no idea who she was.

Vickie and Ainsley had both accused her of spending time with Robert because there was no danger of falling for him. Ace, on the other hand. . . She glanced across the table. Ace might as well have a CAUTION: DANGER sign flashing on his forehead. Suddenly, looking into the beautiful brown eyes of the man opposite her, she knew what she had to do.

CHAPTER 40

Kristy had always hated breaking things off. She wondered if it made her a masochist that she'd rather be on the receiving end than have to do the actual breaking up. Maybe not quite the way Mark had handled it, but a nice "It's not you; it's me" kind of conversation. That would be much easier than having to actually let a guy down. People talk about letting someone down easily. There's nothing easy about it. Rejection is hard to take. And when you're the kind of girl who always considers the feelings of those around you, it's also almost impossible to dish out.

Kristy couldn't even count the number of guys she'd dated a lot longer than she should have, just because she didn't have the heart to break theirs. In fact, in the past, she'd shamefully done things specifically to get on their nerves in the hopes that they'd instigate the breakup.

But she knew this time that wasn't an option. For one thing, she was too old to keep playing the same old games. For another, she couldn't keep Robert hanging on any longer. She did like him. But as much as her mother tried to make him be, he just wasn't right for her.

He'd seemed surprised when she'd called this afternoon. She never called him while he was at work, but figured it would be okay just this once. Especially since after today she didn't intend to call him again.

So they were going to meet for coffee. She needed to go to Jackson anyway. Her empty pantry cried out for a visit to their supercenter, and her wardrobe called out for a visit to the mall. Or at least Kohl's.

Robert had put up a little bit of a fuss when she'd suggested Starbucks. "Five dollars for a cup of coffee. I can brew several pots for that."

She'd finally convinced him by saying she had a gift card that desperately needed to be used. It was true. Except for the desperate part. Honestly, she just wanted to meet him in a public place. But not for dinner. Definitely not at his house. And besides, a venti caramel macchiato would do wonders for her nerves.

She rehearsed her little speech all the way to Jackson. Highway 45 had never flown by so fast. By the time she pulled her Jeep into the parking lot, she didn't feel any more prepared for the conversation than when she left the park grounds.

Robert was waiting at one of the outside tables. He waved her over.

"Hi," she said nervously, hoping he didn't sense the impending conversation. On second thought, maybe it would be best if he did have an idea. She didn't know which way would be worse for him. Either way was bad for her.

"Did you enjoy your day off?" he asked as he held the door open for her.

She inhaled deeply as the sweet smell of coffee filled her senses. If she could bottle up that scent, she would. "I had a nice day. Just kicked around the house. Did laundry. Nothing too exciting."

He nodded.

Once at the counter, she tried to explain the different coffees to him. Mocha, cappuccino, latte. He treated them all as foreign delicacies, especially when he caught sight of the prices that went along with them. Finally, a venti caramel macchiato for her and a plain black coffee of the day for him were ready. They slid their cups into cardboard sleeves, and she followed him to a table outside.

She took a sip. *Courage. Give me a little courage, please.*

He watched her curiously. "Is it good?" he asked.

"The best." She smiled.

Robert started telling a story about a coworker's vacation to Mexico that was filled with mishaps.

Kristy watched him and made the appropriate interested expressions and nods. But the whole time, she couldn't help but try to figure out what it was that made him so wrong for her. Robert was perfect on paper. He was very cute. He was well dressed in a conservative, preppy way. And he was nice. Just an all-around nice guy. The kind of man who would probably stop on the side of the road to help an old lady change a flat tire. Or who would rescue a kitten from a tree. He was just one of those guys. But despite his good qualities, he wasn't for her.

"Would you like more coffee?" he asked when he was finished with his story.

"What? Oh, no thanks. I'm still working on this one." She shifted in the wrought iron seat. "Listen, there was actually something I needed to talk to you about."

He put his cup down on the table, and his green eyes regarded her seriously. "I don't like the sound of that."

She took a breath. "Yeah. Um. I know we've been spending a pretty good bit of time together over the past couple of months." She pressed her lips together, trying to figure out which direction to go in. "And it's been great. I have a lot of fun with you. But I'm not really in a place where I can date someone right now."

She took stock of his expression to see if she'd chosen the correct words. Maybe not. But she plunged on. "I'm just kind of all over the place right now, with the recent breakup and the not knowing where I'll be after Labor Day. So I don't think it's fair to you for me to keep seeing you. You're a great guy, and you deserve someone who can give you their full attention."

She sat back and waited for his response. He'd been totally silent during her little speech.

"Wow. I didn't see that coming," Robert said. "I thought things were going pretty good, actually. Is there anything I can say to change your mind?"

Oh no. She'd hurt him. She could see it all over his face. Maybe she should've eased into it better. Spent a couple of weeks trying to annoy him or something.

"I don't really think so. I'm so sorry, Robert."

He was quiet for a moment. Then he nodded. "Okay. But can I ask you something?"

"Sure." She was so glad to have the bad news off her chest, she'd let him ask her anything at that moment.

"What is it about me? I've heard that same speech over and over again. But no one ever tells me what I've done wrong. They just say things like what you just said. Stuff about needing space or focusing on their career or that they're not in a relationship kind of place right now. What does that mean?"

And she hadn't seen this coming. The easy thing to do here would just be to say he was great and that the right girl would come along and they'd be perfect together. But Kristy wanted to give him more than that. He was a great guy. And with a little help, he would make some woman very happy.

"You really want to know?"

He nodded. "Lay it on me." He smiled. "I don't want to have to hear the 'You're a nice guy, but. . .' speech again for a while."

212

"Okay. Here goes." She bit her lip, trying to figure out where to start and hoping she wouldn't end up making him feel worse about himself. "Consider this your tutorial about the female species," she began.

CHAPTER 41

did it. He's so sweet. I wish I did like him that way." Kristy paced around the backyard, clutching her phone. "It would certainly make my life easier." She bent down and threw a stick for Sam to fetch.

Vickie chuckled. "Easy doesn't seem to be your lot in life."

"I wish you lived closer, though. Believe me, I would fix you two up in a heartbeat." And she would. It had actually crossed her mind early on that Robert was more suited for her friend than for herself.

"Oh, thanks. He's not good enough for you, but he'll do for me." Vickie feigned hurt.

Kristy took the stick from Sam and patted his head. "Good dog," she whispered and tossed it again. "Don't be silly," she answered Vickie. "He's plenty good enough for me. We just don't have that kind of spark."

"I know. I'm just giving you a hard time."

"You won't believe what happened when I told him."

"What?"

"He asked me to tell him what he's doing wrong."

"Whoa." Vickie sounded impressed. "Wouldn't it be cool if every guy cared enough to ask?" Her voice trailed off.

"It really would." Kristy couldn't help but think of Ace, who seemed to know instinctively what she would like or dislike.

"What about us?" Vickie asked. "We care. Don't we need someone to give us relationship advice, too?"

"How about this? Every man should come with a handbook. Every woman in his life—mother, sister, ex-girlfriend, or whoever could add to it. He should have to give it to you upon meeting. Then you could add stuff to it and send it out with him everywhere he went. It'd make things much easier for everyone."

Vickie laughed. "Why don't you get started on that? You can call it saving the world, one man at a time."

"Well, if there were one man who came with a handbook, I can tell you who I'd like it to be." In a way, Kristy hated that every thought brought her back to Ace. But ever since lunch with him, Kristy had been trying to figure out what was going on between them.

"If you're talking about Ace, it doesn't sound to me like he needs one. I'd say his feelings are pretty clear."

"Maybe." Kristy picked up a tennis ball and threw it across the yard for Sam. "We have opened up to each other a lot. And I do enjoy spending time with him."

"Why do I think there is a 'but' coming here?" Vickie asked.

"You know me too well." Kristy laughed and took the tennis ball from Sam. "But the things I said to Robert were actually valid. It's too soon. And besides, who knows where I'll be in September?"

Vickie sighed. "Don't be a defeatist. Something could open up there. You never know. And it sounds like not all the things you said to Robert apply to Ace. I don't hear you saying he isn't right for you or that there isn't a spark. So since you omitted those things, does this mean that you're finally ready to confess that there might be something between you and Ace?"

Kristy froze with the tennis ball in midthrow. She wasn't sure what she felt for Ace. When he'd brought her the sparkler bouquet, the butterflies in her stomach told her that she might be falling for him a little, despite her protests about love. And the other day at lunch, hearing him pray specifically for her—that had sent her over the edge. He was a keeper. Except that she wasn't sure she was ready to trust her feelings yet. Sam leaped up on her, and she threw the ball. She grinned as he chased after it. The way he ran and got the ball and brought it back over and over reminded her of this conversation with Vickie. "If I just say maybe, will you let me off the hook?"

Vickie sighed. "For now."

"Thanks."

"Any other news from Shiloh other than your crazy life? Ironic, isn't it, that Shiloh means 'place of peace.'" Vickie's voice danced with mischief.

"Oh, aren't you the funny one? Actually, the vandal struck again this week. But this time it was personal."

"What do you mean?"

"When I got home last night, all of my lawn furniture was turned upside down. Even on my deck." Kristy shook her head at the memory. "Nobody believes a raccoon or cat did that, so it almost has to be the vandal. Hank figures the guy must be getting nervy to come down to the residential area. So we're going to be on the lookout again tonight." As much as she hated to admit it, it was starting to make her uneasy. She wouldn't want anyone to know, but she'd slept with her lights on last night.

"Does this mean more time alone with Ace? I love it how these little stakeouts have turned into minidates for you guys. And you're both getting paid. I hope Mr. Bramblett doesn't find out how much fun you're having, or he'll separate you."

"They aren't dates. Far from it. Sometimes we have fun, but mostly we're just passing the time."

"Whatever. I hope you have fun tonight. Dress cute." Another laugh from Vickie before they said good-bye.

Kristy knew she'd never fully be able to explain the love/hate relationship she had with the time she spent with Ace. He made her look inward sometimes, even when she didn't want to do so. It was as if he were a mirror for her that sometimes showed things she didn't want to admit to—such as just how broken she was.

Or what an idiot she'd been to almost settle for marrying Mark.

CHAPTER 42

"Can you believe this guy has gotten four monuments?" Ace looked out across the park.

"I really thought we'd have caught him by now." Kristy put her face close to the open window, trying to feel if there was a breeze. There wasn't.

"First the Tennessee, then Missouri, then Kentucky, then Texas. There aren't any common denominators for them that I can see." Ace shrugged. "I guess it's just totally random."

Kristy leaned back against her seat. Tennessee, Missouri, Kentucky, Texas. Was there a pattern they didn't see? Kentucky and Missouri had soldiers who fought for both sides. Tennessee and Texas were mostly Confederate. She thought for another minute. An idea began to form, and once it did, she couldn't shake it.

She sat up straight. "Can you take me back to the visitor center?"

Ace looked over at her. "Mr. Bramblett will be fit to be tied if he finds out. Do you need a restroom break or something?"

She shook her head. "No. I need to check something, actually. There is a book in Hank's office that lists each monument and marker on the park. I'd like to look at it."

He started the truck without question. "If you say so."

Within minutes, they pulled into the parking lot.

Kristy jumped out of the truck and ran to the back door. "You can wait here if you'd like," she called over her shoulder to him.

He walked in the door just as she was disarming the alarm system. "Curiosity got the best of me." He followed her up the stairs leading to Hank's office. "It's kind of creepy in here at night, isn't it?"

She laughed. "Ask Owen about that sometime. There are legends of Shiloh ghosts dating back to when the park was established. We used to have a ranger who believed the legends. Owen pranked him good one night."

Ace chuckled. "I'll be sure and ask him. I'm sure it's a story he'll love to tell."

"I've never heard a grown man scream so loudly." She turned the creaky knob, and they were standing in Hank's overcrowded office. She had no idea where the light switch was. She stumbled over a stack of books on the floor, and a pair of strong hands caught her around the waist and kept her from falling.

"Careful," Ace whispered.

His breath on her hair made her shiver. She ran her hand along the wall until her fingers made contact with the switch. Suddenly light filled the room.

"Which book are we looking for?" Ace asked, gazing around at the shelves along the walls. Books covered every available surface in the room.

"It's like an oversized ledger. I'm not sure where he keeps it. I've only looked in it a couple of times." She scanned the bottom shelf where a lot of larger books were stacked. Finally, she saw it. A blue book that looked like it might be someone's scrapbook. And she guessed it sort of was.

She pulled the book out and laid it across Hank's desk. She

would know quickly if she was correct. "Can you find me a piece of paper and a pencil?" she asked Ace.

He handed her a yellow legal pad and a Shiloh Falls Golf Course pencil.

"Okay, we need to list all the monuments."

"There are hundreds. We don't have time to do that."

"No. Just the large ones. Let's try just the state monuments first."

"Okay, well, the ones that have already been vandalized: Tennessee, Missouri, Kentucky, and Texas," he said.

She wrote quickly. "Okay, and then there's Alabama, Illinois, Wisconsin. . ." She trailed off.

"Arkansas is out at the Hornet's Nest. And, of course, Iowa and Michigan are on the main tour route."

Kristy jotted those down. "Any others?"

Ace scratched his head. "Surely there are more than just those. I know there were more states represented here. How about Indiana?"

She shook her head. "Remember, it was up to each state to put a state monument up. Indiana has monuments, but they're for individual regiments, not the state."

He looked at her in amazement. "You sure know your stuff," he said admiringly. "I could work here forever and probably not know as much about it as you do."

She shrugged. "I love this place. It's easy to learn about something you love."

He gazed at her. "Yes, I guess it is."

"And we should probably also include the Confederate Monument. Even though it isn't technically a state monument, all the southern states are represented."

He jotted it down.

"Okay, now we're looking for the dates each of these monuments was erected." She handed him the legal pad and pencil. "I'll find the date; you write it down."

He nodded.

Kristy quickly flipped through the ledger, calling out the dates for each monument.

Finally, the task was complete. She looked at the legal pad. "See? It's just as I thought. The vandal is working backwards by date."

Ace looked puzzled. "Huh?"

She pointed at the legal pad. "The Tennessee monument was the last one to be brought to the park. It was dedicated in 2006. And it was the first one hit by the vandal." She tapped on the paper again. "Before that, the Missouri monument was dedicated in 1975. And that was the second monument vandalized. Don't you see?" She couldn't keep the excitement out of her voice.

Ace grabbed the paper. "Yes. That means. . ." He scanned the list. "The next monument hit by the vandal should be the Confederate Monument. It's been at the park since 1917."

"Let's go," she said and grabbed the list.

◎◉◎

Brilliant. That was the word he would use to describe her tonight. Watching her in action as she connected the dots and figured out the vandal's pattern had made him fall for her even more. And he hadn't realized that would even be possible.

For the millionth time, he told himself to back off. Not only was she his coworker, but she was also seeing someone else. And Ace had too much integrity to come on to someone else's girl. Even if he didn't think Robert was right for her.

Kristy had radioed the others as soon as she reached the truck. The men were elated to finally have a lead. They'd decided to cover all their bases, though. In case the vandal decided to skip the Confederate Monument and go right to the next state monument on the list, Mr. Bramblett wanted rangers stationed there as well.

The problem was that Arkansas and Michigan were next on the list and were dedicated in the same year.

After a moment of silence—Ace could imagine the discussion going on between the two boss men—the radio crackled to life. "Listen up, troops," Mr. Bramblett boomed. "We're going to divide and conquer. Owen, you cover the Michigan Monument. Ace and Kristy, the Confederate Monument. Hank and myself will be at the Arkansas Monument. Any sign of mischief, notify me immediately."

Ace slowed down as they passed the Confederate Monument. "You know, this was the first monument we staked out," he said as he pulled over to park a few hundred yards away from where the monument stood. The truck should be undetected.

She laughed. "I know. We've come a long way since then."

"Yes. Back then, I was pretty sure you hated me."

"And now?" she asked.

"Now I think we're. . ." He trailed off. "Well, let's just say I think we're closer than I ever thought we'd be."

"I agree. And I'm sorry about the cold shoulder I gave you at the beginning of the summer."

"You needed someone you could take out your frustrations on. I can see why I fit the bill."

They made their way to the edge of the woods. The Confederate Monument seemed to glow in the moonlight. From their vantage point, they'd be able to see any movement near the monument.

"That's still no excuse."

"You think this is an okay spot?" he asked.

She nodded. "I just wish we'd brought chairs or a blanket to sit on or something."

He laughed. "Guess we'll just have to rough it."

They sat down at the edge of the tree line, eyes glued to the monument.

Ace motioned behind them. "You know, this is actually where

222

General Wallace spent the night on the battlefield. Can you imagine? It's amazing he survived through the night."

"It really is," Kristy said.

"I've always thought his survival was due largely to thoughts of his wife."

She snickered. "You really *are* a hopeless romantic."

He turned toward her. "C'mon, think about it. As connected as they were, don't you think he guessed Ann went against his wishes?"

"So you think he knew she'd be waiting for him?"

Ace nodded. "And that thought kept him alive."

Kristy sighed. "I don't know about that, but I think about that night a lot. I know it's strange that I spend so much time thinking about 1862." She smiled. "But I can't help it. After that first day of battle, it rained and stormed something awful. I sit out here sometimes and think about all those men, lying out here wounded and dying, crying out in the rain."

"And you know what all the eyewitness accounts and journals say? Those men were calling out for their loved ones. But so many of them died all alone. General Wallace was definitely one of the lucky ones." He glanced over at her. "Good thing Ann's love was so strong that she was determined to make her way to her husband despite the odds."

She was quiet for a moment. "Are you trying to pull me back into a conversation about true love?"

He grinned. "Just wondering if you came up with a modern-day example yet."

She cut her eyes at him. "Actually, yes, I have. So now you can stop worrying about me."

CHAPTER 43

Kristy had spent a lot of time since the Fourth of July thinking about love. People loved each other in so many different ways. A mother's love seemed to be the sacrificing kind. A father's love typically was more protective. Even though her own dad hadn't been proof of that. She pushed that thought away. Then there was God's love, which was perfect.

She'd considered the love she'd had with Mark. Selfish and jealous. The Bible said love was patient and kind. Many waters couldn't quench it. But it hadn't taken much to quench Mark's love for her. Or hers for him, either, to be honest.

She thought about all the relationships around her. Her parents might've had love at one point, but it wasn't the sticking kind. The commitment to remain through the hard times was absent.

But there was one relationship she could think of that seemed pretty close to the one Paul described in Corinthians. Ainsley and Brad. What they had was special. All you had to do was spend time around them, and you just knew you were in the presence of true devotion. The night before Kristy's almost-wedding, Ainsley had offered marital advice. "Keep God in the center. If both of you look to Him to be the example, you'll never go wrong. Pray together. Sure, there'll be tough times. But it's hard to be mad at someone you are praying for daily."

"Well? Who is it?" Ace asked softly.

"My friend Ainsley and her husband, Brad," she said. "Ainsley and I worked together as seasonals during college. She's a ranger now at the Grand Canyon. Brad is a firefighter. They're the epitome of the perfect couple, if ever there was one. Best friends, totally in love. They've got it all." She stretched her legs out in front of her and leaned back on her arms. "So there you have it. I was able to come up with one modern-day example."

He grinned. "I thought you could come through with one if you tried."

She rolled her eyes. "Are you happy now?"

"Actually. . .no." He looked at her, a serious expression on his face.

Uh-oh. Something told her things were about to get interesting.

"Listen, Kristy." He took a deep breath. "Are you serious about that guy from church?"

"His name is Robert. You know that. You've met him. Why do you always call him 'that guy from church'?"

"Sorry. I guess maybe I'm a little jealous."

Her mouth suddenly felt like cotton. "I ended things with Robert a few days ago. He was a great guy." She looked over at him. "But it was the right thing to do."

"I can't say that I'm sorry to hear it."

"Why is that?" she asked. She was pretty sure she knew, but she wanted to hear him say it.

"I've wrestled with this for quite a while now. And if you had told me things were going well with Robert, I would've just kept quiet." He shifted on the cold ground. "I just want you to listen. I don't want you to say anything back. Okay?"

She nodded, wondering what was coming next.

"Every minute I've spent with you has been special. If I had a highlight reel of the past months, you'd be in every one. I know that you've been through a lot. And I know that you say you don't believe in true love. But I believe enough for both of us. And if you can just give me a chance, I think I can show you that happily ever after does exist."

Her heart pounded against her chest. It was hard to keep denying that there was something between them. She gave him a slow smile, unsure of what to say.

Before she could say anything, he leaned forward. With one hand softly cupping her face, he pulled her closer to him.

She closed her eyes just as his lips met hers. His kiss was timid at first, then bolder. For a long minute, she was lost in the kiss. She'd read about kisses like this in books, seen them in movies, but she could honestly say she'd never experienced one for herself. Until now.

A rustling noise broke through the fairy tale moment, and Ace jerked his head up. Kristy glanced in the direction of the Confederate Monument and pointed. She could just make out the shape of a figure climbing the stone steps that surrounded the statue.

Ace pulled her close. "You radio the others. I'm going to apprehend this guy," he said in her ear.

For a moment, their eyes locked. "Be careful," she whispered.

She pulled out her radio, careful to turn the volume down before she pressed the button. She didn't want to alarm the vandal of their presence. For a split second, she forgot her call number. *Oh well, forget procedure.* She mashed the radio button and whispered, "Arnie, he's at the Confederate Monument."

Kristy watched as Ace crept toward the figure. The vandal was standing in the center of the monument, pulling cans out of a bag. It killed Kristy just to sit there, but she knew she had no choice. She was in no way supposed to be involved. She was eyes and ears only, as Arnie had said so many times. In fact, it was highly unusual that she was even allowed to be involved at all. It showed how desperate they were to catch the guy.

Snap. Someone stepped behind her, their foot making contact with a fallen tree limb.

"Kristy," Arnie whispered. "Where's Ace?"

She pointed to where he stood, partially hidden. The vandal was still trying to get the cans open.

"I can't believe it," the boss said.

"That we finally got him?" She looked up at Arnie. His bald head seemed to shine in the moonlight.

He shook his head and brought his gaze back to the monument. "That we caught two vandals in one night."

She gave him a puzzled glance but didn't have time to ask him what he meant, because Ace chose that moment to confront the vandal. Her eyes widened in horror. The vandal sprinted off, but Ace was quicker. In less than a minute, the vandal was on the ground in handcuffs.

She stood and heard a noise behind her that sounded a lot like. . .sobbing. She spun around to see the silhouette of Hank holding a bag in one hand and roughly herding a slight, obviously handcuffed figure with the other one. Kristy glanced from one vandal to the other. She'd been joking when she'd said maybe the vandal was a woman, but Hank's culprit was so much smaller. Maybe the two were a couple.

Before Kristy could comment about the small stature of the second vandal, a flash of blue lights alerted them to Owen's arrival from the Michigan monument. He jumped out and ran to Ace, who was leading the glowering prisoner to the car.

As Ace led the culprit past the spot where she stood, Kristy finally caught sight of the man's face. She was certain he'd attended her cemetery walking tour a few weeks ago. He'd peppered her with questions afterward about the history of the cemetery. But it hadn't seemed unusual, so it never crossed her mind to report him as suspicious. He'd just seemed like an inquisitive park visitor.

Owen opened the back door of the patrol car and stood aside as Ace led the cuffed man past him. At the sight of the prisoner's face, Owen looked startled. "Mr. Miller?" he said to the scowling man. "Is that you?"

The man grunted in Owen's direction as Ace guided him into the backseat and slammed the door.

The sobbing grew louder behind her as if the second vandal panicked at seeing the first one put into the police car. Kristy turned toward the sound and gasped as moonlight fell on the familiar tear-streaked face. "Zach! Have you been helping spray-paint monuments?" she exclaimed.

"N–no," Robert's brother sobbed, looking more like a little boy than a teenager. "Tonight was the first time I messed with the monuments. And it's not paint." His wild eyes pleaded with Kristy to believe him.

Hank frowned, and he held out the bag to Kristy. "They are cans of something. Looked like paint."

She held the bag open. Hank pulled out a flashlight and shone the light on the contents then harrumphed. "Silly String."

"I'm s–sorry." Zach continued to cry. "It was just a joke."

She and Hank exchanged glances. "I know him from church. Can you uncuff him and let me take him back to the visitor center?"

"Fine." Hank's voice was gruff, but she thought she detected some relief that he wasn't going to have to deal with the kid. "See if you can get to the bottom of it." He motioned toward the patrol car where Ace and Owen stood. "We'll handle things out here."

Hank took the handcuffs off Zach. "Listen, son. You go with Kristy. No funny business, though. She's gonna take you back to the visitor center and ask you some questions."

"Yes, sir," Zach said quietly.

Kristy motioned toward the truck. "I'm parked over here."

She had no idea what had gotten into Zach. She might not know him very well, but she was fairly certain this was uncharacteristic. She just hoped she could convince Arnie not to press charges.

CHAPTER 44

"Hello?"

"Robert. It's Kristy." She hated to make this call. But she had a feeling he would be able to deal with Zach better than anyone else could.

"Hey. I didn't expect to hear from you again."

"And I wish it were under different circumstances. Listen, I have Zach here at the visitor center. He was caught tonight attempting to vandalize one of the monuments."

Complete silence on the other end.

"Robert?"

"I'm sorry. I just don't know what to say. Are you telling me that *Zach* has been the person vandalizing the monuments all this time?"

She peeked in the yellow office where Zach sat, a dazed expression on his face. She guessed handcuffs and patrol cars weren't what he'd expected tonight.

"Actually, no. The real vandal was caught tonight as well. Zach was actually about to Silly-String the Michigan Monument. It wouldn't have caused damage, just a little extra cleanup." She sighed. "But he's also confessed to me that he's been the one doing things at my house these past weeks, too."

"What kinds of things?"

"Remember when I told you about the random stuff that was happening? Pulled-up flowers, tipped-over trash cans, and then all my patio furniture was turned upside down the other night. Well, it was Zach."

"I don't know what to say."

"I'm hoping you'll say that you'll come and get him. I think this would really upset your mom. Especially since Owen will be here soon."

"I'm actually already on my way. Mom called me about an hour ago, worried. Zach wasn't answering his cell, so I was coming to help her look for him. Give me fifteen minutes and I should be there."

"Thanks."

She stepped to the door.

Zach turned his tearstained face toward her.

"I just spoke to your brother. He'll be here soon."

He nodded.

She sat down in Ace's desk chair. "What got into you, Zach? Do you want to tell me about it?"

He stared at the floor, refusing to meet her eyes. "Just mad, I guess."

"At?"

He shrugged. "I dunno."

She was no Dr. Phil, but she'd give it a shot. "Zach, I'm going to try my best to keep Arnie from pressing charges against you. But I'm going to need you to explain this to me." Tough love might be her best bet.

He thought for a second.

Maybe it was the fact that he'd already been handcuffed once. Or maybe it was seeing the vandal wrestled to the ground and put into the patrol car. But he finally seemed to accept that he needed to state his case.

"Robert kept canceling on me. Because of *you*." He frowned. "I guess I just wanted you to feel bad." He sniffed. "I tried to get you not to want to go out with him in the first place."

She stared at him for a second as things clicked into place. "Wait a minute. Do you mean when you called me pretending to be him?"

He nodded. "After we met you at church that day, my mom kept talking to him about you. She really wanted him to ask you out." He shrugged. "I figured if you had a reason not to like him, maybe you'd never go out with him." His eyes filled with tears. "I know it was stupid. But I remember when my dad first started dating. All of the sudden he never had time for me anymore."

"And you didn't want the same thing to happen with Robert."

He shrugged. "I know doing all that stuff to your house was dumb. I was just mad."

And strangely, she understood. She remembered what it had felt like when her dad canceled on her—when it happened more and more—and she knew it had something to do with his "new" family. She'd have liked to tip over their trash cans, too. And she knew that since Zach's own father had dropped out of his life, Robert was the only father figure he had.

"Okay. I get that. It wasn't the right thing to do, but then, you already know that." She leaned forward in the chair and propped her elbows on the desk. "But why Silly-String the Michigan Monument? That's a lot different than just tipping over my lawn furniture."

He looked uncomfortable. "I knew that was a stupid idea."

"But you did it anyway?"

He sighed. "You know my mom's seeing that Owen guy?"

Probably not the best time to tell him she'd had a hand in the introduction. "Yes."

"I heard her talking to a friend. She said if stuff kept happening out at the park, they'd never find time to go out again."

And now it made sense. "So you were going to make sure that things kept happening?"

"Yeah, but it wouldn't have been permanent or anything. You can just wipe Silly String off."

She looked at him sternly and shook her head. "Zach, this is a national park. You don't just go around spraying monuments with Silly String."

He nodded. "I know."

She sighed. This was like pulling teeth. "And have you thought that maybe Owen is a good guy? And that your mom could probably use a friend?"

The scowl on Zach's face told her she'd overstepped the boundaries. He regained his stony silence.

She heard the back door open and got up. "You stay here," she told him, pulling the office door closed behind her.

Ace and Owen were in the hallway.

"What's the word?" she asked them.

"Have you met Jerry Miller before?" Owen asked.

She shook her head. "Sort of. I've seen him around town before, and he came to one of my cemetery walking tours not too long ago. What was his motive?"

"His dad's a veteran in poor health. They live in Adamsville. Jerry came out here a few months ago, wanting to get his dad on the list to be buried in the National Cemetery," Owen explained.

Kristy frowned. "But it's full, except for the widows of veterans who are already resting there."

"Exactly. And that's sort of the problem. Jerry saw a fresh burial a few weeks ago, so he got it in his head that we were lying to him about the cemetery being full. I guess he's been through a lot, and seeing the fresh grave just set him off."

"So he decided to get revenge by damaging the monuments,"

233

Ace said. "And you were right on the mark with the years. He'd gotten a list of monuments from somewhere. I think he said off the Internet. He just went down the list."

"And the list was in reverse chronological order," Owen surmised. "Boy, I feel stupid. I was the one he talked to about the National Cemetery. I knew he was angry when he left. But I didn't think about it again, even after the vandalism started. He just seemed so unassuming." Owen shook his head. "Guess you just never know about people, do you?"

"What about our other suspect?" Ace asked. "What was the deal with the Silly String?"

Kristy looked at Owen nervously. "It's Zach Aaron," she said, her voice a whisper.

Ace looked confused. "Who?"

Owen rubbed his head. "Dorothy's son. My friend. You know."

Ace looked at Kristy with wide eyes. "Robert's brother?"

Kristy nodded somberly. "Turns out, he's the one who's been pulling pranks at my house." She motioned toward Owen. "But once Dorothy and Owen started seeing each other, he decided to move on to bigger things."

"Did you call Dorothy?"

She shook her head. "I called Robert, actually."

Ace shot her a questioning look.

She shrugged. "I thought he should know."

Owen looked thoughtful. "Maybe I should call Dorothy and fill her in." He looked at his watch. "It's nearly ten. She's probably worried sick about him."

He left Kristy and Ace standing in the hallway.

"Robert should be here any minute."

"Great."

He could be so frustrating. She'd already told him she'd ended things with Robert. Yet he seemed irritated that she'd called him.

234

The phone in her hand buzzed, and she looked at the screen. "It's him. I'm going to go let him inside."

She opened the back door. Robert was just climbing out of his Honda.

"You can come in the back," she called.

He strode toward her, a tense expression on his face. "Thanks for calling."

She stepped outside and shut the door behind her. "I think he's pretty upset. As it turns out, he was trying to get me back for taking up so much of your time. And then when your mom started spending time with Owen. . ." She trailed off. "Well, I think that just made it even worse. It seems that he had a personal vendetta against the park because the rangers keep horning in on his family."

Robert sighed. "I should've done a better job of being there for him. I feel very responsible for this."

She shook her head. "I think he just feels displaced. I've been there. I was about his age when my dad left. It can be really tough."

"Do you know what will happen to him as a result of the vandalism?"

"Since he didn't actually do anything to park property, I doubt there'll be any consequences. And as far as my house goes, he didn't do any real damage. So I'm pretty sure we can just let it slide. I'll have to confirm it with Arnie, though."

Robert nodded. "Can I see him now?"

She opened the back door and motioned for him to follow her to Ace's office, where Zach waited alone, his head in his hands. He looked up at them, fear and regret evident in his eyes.

"Take your time," she said softly to Robert. "I'll be out front."

She closed the door behind her and followed the sound of voices. Owen and Ace were standing in the museum section of the visitor center.

"Long night, huh?" she asked as she joined them in front of a cannon.

Owen leaned against a glass case holding muskets and bayonets. "Definitely." He rubbed his eyes. "And I called Dorothy. She said Robert had called and filled her in. She was very apologetic about everything."

"Sounds like Zach has some issues," said Ace.

For some reason, his comment brought up Kristy's defenses. "His world has been torn apart fairly recently. He just handled his anger in the wrong way." She turned toward Owen. "Will he be in any kind of trouble?" she asked.

"I called and talked to Arnie about it. Since he didn't do any damage to the park, he's off the hook." He eyed her. "But if you want to file a complaint with the police about what he did at your house, that's your decision."

"I don't think that'll be necessary. I'm pretty sure Zach has learned his lesson."

"Plus, you're not seeing his brother anymore, so that should ease his mind," Ace piped up. "Right?"

"Right," she said, suddenly wiped out. Her head still spun with Ace's declaration of a couple of hours ago. She only knew one thing for sure. She wasn't going to deal with it tonight. Hopefully Ace would remember that love is patient.

And if he didn't remember that? She gave him a tired smile and said good night. Well then, that would prove her point that true love might not exist.

For some reason that thought didn't thrill her.

CHAPTER 45

Ace was exhausted. All he wanted to do was fall into bed. But he needed to finish the book he was reading about Civil War generals. He climbed into bed and forced himself to keep his eyes open, but the book in front of him may as well have been written in another language.

His mind kept wandering back to the kiss he and Kristy had shared. Had he been a fool to let her know how he felt about her? His instinct told him she felt the same way. Especially after the way she'd kissed him. That was some kiss. He just wished she'd had a chance to tell him what she thought. He knew he'd told her she didn't have to say anything, but he'd secretly hoped she would tell him that she felt the same way.

When they'd finally left the visitor center, she'd been preoccupied. She walked out with Robert and Zach, and he'd overheard her telling them not to worry about what had happened.

He'd hoped for a private good-bye, possibly another kiss, but by that time, Owen, Hank, and Arnie had been milling around in the parking lot talking and recapping the evening.

He closed the book with a snap. May as well give up on trying to learn anything tonight. The way his research was going, he wasn't going to meet his deadline. Maybe now that the vandal had been caught, he'd get back on track.

Ace had just clicked off the lamp when he heard a banging at his door.

He pulled on some sweats and ran barefoot to the window.

Kristy was standing on his front porch, pounding the wooden door.

Crying.

He threw the door open and pulled her inside. She fell against his chest, great sobs coming from her. He circled his arms around her and held on tight.

"Shhh. Whatever it is, it will be okay." For a long moment, he held on to her, her sobs never subsiding. Finally, she seemed to pull herself together and her cries lessened.

He led her over to the couch. "Can I get you something? Hot tea? Hot chocolate?"

He wasn't sure why hot beverages were supposed to make people feel better, but every time there'd been a disaster in his family, his mother had always offered them.

"Maybe just some Kleenex?"

"Of course." He grabbed a box off an end table and handed it to her.

She plucked a tissue from the box and began mopping the tears from her wet face.

"Do you want to tell me what happened?" He sat down next to her, unsure of what he should do. Crying women had never been his forte. And Kristy looked so pitiful. He thought he felt his own heart hurt a little bit just seeing the pain on her face.

"It's Brad. My friend Ainsley's husband."

He nodded. She'd told him about them. Whoa. That conversation was earlier this evening. It seemed like a year ago.

"I had a message when I got home. Ainsley is devastated, of course. He was killed while fighting a fire this morning. I'm not sure of all the details. Just that there were two men killed and he was one of them." The tears began to flow freely down her face again. "I finally got in touch with Vickie. We're going to fly to Arizona tomorrow and stay until the funeral."

He nodded.

"She's like a sister to me. Closer than a sister, actually." She wiped her eyes.

He thought of her biological sister and understood the sentiment. "Is there anything I can do?"

"Pray with me."

He grabbed her hand and bowed his head.

"Heavenly Father, please look down on Ainsley tonight. Heal her as only You can. Give her the strength she needs to face this tragedy, and the wisdom to turn to You for comfort. Lord, please be with Kristy as she travels. Keep her safe on her journey. In Jesus' name. Amen."

Kristy squeezed his hand. "Thanks. It would mean a lot if you'd keep her in your prayers these next few days."

He looked down and realized he was still holding on to her hand. "Of course." He pulled her to him and kissed her on the forehead. "I'll keep you in my prayers, too."

She gave him a teary smile. "And do you think you can keep Sam for a few days? I hate to ask you, but I don't have time to call to have him boarded. I've got the first flight I could get out of Memphis in the morning. If he ends up too much trouble, just call me and I'll have Mom come and get him."

"Don't worry about it. I get lonely here all by myself anyway. Sam and I will get along great."

She nodded. "I can't thank you enough." She stood up.

"You don't have to. I'm just glad I can help you in some way." He reached out and brushed away a wayward tear.

She looked up at him, her lips trembling. "You could hug me again."

He smiled. "I'd like nothing better." He pulled her to his chest, wishing he could take away some of her pain.

"I'm terrible in these kinds of situations," she said against him. "I never know what to say and am always afraid of saying the wrong thing."

He smoothed her hair. "The best thing you can do is just be there. Let her take the lead. If she wants to talk about him, let her. If she wants you to take her mind off of things, do it. You can't make her grief go away, but you can grieve with her."

She pulled out of his embrace. "Thanks. For everything."

He followed her outside to her Jeep. "Do you want me to come pick Sam up in the morning?"

"If you don't mind, that would be great. There's a key hidden underneath the mat on the back deck. It unlocks the back door. There's a tub of food in the kitchen, and I'll set out some bones."

He nodded. "Be careful. And if you think about it when you get there, call me and let me know you're safe."

"Sure." She climbed in the Jeep.

Ace stood and watched her drive off; then he walked back inside shaking his head. What a night.

CHAPTER 46

An overly perky flight attendant stood in the aisle, demonstrating the proper use of an oxygen mask. Even though she knew the drill, Kristy tried to pay attention. Better safe than sorry. Flying had never been her favorite thing. She said a silent prayer for a safe trip and leaned her head against the cold window.

Exhausted didn't begin to describe how she felt. She'd had to get up before 6:00 a.m. in order to get to Memphis to catch the flight. At least it was nonstop to Phoenix.

Vickie had called this morning with more details. Ainsley would be staying at her parents' house in Flagstaff for several days. It was too tough to be at the home she'd shared with Brad. Vickie's flight from Washington would arrive in Phoenix just a little after Kristy's.

Tap, tap, tap. The man next to her nervously tapped his fingers against the armrest as the plane began to move. Between the incessant tapping and the crying baby a couple of rows back, Kristy was wishing for her iPod. Of all the things to forget. Although with everything on her mind, it was a wonder she'd even remembered her luggage.

She draped her fleece jacket over her legs. The next time the flight attendant went by, she'd ask for a blanket. It could be one hundred degrees outside, but in an airplane, she still felt like an ice cube. She shifted in the seat and attempted to stretch her legs.

With all the commotion of yesterday, Kristy had barely had a second to be still. But now that she had nothing to do but sit and watch the clouds roll by, she was flooded with thoughts. The kiss with Ace. Catching the vandal. Finding out Zach had been taking out his frustrations on her house. And now Brad's accident. She tried to gauge her feelings on everything, but they were too tangled.

She settled as far as she could into the crook of the seat against the side of the plane. She closed her eyes and listened to the roar of the engine. The sound finally began to lull her racing mind into calmness. And after a few minutes, she finally drifted off into a much-needed sleep.

☯

"I'm so glad to see you." Kristy embraced Vickie at the Northwest gate. She stepped back and looked at her friend.

Vickie's shiny brown hair was cut into a smooth pageboy style. The blue and gray argyle twinset and gray slacks perfectly set off her petite figure. Vickie always described herself as "too buttoned up," but in reality, her style was classic.

Kristy caught sight of the single strand of pearls around Vickie's neck and smiled. Even in the midst of chaos, her friend was completely pulled together.

"I'm glad to see you, too, although being glad about it makes me feel guilty." Vickie pulled up the handle of her navy blue wheeled bag.

"I know what you mean." Kristy shook her head. "My heart is breaking for Ainsley, but I guess it hasn't really sunk in yet."

Vickie nodded. "Me, too." She motioned toward the rental

car sign. "This way. I made the reservation for a car rental. Hope that's okay."

"Fine by me. I'm just glad to be traveling with the planner."

Vickie laughed. "Yes, rental car and hotel are booked. Maps are printed. I even have a list of local flower shops. Remind me to call one as soon as we get to Flagstaff so we can have a plant sent to the funeral home."

"You are amazing. I think you really missed your calling. You'd for sure be a great event planner. Or personal assistant. Or anything that requires organizational skills."

"No, thanks. I love what I do."

Kristy smiled. "I know. I'm just teasing." She watched as her friend made the arrangements at the rental counter. Vickie hadn't changed at all since college. She was the dependable one. The girl who was always elected secretary of organizations and kept her closet arranged by color. On the road trips they'd taken with some of the girls from their dorm, meeting cute boys was on everyone's agenda but Vickie's. She always had her nose in a book—usually a classic—and didn't even notice that there were boys around, much less cute ones.

Despite their differences, Kristy and Vickie had become fast friends, and their friendship had carried on through the years. And even though they were about to embark on a sad trip, Kristy was glad to have her friend by her side.

After fifteen silent minutes, Kristy couldn't stand it. "Vick?"

"Yeah?"

"I think it would be okay for us to catch up. If anyone loved a good reunion, it was Brad."

"You're so right. It's hard to believe he won't be there to greet us."

"So how do we do this?"

"I have no idea." Vickie sighed. "All the etiquette books in the world don't prepare you for how to help someone who's lost the center of their universe." She smoothed her perfectly straight hair. "But you're right. Brad wouldn't have wanted us to be stoic for the entire trip. Remember how he used to make fun of the three of us, laughing so hard we could barely breathe?"

Kristy nodded. "Last time we were at their house, he told me he'd invested in special ear plugs to drown out the laughter so he could get some sleep. Said he didn't understand why with us everything that happened after 10:00 p.m. was automatically funnier."

Vickie laughed. "Okay then. No more silence. Fill me in on what's been going on with you."

Kristy exhaled and peered out the window at the dusty landscape.

Vickie glanced at her through oversized dark sunglasses. "Problem?"

"Not really. There is a new development with Ace, though."

"What's that?"

"He finally told me how he feels about me."

"And was I right? He's crazy about you, isn't he?"

Kristy smiled. "It seems that way. And. . ." She broke off. "We sort of kissed."

"Sort of kissed?" Vickie said. "I may not have much dating experience, but can you explain to me how you 'sort of kissed' him?"

Kristy laughed. "Okay. We definitely kissed. It took me by surprise, actually. It was the first time a guy has just kissed me without asking first."

"They usually ask your permission?" Vickie was incredulous.

"Yeah, at least the first time they do. Apparently I give off that kind of vibe."

Vickie shook her head. "At least you have guys wanting to kiss you," she said glumly.

She often referred to her inexperience like it was shameful, but Kristy had always thought it was sweet. She knew her friend hoped to find a love of her own someday. And when she did, it would be a big one. The kind that would last.

"Stop it." Kristy examined her friend's heart-shaped face. Vickie's translucent skin and tiny features always reminded her of a porcelain doll. "There are a million guys out there who want to kiss you. They just haven't had the courage to do it yet."

"Sorry. I get so impatient sometimes. I know the Lord has a plan for me. But it's hard not to feel like I'm the only person in the world who hasn't been in love. And I don't want a million guys. Just one." Vickie gave a tiny smile.

"Love isn't always easy, you know." She remembered the conversation she'd had with Ace about true love. "Nothing worth anything ever is."

CHAPTER 47

Patricia Garrett met them at the car, wearing a gingham apron over her black dress. She dusted her flour-covered hands on the apron and held them out to them.

"Girls," she said, pulling them to her. "So glad you could come. I know she'll be comforted just knowing you're here."

"How is she?" Vickie asked quietly as they followed Ainsley's mom into the brown brick house.

"About as you would expect. She's in the basement right now, but I don't think she's sleeping." She led the way down the hall. "I'm baking bread right now." She threw them an apologetic look over her shoulder. "I needed to do something to keep busy."

"Do you think it would be okay if we go see her?" Vickie asked.

"Please." Mrs. Garrett pointed to a wooden door just off the kitchen. "Right through there. Be careful on the stairs."

Kristy followed Vickie through the door and down the stairs. She dreaded seeing her friend.

They reached the bottom of the narrow staircase and stepped into what looked like a studio apartment. In the corner of the room, in the middle of a four-poster bed, sat Ainsley. Her arms were wrapped around drawn-up knees, her curly red hair unkempt.

Vickie went to her immediately.

"I'm so sorry," she said as she wrapped her arms around Ainsley. "What can we do?"

Kristy hung back. She knew there was nothing they could do. She felt out of place. How did Vickie always know what to say in every situation? "Yes, please. Is there anything we can do to help you?" she said in a muted tone.

Kristy awkwardly perched on the end of the bed, waiting for Ainsley to speak.

Ainsley's red-rimmed, amber-colored eyes filled with tears. "I'm just glad you guys are here." She took a shaky breath. "I don't know what you can do, though. Just listen, I guess."

Vickie sat down on the other side of the bed. "We're here. Whatever you need."

Ainsley swallowed hard. "I just keep thinking it's a bad dream. Everything is all cloudy and dull. He was the other half of me. And now. . ." She trailed off. "It's like my arm has been cut off. And my leg. And my heart." Tears began to drip onto the quilt she was wrapped in.

Kristy patted her leg. She couldn't fathom the pain her friend was feeling.

"And you want to know the irony?" Ainsley shook her head. "The day of the accident was the happiest day of our lives."

Vickie and Kristy exchanged confused glances.

A tiny smile broke through the still-falling tears. "That was the day we found out for sure that we're pregnant."

Vickie let out a squeal that resonated very loudly in the quiet of the basement. "You're pregnant?"

Kristy was silent. This was even worse than she'd expected. Not only had her friend lost her husband, but now she was about to become a single parent?

"Yes," Ainsley whispered and placed her hand on her belly. "Finally pregnant."

Kristy felt Vickie's eyes on her and met her gaze. Vickie's widened eyes told her that she needed to respond to the announcement.

"Wow. A baby." Kristy played with the quilt's frayed edge. "That's great news."

Ainsley let out a small laugh and grabbed her hand. "It's okay, Kris. You can be happy for me. I'm having to learn that deep happiness and deep sadness can coexist." Her voice grew stronger as she spoke of her news. "I had actually planned on calling both of you after the doctor's visit to share the news. I'd done a home test but wanted real medical confirmation before I told anyone. But then. . ." She stopped.

They knew what had happened then.

Ainsley brushed a springy red curl out of her face. "I just keep telling myself that at least he knew. At least he got to see that little blip of magic on the ultrasound screen. And now, somehow, it's helping me get through it knowing that I'll always have a little piece of him to hold on to."

Kristy closed her eyes, fighting back her own tears. She felt guilty now for not seeing the positive side of Ainsley's pregnancy. Of course it would help her deal with losing Brad.

God really did look out for His children, even when they didn't realize it.

◎◑

"Which bed do you want?" Vickie asked once they were back at the hotel.

"You choose. As long as the sheets are clean, I don't care."

Vickie laughed. "I never assume that the sheets are clean." She opened her suitcase and took out a perfectly folded sheet set.

Kristy's eyes widened; then she threw back her head and

248

cackled. "Oh, I so needed that today." She couldn't quit snickering as she watched Vickie pull the ugly motel bedding off the bed and replace it with the linens she'd brought from home.

"Glad I amuse you. But I saw that special on *20/20*. I'm not taking any chances."

Kristy shook her head. "What, no pillow?"

Vickie smirked and unzipped the outside pocket on her bag. She pulled out what looked like a deflated pool float. "It's an inflatable pillow," she explained in response to Kristy's questioning gaze. "Blow it up, put a case over it, and voila. A clean pillow." She popped out the plastic nozzle, and soon her crisp white sheets had a little inflatable pillow on top of them.

Kristy shook her head. "You never cease to amaze."

"Thanks." Vickie, looking very proud of herself, sank down onto her freshly made bed. "So how do you think she's really doing?"

"No idea. If it were me, I probably wouldn't be able to carry on a conversation. But she seems to be dealing with it as well as she can. I think it's good that her parents are close by. At least she can stay with them for a little while until she's ready to face their house again."

"And the news of a baby is such a blessing."

"Can I make a confession?"

"I love confessions." Vickie grinned.

"When she first said she was pregnant, I wasn't sure what to say. I didn't see how it could be a good thing. You know?"

"And now?"

"After I heard her talking about having a little piece of him still with her, I realized what a divine gift the baby is." Kristy shook her head. "If I know anything about Ainsley, it's that she will be a wonderful mother. And I think going through the pregnancy will give her something to focus on besides her loss. Don't you?"

Vickie nodded. "Yes. This way, she has motivation to get out of bed and to keep herself healthy. It's definitely a blessing."

"I know that she's still going to grieve. I don't think you ever really get over something like that. He was her world. If not for she and Brad, I wouldn't have ever even let the term *soul mate* enter my speech."

"So does that mean that now you believe in soul mates?"

Kristy leaned back against the stack of pillows. "Let's just say that I'm closer to believing than I've ever been. I still have my moments of doubt, though."

Vickie made a futile attempt to fluff her tiny pillow. "Well, I believe in them."

Kristy snorted. "You probably still think Prince Charming's gonna ride up on a white horse and carry you away, too, don't you?" Vickie's romantic notions had been honed by a lifetime love of Cinderella and Jane Austen novels. With the occasional chick flick thrown in for good measure.

"Maybe not a horse. More like a white Volvo or something." Vickie grinned.

CHAPTER 48

Sam's hatred of the leash was evident after just a few steps. For such a small dog, he sure was stout. Ace gave the leash another tug. "Come on, little guy. We're almost there." They'd only been walking five minutes. But Sam couldn't be coaxed along any farther. He sat back on his haunches and regarded Ace.

"Fine." Ace scooped the dog into his arms and carried him the rest of the way to the mortuary monument of W. H. L. Wallace. He sat down on the corner of the concrete step and put the dog on the ground. Sam scampered out as far as the leash would allow and collapsed, panting as if he'd been on a ten-mile hike.

Ace grinned at his canine companion. "You just might be the most spoiled dog I've ever met." He stood up and looked at the monument. It was comprised of a large concrete square with General Wallace's name on it. Two steps led up to the monument itself. In each of the four corners was a pyramid of cannonballs. In the center, a shiny black cannon tube faced the sky. Even though General Wallace hadn't actually died on the battlefield, the wound that had eventually ended his life happened right on this spot.

Life sure did throw curveballs sometimes. Ace often wondered what might've happened if Caroline had lived. Would they be together now? As much as a part of him wanted to believe that they would, deep down he knew better. He'd loved her, sure. But all the talk lately about true love had made him realize something. Caroline, even though she was his best friend, wasn't his true love. He'd miss his friend forever. But he took some solace in knowing she'd want him to be happy.

And with Kristy. Wow. The thing that took him most by surprise was how he felt when he was with her. She could be his best friend. Easy. But she could also be more. The memory of their kiss was evidence of that. He couldn't wait for her return. And once she returned, if she still needed some time to grasp what was happening between them—well, he could give her that.

☯

Funerals were never easy. Kristy had been to a few rare ones that seemed more like celebrations of a life well lived than sorrowful occasions. But each of those had been an instance where the deceased was far advanced in years and had lived a happy life. In a situation like Brad's, there was a feeling of heartbreak and the sadness of a life cut too short.

Watching her dear friend endure the pain of saying good-bye to her husband was even harder to bear than she'd anticipated. She'd clung tightly to Vickie's hand, her eyes traveling between the large photo of Brad that sat atop the mahogany coffin and the back of Ainsley's head as she sat in between her parents.

"It was a lovely service," Vickie remarked as she flipped on the headlights of the rental car. She followed a red minivan into the long processional of cars leaving the church.

Kristy nodded. "The preacher did a wonderful job."

They were silent for a moment.

"He really would've hated that, wouldn't he?" Vickie asked.

"Totally. He probably would've wanted us to tell funny stories about him."

Vickie smiled. "Maybe we can do that later, once we're used to him not being here anymore."

"The only comfort I have is knowing that Brad was a Christian."

"I know what you mean. That at least makes it a little easier."

Kristy looked out the car window, glad the day was overcast. Bright sunshine would've somehow been too much to handle.

⊙ɔ⊚

"More coffee?" Mrs. Garrett asked.

"I'm fine, thanks." Kristy scanned the crowded living room for a familiar face. She finally spotted Vickie speaking softly to an elderly woman. She made her way over.

"Your grandson was a wonderful man," Vickie was saying, patting the woman's arm. "We were all better for knowing him."

Kristy nodded her agreement.

"And you must be Ainsley's other college friend, the one who lives in Tennessee?" The woman looked at Kristy through red-rimmed eyes.

"Yes, ma'am. I'm Kristy O'Neal." She extended a hand, and the older woman took it in hers.

"I'm Martha Bledsoe, Brad's grandmother." She dabbed her eyes with an embroidered handkerchief. "We're all just devastated."

"I'm so sorry."

Mrs. Bledsoe spotted someone across the room and excused herself.

"Have you seen Ainsley?"

Vickie played with the single strand of pearls around her neck. "Not lately. She might've gone back downstairs. I can see how this could be a little overwhelming."

"You're probably right. Do you think it'd be okay if we went to see?"

"Sure. She might want the company."

They scooted through the crowd to the basement door.

"Oh, good. I was just coming to find you," Mrs. Garrett called to them before they could descend the stairs. "I think Ainsley is probably down there. This was just too much for her." She held up a box. "Could you take this to her? One of Brad's colleagues dropped it by. Said it was stuff from his locker. I thought it might make her feel better to look through it."

Kristy took the box. "Sure." She followed Vickie down the stairs.

Today Ainsley was sitting on a blue plaid couch. Her red hair was pulled into a bun, but corkscrew tendrils escaped. She still wore the plain black dress she'd had on at the funeral.

She looked up at them through puffy eyes. "No one tells you how to act," she said. "When all these people, these well-wishers, keep saying the same things over and over. 'We're so sorry for your loss,' or 'He was so young'. And I don't know what to say back. Because nothing they say makes it okay or makes it hurt any less." She motioned to the dark, empty room around her. "So I figured I'd just be better off to come down here. I think I make people uncomfortable anyway." She managed a brave smile. "But I hoped you guys would find me."

Kristy sank down in the overstuffed recliner opposite the couch, clutching the box.

"One of Brad's coworkers was here," Vickie said, sitting down beside Ainsley. "He brought the contents of his locker."

Kristy held up the box.

"But you might want to wait a few days before you look at them."

Ainsley looked interested. "No. I'd like to see it, actually."

Kristy handed the box over.

Ainsley lifted the lid and began pulling out the contents. She set the tattered wedding photo on the coffee table. "This was his favorite. He loved the way I was looking at him instead of the camera." She smiled. "He'd just made a wisecrack about the photographer, and I looked back at him just as the picture was snapped."

Kristy remembered their wedding day like it was yesterday. Such a celebration of love. It wasn't fancy, and it didn't come with all the bells and whistles of some weddings. She'd left the church that day thinking the ceremony was more about the marriage than the wedding. It had been refreshing compared to some of the extravagant weddings she'd been to.

Ainsley looked up at them, fresh tears in her eyes. "I was lucky to have had him for as long as I did."

They both nodded.

"I've known the kind of love most people only dream about." She covered her stomach with her hand and smiled tearfully.

She reached into the box and came up with an envelope stuffed so full it wouldn't close. She pulled out a stack of letters bound together by a rubber band. Flipping through them, she wrinkled her brow. "These aren't Brad's," she said.

"Do they have a name on them?" Kristy asked, glancing over her shoulder.

Ainsley flipped through the stack. "It looks like each one is only addressed to 'The Man of My Dreams' and is signed 'Love, me'."

Vickie looked puzzled. "And they aren't from you?"

"These aren't Brad's," Ainsley said again, shaking her head.

Kristy and Vickie exchanged glances.

Kristy reached over and took the stack of letters out of her friend's hand. "Then we'll just see to it that they get returned to the right person."

Ainsely nodded. "Good."

Kristy stuffed the stack of letters back in the envelope and projected calm for her friend's sake. She needn't have bothered putting up a good front, though. Ainsley had forgotten the letters already and was back to looking at the pictures and cards spread out in front of her.

Kristy stared at the envelope in her hand. Was there a lie lurking at the bottom of every declaration of love?

CHAPTER 49

I can't believe you brought those with you to the hotel," Vickie chided her.

"Why? She said they weren't his. So don't you think it's okay to look through them and see who they belong to?" Kristy looked up from the bed where she lay on her stomach, reading the letters one by one.

"It isn't our business," Vickie said, pulling some Crabtree & Evelyn lotion from her bag and smoothing it on her hands. "Besides, it's tacky to read someone else's love letters."

Kristy pushed herself into a sitting position and crossed her legs akimbo. "Listen to this. 'The time we spend together is magic. You are an incredible man. It would take an eternity for me to tell you how much I love you.' " She threw the letters down on the bed. "Not only are these poorly written, but they're also proof that Brad wasn't the devoted husband we thought he was," she said angrily.

Vickie gasped. "You don't know that for a fact." She chewed on her bottom lip. "And don't you dare utter a word of your suspicion in front of Ainsley or anyone in her family."

"I'm not completely without tact. I'll try my best not to put my foot in my mouth. Besides"—Kristy folded the letters together and bound them with a rubber band—"don't you think she'll come to the same conclusion at some point?"

"No. You saw her today when she saw them. There wasn't an ounce of doubt in her voice or on her face."

Kristy shook her head. "I guess at this point, her complete trust in him will protect her from the truth."

Vickie eyed her suspiciously. "Just make sure that you take those letters with you tomorrow when we go say our good-byes. Don't tell Mrs. Garrett what's inside, either. There is no need for the others to suspect. That wouldn't do anyone any good."

"I'd already planned on handling it that way." Kristy pulled back the bedcovers. "Don't worry. I promise not to make some kind of etiquette faux pas."

But as she drifted to sleep, Kristy couldn't help but have a sick feeling in the pit of her stomach. Ainsley and Brad had been the ideal couple. And knowledge that there might've been a secret side of Brad shook Kristy to the core.

⊙୭⊙

Ace paced behind the front desk of the visitor center. Kristy should be in the air right now. He'd said an extra prayer for her safety this morning, but he couldn't help but let worry cloud his day.

He tried to tell himself that planes were safer than cars, but then he started thinking about her fighting Memphis traffic and worried even more. He knew a lot of his worry stemmed from Caroline's accident. It had been such a wake-up call for him that life was fleeting.

One minute a person could be standing next to you, telling you their plans for the future, and the next you could be standing over their grave, clinging to only the memory of their past. Things just happen so quickly.

He'd spoken to Kristy this morning, right before she got on the plane. He felt like an idiot for calling. But he just needed to hear her voice. The intimate moment they'd shared last week was still replaying in his mind. And it was strange, but the moment that meant the most to him wasn't the kiss. It was the fact that when she needed someone to comfort her during a tough time, she'd chosen to share it with him.

He knew her well enough to know that moment spoke volumes about how much she trusted him. Maybe she didn't trust him completely yet. He could understand that after what she'd been through. But it showed him that she was at least on the road to trusting him.

And nothing would make him happier than the chance to earn that trust.

CHAPTER 50

Kristy felt a sense of relief as she turned beside the park entrance sign. She couldn't get home soon enough. All she wanted was to wash the plane germs off herself and fall into bed. In between her nice clean sheets.

When Ace had called this morning as she was boarding the plane, he'd told her that Sam would be waiting on her when she got home. She was glad. She didn't want to have to drive over to Ace's to pick the dog up. She had a feeling Ace would want to talk about her trip. She also had a nagging feeling that he was ready to talk about what had happened between them last week.

And the only thing she was sure of, besides Brad's infidelity, was that she wasn't ready to talk about her feelings yet.

She'd finally admitted to Vickie on the car ride to Phoenix just how much those letters had bothered her. "They were the only real-life, modern-day example of happily ever after I could come up with, and now I find out that it was all a sham," she'd said.

Nothing Vickie could say made her feel better. Not even when Vickie promised that she would at least think about signing up with an online dating service, and Kristy had been trying to get her to do that for years.

She parked the Jeep in the driveway and pulled her suitcase out of the back end. Sure enough, there was Sam in the window, his whole body wagging with happiness.

"Hey, little guy. Did you have fun with Ace?" She knelt down on the floor and let Sam give her puppy kisses. "Come on, let's go outside."

At her words, Sam ran to the back door, eagerly waiting for it to open.

Kristy unlocked the door, and he ran outside.

As she walked into the kitchen, she cringed. Her list. Her anti-Mark list was prominently displayed on the fridge. Had Ace seen it?

She flipped the light on and saw a shiny silver gift bag on the counter. That definitely wasn't there when she left. She went over and peeked inside. Gourmet hot chocolate mix, bubble bath from Bath & Body Works, and the newest John Grisham she'd mentioned she was looking forward to reading.

She set her prizes on the counter and spotted a card in the bottom.

Kristy, I know it was a tough trip. Here are a few things that I hope can melt away your stress. I missed you and can't wait to see you tomorrow. Ace

She thought back to the advice she'd given Robert about getting to know a prospective girlfriend. Ace certainly knew her well. He'd paid attention to her.

She just wasn't sure she was ready. She glanced at the list on her fridge. Was she ready to risk her heart again? How could she know for sure?

☙❧

Ace was at work extra early. He'd been so excited this morning, because he knew she was back. He looked impatiently at his watch. Of course, there was no need to be here early. She usually didn't make it until 8:00 a.m. on the dot, and sometimes that was even pushing it. He smiled.

"What are you grinning about?" Owen asked.

"Oh, nothing," Ace said, embarrassed.

Owen chuckled. "I figured you were just happy because Kristy'll be in today."

"Oh, is she coming back today? I'd forgotten." He tried to keep a straight face but lost it and burst into laughter.

Owen joined in. "So I take that to mean you'll be at the picnic together tonight?"

"That was the plan before she left town. I'm hoping we're still on." He grinned. "How about you? You bringing a date?" He leaned against the front desk, glad there weren't any visitors yet.

The older man nodded. "Dorothy's coming with me. She tried to back out, said she was embarrassed about Zach and the Silly String. But I told her nobody held it against her."

"Has he warmed up to you any more?"

"Maybe a little. I took him fishin' yesterday. Let him drive the boat." He shrugged. "That seemed to win me some points. Though I hate to bribe him."

"No harm in that. Once he starts to get to know you, he'll come around."

"I hope so. Can't help but feel for him, though. That's a tough age, even without all the changes he's had to get used to."

Ace wondered if every age could be considered a "tough age." It sure seemed that way to him sometimes.

"Can you handle things out here?" Owen put his hat on top of his head. "I need to run over to the administration building."

Ace nodded. "Take your time."

Owen walked through the swinging doors and into the office area. In a second, Ace heard the back door close. A moment

262

later, it opened again.

"Did you forget something?" He stepped through the swinging doors, and there she was. Kristy. "Oh. It's you." His heart beat a little faster at the sight of her.

"Sorry I'm running late." The dark circles underneath her eyes gave away her exhaustion. Even so, he had to resist the urge to pull her into his arms right there.

"Not a problem." He grinned. "I'm glad you're back."

She nodded. "Me, too. And thanks for the gifts. And for keeping Sam." She finally gave him a tiny smile. "I can't thank you enough."

"Tell you what. Say you're still going to be my date to the picnic tonight, and we'll call it even."

"It's a deal."

The bell on the front door rang. The first visitor of the day had arrived.

"I'll take care of them." He motioned toward the front desk.

She slowly made her way into the seasonal office. Something was different.

"Hey."

She stopped in the doorway and turned to face him.

"Are you okay?"

She nodded. "Just tired, that's all."

He stepped through the swinging doors to greet the visitors, but he couldn't shake the feeling there was something wrong with her besides exhaustion. Of course, she had just been through an emotional time with her friend. That was probably it. She'd be back to her old self in a few days.

CHAPTER 51

"So this is the famous potato salad recipe, huh?" Ace picked up a tattered piece of paper from his kitchen counter and looked it over.

Kristy glanced over at him and nodded. "I called and got it from my grandma. She promises it'll be the best anyone has ever tasted. And it probably would be, if *she* were the one making it." She picked up a bowl of freshly scrubbed potatoes from the sink and began laying them on a cutting board he'd fished out of the cabinet for her.

Cooking in his kitchen seemed so personal. And while just a week ago she'd thought she might be ready to get personal with him, now she wasn't so sure. Especially in light of what she'd learned about Brad. Maybe there was no such thing as trustworthy.

"I think anything you cook will be perfect." Ace leaned against the counter and crossed his arms. She could feel his eyes on her, and the blush she felt creeping across her face irritated her. "Don't watch me cook. The least you can do is make yourself useful. How about you start getting the rest of the ingredients out of the fridge? They're in a brown grocery bag in the bottom."

His nearness was suddenly unnerving to her, despite the fact that they'd worked together all day. She'd tried all day to avoid being alone with him, because she still wasn't sure how to proceed. On the one hand, she was afraid of getting hurt again. But on the other hand, she'd missed him while she was gone. It had come as a total surprise. If she hadn't been staying with Vickie, she knew she would've given in to the temptation to call him each night she was there.

"I happen to enjoy watching you. You're a cute cook." He grinned as she narrowed her eyes. "Fine, fine. I'll help." He pulled the bag from the bottom of his fridge, set it on the counter, and began pulling out items and lining them up near where she was working.

"Thanks." Kristy tried to concentrate on the task at hand. Chopping potatoes and putting them into the bowl. In a second, though, she felt Ace watching her again. She looked in his direction, a rogue strand of blond hair falling in her face.

"Here, let me," he said softly. He reached over and tucked the hair behind her ear, his hand lingering on her jaw. "I hope you know I meant what I said the other night, Kristy."

He said her name with such a sweetness, she couldn't help herself. She dropped the knife into the bowl and turned to face him. He cupped her face with his hand, and she stared up into his brown eyes, her heart pounding. When he'd kissed her before, it had been dark. But kissing him in broad daylight. . . That would be admitting that she felt the same way he did, wouldn't it? She didn't turn away, though, even as he lowered his mouth toward her. The phone jangled next to her, and they both jumped. She laughed nervously.

"Saved by the bell," he whispered with a wink, "but not for long." He grabbed the cordless phone off its holder. He glanced at the caller ID and straightened up. "I'll just take this out on the patio." He rushed out the side door, and Kristy could hear the beep as he hit the answer button.

Well, that was strange. Who could be calling who had him so flustered? She shrugged. Surely he'd tell her once he was through. She glanced around the kitchen, wondering where she could find a large pot to put the potatoes in. After peeking in all of the bottom cabinets and finding nothing, she grabbed a step stool to help with the climb to the top cabinets. She put one foot on the stool and a knee on the counter. She felt the wet puddle of water just as her knee slipped. Her flailing hands grasped for whatever she could reach. As she made contact with the speaker button on the phone set, she finally lost her balance and tumbled to the tiled kitchen floor. Ace's voice filled the room.

"Tomorrow will be fine. I can be in Nashville around lunchtime."

"Lunch sounds great." An unfamiliar female voice caused Kristy to sit upright on the floor. "Can I choose the restaurant?" the woman asked.

"Not if you're going to make me try escargot again." Ace chuckled.

"Where's your sense of adventure?" The woman's tinkling laugh seemed to cover Kristy like a blanket. She couldn't believe her ears.

"My sense of adventure is just fine. But how about we try the Pancake Pantry this time?"

"That sounds great. I'm looking forward to it, Ace. See you around noon on Saturday. And you have my cell number in case you need to contact me before then, right?"

The familiar way the woman said his name let Kristy know this wasn't a casual acquaintance. Not that casual acquaintances tried to force each other to try new foods. Still stunned by what she was hearing, she finally picked herself up off the floor.

"I've got it. And I'm looking forward to it, too. See you soon."

As they said their good-byes, Kristy rushed to the phone console and hit the speaker button. The voices that had filled the room were finally quiet, but Kristy's thoughts prevented her from being left in silence.

Unbelievable. He says he has feelings for me, but he's meeting some chick from Nashville for lunch? First my dad, then Brad, now Ace. They're all the same.

She leaned her head down on the counter and sighed.

"What's this? Has the cook gone on strike?" Ace's cheery voice jerked her upright.

Don't let him know that you know. Just see what he says. Maybe Miss Tinkling Laugh is his sister.

She turned toward him and gave her best smile. "Important phone call?"

"Nah. Just a friend of mine needing some information." He set the phone back on the console and peered into the bowl of potatoes. "Looks like all the chopping is finished."

Kristy stared at him, her brain refusing to work. "I needed a large pot, but I couldn't find one."

Ace pulled one out of the top cabinet and handed it to her. As she filled the pot with water, she tried not to look at him. She could sense him shifting from foot to foot behind her.

"Everything okay?"

She shrugged. "What's not to be okay?"

"O–okay. . . ," he said slowly. "I guess I'll run and change."

She nodded without turning around. Although Kristy had already gone home to change into picnic attire, Ace still had on his ranger uniform.

"I'll just finish making the potato salad," she said coldly. "It's not like you were much help anyway."

Ace took a step into her line of vision, and even though she could feel his eyes on her face, she refused to meet his gaze. Finally, he walked out of the room.

She shook her head. How stupid she was to think he was actually falling for her. All his talk about true love and trust.

The end-of-season picnic was in full swing by the time they got there. Ace led her over to where the tables were set up, buffet style, and scooted over a bowl of pasta salad so she could set her dish down. Owen waved them over to where he and Dorothy were seated.

"So glad to see you again, Kristy," Dorothy said after they'd hugged and sat down. "Your mom told me about your friend's husband. I'm sorry."

Kristy nodded. "Thanks. It was a hard loss for her. And she's expecting a baby, too, so that makes it even worse." *And then there's the fact that her husband was cheating on her, even though she refuses to believe it.*

"God will get her through, if she'll let Him," Ace said from behind her. "I know that hopeless feeling, though. It's almost like you wake up in someone else's life."

"Your situation wasn't exactly the same as hers is." Kristy's harsh words came quickly. "She lost her husband, her best friend, the father of the child she's carrying. And you don't even know the whole story, so don't act like you have all the answers."

Owen cleared his throat. "So what did you guys bring? We decided just to pick up a couple of pies from the bakery in Savannah."

Kristy looked at the expression on Owen's face and regretted her sudden explosion.

Ace, however, wasn't going to let it go. "What is that supposed to mean? Are you angry at me for something?" He glowered at her a little, and even though there was an audience, she had to fight the urge to outright accuse him of two-timing her.

"Sorry. I'm still upset about the situation." She smiled tentatively at Owen and Dorothy, who were watching her with interest. In her heart, Kristy knew she was just trying to pick a fight. It didn't matter what it was about.

Their awkward moment was finally interrupted by Hank. "Ladies and gentlemen, first I want to thank you for a great summer season. We've had some real challenges this summer, and I'd like to personally thank each of you for working hard to keep your Shiloh Park truly a place of peace." The crowd clapped. "And now, Superintendent Bramblett will come forward and give us his yearly wrap-up."

As Arnie went to the podium and droned on about the fantastic summer season they'd had at Shiloh, Kristy's mind wandered. Not only was Ace meeting a mystery woman tomorrow in Nashville, but also Kristy's job would be over soon. They might be able to justify keeping her for a week or two after Labor Day, but she knew it was time to start looking elsewhere. And frankly, she had no idea where to look. She'd thought she was over this patch in her life where she felt adrift in a strange sea of hopelessness, especially after the good summer she'd had. And she hated to admit to herself just how much Ace had to do with that. He'd given her hope, made her believe she deserved good things. And now. . .now he was turning out to be just one more in a long string of disappointments.

The audience clapped and cheered, and Kristy shook herself back to reality and joined in, choosing to ignore Ace's questioning glance. Hopefully he was the only one who'd noticed her spacing out during Arnie's speech.

Ace pulled her aside before she could join the line for barbeque.

"What's the deal? Are you okay?"

"Sure." She tried to keep her voice even. "Hey, do you want to go to Hagy's for lunch tomorrow?" *Let's see what kind of excuse he gives.*

Ace scratched his head. "Oh, I meant to tell you. I'm going to Nashville tomorrow."

"Nashville? Why?"

He frowned. "Well, among other things, I need a new laptop."

She scanned his face for signs of lying. None. He was good. "Why don't you just go to Jackson or Memphis? It'd be closer."

"I know. But I've not spent much time in Nashville, so I thought it would be a nice way to spend my day off. I wish you could come."

I'll bet you do. I'm sure your little mystery girlfriend would appreciate me tagging along on your lunch date. "Too bad I have to work. But I hope you have fun." She could barely keep from blowing up at him. Really letting him have it and telling him that the jig was up. She knew the truth. She wouldn't be made a fool again.

As Ace walked her home after the barbeque was over, he grabbed her hand.

"Don't you think we should talk about things?" he asked. "You're certainly keeping a guy hanging." He laughed as they walked up her driveway. "I mean, I know I said you could take some time to think about how you felt, but I'm feeling awfully exposed here." He spun her toward him and pulled her close. "And I think we have some unfinished business."

He leaned toward her, but she pulled back. "Tomorrow. We'll talk about it tomorrow." She managed a shaky smile. "Be careful in Nashville."

Kristy went to bed with an unsettling thought. The feeling in the pit of her stomach was no longer only anger. It was anger mixed with jealousy.

○

Ace felt awful. He hated keeping his meeting with Diana from Kristy. But he wanted to wait and see how their lunch went before he came clean. And he did need to get a new laptop. His

270

old one was worn out from all the use it had been getting lately. So it wasn't as if he was lying, just not telling the whole truth. But once he got back from Nashville, it would be time to fill Kristy in.

CHAPTER 52

Kristy's pale reflection stared back at her from the mirror. Sick day? She thought about it for a few minutes then looked at the clock. She could still catch Owen before he left his house. But if she called in sick, she had a feeling she would just spend her day wondering what Ace was up to and who the silky-voiced woman was. And what they were doing.

The decision was easy. Throw herself into the day and hope it turned out to be a busy one.

"Morning." Owen nodded at her as she came through the door. "Did y'all have fun at the barbeque last night?" He peered at her over his coffee cup.

Kristy wondered briefly if she should apologize for her outburst but decided against it. "Yes. How about you and Dorothy?"

Owen's face lit up. "We had a good time. She's a nice lady."

Was he blushing? As awful as Kristy's luck with love was, she could still be happy for her friend. "She is that. I think y'all make a cute couple."

"I didn't know how lonely I was until I met her."

Kristy thought about her own life and how empty it had become before Ace came along. "I know what you mean. I'm glad you found one another. And how is Zach taking it?" She was worried about him, despite the feelings he'd harbored against her. She knew from experience that sometimes it makes you feel better to have someone to direct your anger at, even if that person doesn't deserve it.

"I think he's finally coming around. He seems genuinely sorry for everything that went on out here. And I've promised to take him to a UT football game at Neyland Stadium once the season starts. He's pretty excited about it."

From the sound of things, Zach wasn't the only one excited about it. Kristy had always thought Owen would make a wonderful father. It looked like maybe he was at least going to get the chance to be a father figure.

The day kept dragging on. Because it was their last day, Matthew and Mason were in high spirits, cracking jokes and acting silly. But not even their antics could pull her out of the depression she felt herself falling into. She wasn't sure whom she was angrier with—Ace for not telling her the entire truth about what he was doing today, or herself for starting to trust him. She knew one thing, though. It wasn't worth it. She'd seen the rug ripped out from under others. How her mom had struggled when her dad left them. How she had fallen apart when Mark had left her standing at the altar. And she could easily look into the future and see how awful it was going to be once Ainsley finally came to grips with the truth about Brad's infidelity. For all of Ace's grand talk about historical loves, he couldn't follow through.

"You look like you could stand some fresh air." Owen stepped to the office door. "Since it's nearly five, why don't you go with Mason to get the cemetery flag?"

She rose slowly and put her hat atop her head. "Sure." Lowering the cemetery flag was one of her favorite things. At the end of the day, the cemetery was deserted and peaceful, and going through the ritual of lowering and folding the flag always felt like the perfect cap to the day. But not today. Instead of calming her, the cemetery filled her with sorrow.

"Are you okay?" Mason asked her as they set off toward the cemetery gates.

She managed a weak smile. "Just a lot on my mind, that's all."

"Oh." He was quiet for a moment. "Well, usually when I have a lot on my mind, it helps me to talk to Matthew." He shrugged. "Sometimes just saying it all out loud helps me to figure it out. Maybe you should tell someone your troubles."

Such a good kid. She'd grown quite fond of him. His brother, too, but Mason's sweet shyness had stolen a piece of her heart. She smiled. "That's a great idea, Mason." The irony was, the person she'd gotten used to telling her troubles to was the person who'd caused her troubles this time.

"Since this is your last day here, why don't you do the honors?" she asked.

Mason solemnly undid the ropes and slowly began to lower the flag.

One lone man stopped his perusal of the headstones and stood at attention. Kristy noticed a single tear trickling down his lined face. Based on his age, she guessed he was a Vietnam vet.

They silently folded the flag until it was a small triangle.

"Afternoon, sir," Kristy said to the visitor, who still stood at attention.

The man wiped his eyes and nodded at her.

"Thanks for taking care to fold it correctly. That flag is a beautiful sight, even flying over a sea of headstones."

Kristy smiled at him, ashamed of herself for begrudging the task. Just goes to show that you never know who might be watching, whom you might be able to touch.

Mason tucked the flag underneath his arm, and they headed back to the visitor center. Finally, the day that seemed to drag on forever crept to an end. As soon as the second hand on the big clock over the front desk ticked five o'clock, Kristy said her good-byes to the twins, grabbed her hat and purse, and began the short walk home.

"Have a good weekend!" Owen called to her as the door closed behind her.

A good weekend wasn't likely on her agenda. She wondered again, as she'd done a million times since the day started, what Ace was doing.

☯

Ace checked his watch again. Kristy was home by now. He considered calling to see how her day had gone but thought better of it. She'd acted so oddly last night at the picnic. He was beginning to think maybe he'd imagined the spark between them. Had he been a fool to confess his love for her so soon?

He maneuvered his blue extended cab Chevy around a slower car and hit the cruise button. He'd be back to Shiloh soon. He was nearing the Lexington exit. Sure enough, there was the sign for Shiloh. He breathed a sigh of relief. Even after just one day in the city, he couldn't wait to get back to the peaceful town. And after the tedious meeting he'd had with Diana, he was more than ready to relax. Things had gone well, but there were challenges still to be dealt with before he felt free to share the details. He'd be glad when he could let it all out in the open—and especially let Kristy in on the secret he'd been carrying around all summer. But would she be supportive? Only time would tell.

CHAPTER 53

Kristy paced back and forth across her living room. Despite the small space, she felt like she was walking miles. Ace was on his way over. He'd called from his house and asked if he could stop by. Said it was time for them to talk about the other night. He hadn't mentioned much about his day, though.

The ringing bell brought Sam running, and Kristy threw open the door. His blue button-down shirt and khakis were dressier than she was used to seeing. Had he actually dressed up to meet his lunch date?

"Aren't you going to invite me in?"

"Oh. Sorry." She opened the storm door, and he stepped inside. He immediately pulled her into his arms for a close hug.

She stiffened, willing herself not to get lost in his embrace.

He inhaled deeply as he released her. "You smell nice."

"Thanks." She hated the feeling of dread in the pit of her stomach. She'd almost trusted him with her heart. And as it turned out, he didn't deserve it after all.

He followed her over to the couch and sat down, Sam immediately jumping in his lap.

"So how was Nashville?"

"Crowded." He stretched his legs out in front of him. "Living here, it's easy to forget what it feels like to be stuck in traffic." He absently stroked Sam on the head. "I did have a delicious lunch, though. A place called the Green Hills Grille. You ever been there?"

She tried to read the expression on his face. Is this where she should confess that she'd overheard about his lunch plans? No, she decided, it all hinged on whether he would tell the truth, unprompted by her. "I don't think so." She forced a laugh. "You're braver than I am. I hate eating out by myself." Her gaze zeroed in on his eyes. There it was. Guilt. Her heart quickened. She'd been fooling herself to think he was a trustworthy kind of guy.

"I don't know about brave. I was just a hungry man." He stopped scratching Sam, and the dog immediately jumped down and scampered off. "But I did what I went there to do. I got a new laptop. I'm a Mac guy now. We'll see if that makes me as cool as those commercials let on." He chuckled. "Anything happen at the park today?"

She could feel her heart in her throat now. She wanted to cry. To scream. To go back in time and refuse to let herself get close to him. How could he lie to her so easily? If his lunch date had been innocent, he would've told her about it. But the fact that he'd chosen to let her think he'd dined alone. . .well, that pretty much said it all. "Nothing much. Pretty typical Saturday."

He reached over and grabbed her hand. She was torn between tearing it out of his grasp and enjoying the last contact she would have with him. She knew what had to be done.

"Kristy. I told you the other night how I feel about you. It's the complete truth. I love you." He reached over and brushed a strand of blond hair from her forehead, letting his hand caress her face. "I need to know how you feel. You've left me hanging here far too long."

She jerked away from his touch and saw the confusion reflected on his face. "Look, Ace." *Just breathe. No tears. Like ripping off a Band-Aid.* She shook her head. "There's just no way this can work." She saw his jaw tense. "For one thing, we're completely different. And for another, who knows where I'm going to end up? The downside to you having my job, besides the fact that you've ruined the program I worked so hard to build, is that my position is over in two weeks. Two weeks. So while you can sit here, secure in your career, I can't. I'm job hunting right now, and if there is one thing I know I don't want, it's a long-distance relationship." She shifted uncomfortably.

"You never know. Something might open up. And you and I both know you don't want to leave this area." He wasn't grasping what she was trying to tell him.

"No, I don't. But I'm not going to have a choice." She was shivering now. Any warmth she'd once felt from being near him had gone ice cold.

"But what about us? I love you. And I'm pretty sure you're starting to feel the same way about me."

"No. You're a nice guy. I'm flattered that you think you love me. But, Ace, come on. You're in love with the idea of love. Not me. You think life can turn out like a movie or a fairy tale. It can't. Your idea of forever. . .it doesn't exist. At least not for me."

The sadness she felt flood through her body was reflected in his face. She doubted he would've flinched more if she had actually hit him. And as angry as she felt at the entire situation, there was no satisfaction in knowing she'd caused him pain. No matter that he was a liar and possibly a cheater. He was still decent as far as men seemed to go. But she wasn't going to risk her heart again. No more.

"Kristy, please. Consider what you're saying. I've seen the love in your eyes, even when you tried to hide it. Think about the time we've spent together. How can you just walk away?" His pleading cut to her heart. But he wasn't being completely honest with her. That was a deal breaker for her. Even if he was twice the man Mark had been.

She shook her head. "After everything I've been through, I just can't do it." She stood up and resumed her pacing from before. "Besides, you're always going to be pining away for Caroline." She could see her words hit him square in the face.

"Wait a minute. That's not fair. I'm not pining for her. Yes, she was an important relationship in my life, and yes, it has been hard moving forward. But we were never more than friends. What I have with you is totally different. And the fact that you'd even bring it up is really low." He rose from the couch and stepped in front of her, grabbing her by the arms. "What is wrong with you? I know things have been tough lately, with your friend losing her husband, and now you facing your time here being over. But don't make me the bad guy. I'm not responsible for those things."

"Well, in a way, you kind of are." She knew she was bordering on being unreasonable but couldn't stop herself. "I mean, obviously not about Ainsley's situation, but you are the reason I don't have a job come Labor Day."

"Would you listen to yourself? I'm not the reason for that. Blame yourself for not making good decisions. Blame Mark for leaving you high and dry at the altar. But don't put that on me. When I took that position, I had no idea there was someone who felt ownership over it. You quit. And I think it's time for you to finally deal with it."

Sam cowered underneath the coffee table, looking up at them with wide eyes.

"It's okay, little buddy." Kristy bent down to pat the dog on the head. She glowered up at Ace. "I am dealing with it. I deal with it daily, okay? When I see you sitting there with your feet propped up in my office, it is a constant reminder of my bad decisions."

He raked his fingers through his hair. "I don't want to fight with you. I just want you to think about what you're throwing away. This thing between us has real potential. But it's like you can't even see it because your view of things is so clouded over."

Kristy patted her hand over her heart. "See this? It is barely pieced together. Hanging by a million threads. I can't. . .no, I won't. . .risk getting broken again. It isn't worth it. Not now and not ever."

He stared at her for a long minute. "Aren't you afraid that someday you'll regret this? That you'll look back on this moment and wonder what might've been if you'd been able to trust me with your heart?"

She sighed. "See? That's just it. I can't trust you with my heart. I don't trust you at all. And that isn't going to change. I'm sorry."

"No. I'm sorry. Sorry that you have so little faith in me," he said softly. "But you've said enough. I may love you, but I do have some pride. I'm not going to beg. You won't have to worry about me again." He reached down and gave Sam a scratch under the chin. "Good-bye." And without another word, he walked out, closing the door behind him.

Kristy sank to the floor, the tears already beginning to flow.

CHAPTER 54

Two days off and a sick day thrown in for good measure later, Kristy could finally go more than a few minutes without crying. She knew she had to face the world again. But for three days, she'd hidden. She and Sam went to stay with her mom. One look at Kristy's pale face and Nancy had put her straight to bed, never questioning whether the sickness was physical or emotional. Thank goodness for Grandma's famous chicken soup recipe.

"Morning," she called to Owen as she came through the back door.

He stuck his head out of his office, his brow furrowed. "Hank just called. Asked me to have you come straight to his office."

"What's it about?" She didn't want another ambush in Hank's office.

"That's between you and the chief." Owen shook his head.

"Fine. I'll be back in a minute." Kristy marched up the stairs. She had a feeling she knew what her meeting was about. It was time for her to decide if she wanted to try to transfer to another park or leave the service completely. She couldn't bear the thought of being at another park. So it was time to hang up her ranger hat and look for another career.

"Kristy. Have a seat." Hank riffled through a stack of papers strewn across his desk until he found the one he was looking for.

She settled herself across from him, ready to seal her fate. In just one short week, she would no longer be a park ranger. Surely she'd find some other career that made her as happy. Right?

"I guess you already know what this is about," Hank started. "It's unfortunate that we have to lose a good ranger to get a good ranger back, but as they say, them's the breaks." He passed a form across the desk to her. "If you'll sign at the bottom, you will officially be reinstated to your old position."

Kristy froze. Her old position? What was he talking about? "Um, I'm not sure what you mean. What's going on?" All the papers on Hank's desk seemed to swim in front of her, and she tried to focus on his weathered face.

Hank's eyes grew almost as wide as his bifocal lenses. "I thought you knew. Ranger Kennedy is gone. Took all his vacation in one lump and headed up north somewhere." He leaned back in his chair. "You really didn't know? I thought you two had gotten close this summer, but guess I was wrong."

Kristy felt like she'd been doused in ice water. Ace was gone? Without telling her? She struggled to make words. "Oh. Well. Of course. Yes, I definitely want my old position." She shook her head. "I just didn't realize he'd be leaving so soon." A poor attempt at trying to save face, but it was the best she could come up with. She silently signed the paperwork and rose to her feet.

"Feel free to move your things into the yellow office." Hank snickered.

Kristy barely managed a smile. "Sure." She forced her legs to carry her down the stairs.

"Guess you heard the news, huh, kid?" Owen asked kindly. "Ace came by to see me before he headed out. Said it was going to be a shock to you, but he knew you'd be happy to have your job again." Owen shrugged. "He also said something about how you'd be glad to be rid of him, but I told him he was crazy." He looked at her white face. "I was right, wasn't I?"

"What? Oh. I guess things just work out the way they're supposed to. Things are finally back to normal again." The reality of her situation was taking some time to sink in. Her job, her office, her life. All back to the way it used to be. Except that Ace was gone. And somehow that canceled out any bit of happiness she might've felt.

❦

It took every bit of self-restraint he possessed to keep from turning his truck around. But Ace knew that wouldn't solve anything. Sure, he could beg her to change her mind about things. And there was a chance she would relent. But he wanted her to love him without having to be convinced or prodded.

Besides, he was pretty sure the anger she'd released on him the other night had very little to do with him. Whether it was about Mark, Brad's death, or something else, he wasn't sure. But he did know enough to realize there were some things she was going to have to work out on her own. His being there was only going to make it worse.

He'd stopped by the visitor center on his way out, comforted by the knowledge that it was her day off.

"Are you sure, man?" Owen had asked. "Seems a shame for you to skip out of town like this. With a little notice, we could've at least had you a going-away party."

"Sometimes you just have to move on." Ace had shrugged. "The offer to teach history back in Illinois wasn't going to be on the table for long. It just worked out that way."

The truth of the matter was, he'd really had to pull some strings to make it happen. If it hadn't been for all the research he'd done this summer, he probably wouldn't have gotten the offer.

Plus, it helped that he knew the department chair pretty well.

And while he was hopeful about the future, and hopeful that someday he'd see Kristy again, he knew it would be better for her if he just faded away. Now if his feelings for her would just fade away. But he had a feeling those would be sticking around for a long time.

Annalisa Daughety

CHAPTER 55

"Y ou have a visitor at the desk. Says it's urgent." Owen poked his head into Kristy's office.

She looked up from a draft of the new Junior Ranger booklet she was proofing. "Who is it?" She wasn't expecting anyone.

An uncomfortable look crossed Owen's ruddy face. "I really don't want to get in the middle of it. But since we're light on visitors today, maybe you should get out of here and talk to him. Take your time." Owen exited, closing the door behind him.

Ace. It must be Ace. Finally. Kristy breathed deeply. After nearly a month, he'd come back for her.

She glanced in the mirror behind the door. Her looks needed a little help. It had been so long since they'd last seen each other, she didn't want to face him looking all unkempt. The way her green trousers hung on her frame surprised her. Had she lost weight and not noticed? But ever since Ace went away, she hadn't had much of an appetite. Not even Hagy's tempted her much anymore.

She grabbed her purse in search of a brush. There was no way to get the ridge out of her hair from the day's ponytail, but she needed to do something. She brushed out her hair and redid the hairstyle. There. Not winning any awards, but at least it looked smoother. A little powder and lipstick, and she was ready to see him. At least her physical appearance was ready. But her insides were in knots.

She opened the door, trying to figure out what she was going to say. Apologize, for sure. And hopefully he would do the same.

She rounded the corner. The excitement in the pit of her stomach made her feel like she'd had one coffee too many. She eagerly scanned the visitor center for him.

"Hey." A familiar voice startled her. Not the voice she was expecting.

Mark's blond hair was longer than it had been the last time she'd seen him. But his eyes were the same slate blue she remembered. Vickie called them "steely" after the first time she met him.

"Why are you here?" She couldn't help herself from asking.

"You haven't returned my calls. Ignored my e-mails. Kristy, I really need to talk to you." Mark seemed on edge, which was a change from the normally in-control guy she was used to dealing with. He'd always been completely unexcitable. But today he was so keyed up he was practically twitching.

"I'm not sure we have anything to say to each other. You should've called first."

He snorted. "Like you would've answered. I've been trying to reach you for months. I finally figured surprise might be the best tactic to get you to talk."

"I'm pretty sure I can count the number of times you tried to contact me on one hand. So don't act like you've been going to a lot of trouble to reach me." She was irritated. Sure, he'd called a couple of times. But never left a message. And the e-mails had just asked her to call him. Not much meat to the messages. They hadn't deserved a reply.

"Come on, Kristy. I'm here now. At least hear me out." She could see there wasn't a way out. She sighed. "Fine. Let me grab my hat. We can go down to the employee picnic tables. There won't be anyone around."

She passed Owen's office on her way to her own. "I'll be out for a bit."

He looked up from his computer screen. "Sorry I didn't tell you it was him. I was afraid you'd refuse to come out of your office. And if I had to deal with him much longer, I'd have given him a piece of my mind."

She smiled. "It's okay. But can you cover for me for a little bit? I'm hoping this will be a short conversation, but you never know. Is that okay?"

"Take as long as you need." He gestured toward the empty front desk. "Nothing much going on around here today."

She grabbed her hat and keys and forced herself to go back to where Mark stood waiting. Talk about a bad day. He held the door open for her as they silently exited the visitor center. This small gesture, which once would've thrilled her, only angered her now. She didn't want him to do anything nice for her, however small.

"So how have you been?" he began as they walked across the grass toward the picnic tables.

Really? All these months and he wanted to make small talk? What in the world?

"Fine. And you?" Suddenly she felt a little sick. Why was he doing this? He wanted something. Forgiveness? The few wedding gifts she hadn't returned? That seemed more likely. Or maybe he'd finally realized she had his collection of Indiana Jones movies.

"I've been better. Work is good. I actually had to travel to Memphis for meetings this week. I'm playing hooky today so I can see you."

Typical. Two birds, one stone. Classic Mark.

They sat down opposite one another at the table. The cold stone of the picnic bench seeped through Kristy's uniform, sending a chill through her body, and she crossed her arms in an attempt to warm up. She didn't eat there often, since she lived so close. But back in college when she still lived with her mom, she'd spent many a lunchtime here in the seclusion. No danger of an inquisitive visitor down here by the maintenance compound.

"So what brings you here today, Mark? I know it isn't your love of history."

He'd been bored to tears with her job. Every time she tried to tell him a story of something she'd learned about that had happened in 1862, he rolled his eyes. He'd never even attended any of her ranger programs, not once in the entire three years they were together.

"No. It's you. Look, Kristy. . ." He trailed off and reached across the table, grabbing her hand.

She looked down at their hands. Once, she'd thought his would be the hand she held during the ups and downs of her life. During births and deaths and everything in between. But no more. She pulled her hand away.

"Just say what you've come to say, please."

"I still love you." His voice cracked with emotion.

CHAPTER 56

Kristy swallowed hard. Love? He loved her? She opened her mouth, but no words formed.

"Don't speak. Let me. . .let me say what should've been said a long time ago." Mark leaned forward into the picnic table, as if to draw himself closer to her somehow.

"I messed up. And believe me, I know it. I hate what I did, how I treated you." He shook his head. "But I want to make it up to you now, if you'll let me. It didn't take me long to realize what a good thing I had with you. And I'm sorry I didn't see it before. Please. Let's give this another try." He sat back and waited for her response.

She was frozen. Frozen to the spot, frozen in time. How could this be? This chapter in her life was supposed to be over. She'd begun to move on. Yet here he was in front of her, acting as if no time had passed. But she knew better.

"You did have a good thing with me. But you see, I didn't have a good thing with you. Not really. Don't you remember how it was? The fighting, the tension, the general disagreeing on everything from restaurants to TV channels? Have you seriously forgotten all of that?"

"That was just opposites attracting." He smiled.

"No. It wasn't. It was two people who never should've stayed together for so long in the first place. Mark, I'm thankful to you. Thankful you didn't show up at the wedding. And yes, it's taken me a long time to get here. Six months ago, the words you just said would've had me melting. And while a tiny piece of me loves the thought of riding off into the sunset with you, that's just not going to happen. We were so wrong for each other. We brought out the worst in each other. You know that. You have to know that."

"We had some good times."

"I'm not saying there weren't good things about our relationship. But the bad far outweighed the good. If you'd really think, you'd remember."

"Come on, Kris. Give us another chance." He, once again, grabbed her hand from across the table.

She shrugged it off. "Mark, I don't know where this is coming from. Loneliness, maybe. But we aren't right for each other."

"Three years. Three good years." He shrugged. "Why throw that away?"

She sighed. "Mark, do you believe in true love? The kind that lasts through time and space?"

"I guess. And I truly love you." His eyes were pleading across the table.

She nodded. "Yes. And a little piece of me has love for you. But not the kind of love we deserve. I'm through with settling. I'm not the same girl you knew."

She stood from the table and began pacing underneath the tall oak tree. "I've spent years worrying so much about how other people feel that I've forgotten to worry about my own feelings." She stopped in front of where he sat, watching her. "I'm looking for a big love. The kind of love that makes it into history books. The kind that keeps soldiers warm at night, even when they're on a faraway battlefield." She paused. "And you and I don't have that. We're compatible half the time, at best. Most of the time, the best thing we had going for us was that we agreed on a pizza topping. But, Mark, we didn't agree on much else. You mocked my faith. You put down my career choice. And I thought you spent too much time on the golf course. If you had actually shown up at our wedding, we'd have been in for a lifetime of misery."

He reached out and took her hand again. "Are you sure?"

She pulled him up from the bench. "Consider this the best gift you'll ever get. I'm telling you to go. You and I are finished. We did have some good times. But it's time for both of us to move on. So you go find her. Go find your person who will be there with you through your journey. And I'll go find mine."

He stared at her for a long moment. "Can I hug you?"

She nodded.

He pulled her close, and she breathed in his familiar smell. "I forgive you," she murmured.

"What?" he whispered, his lips against her ear.

"Never mind."

She watched as he walked up the hill and out of sight. It was funny. She'd thought her life was all but over when Mark didn't show up to their wedding. But now she saw it had been mostly her wounded pride that was hurt. The pain she felt with Ace gone made her realize that she hadn't really known loss before. And she knew now what she had to do. It wasn't going to be easy. But if she was going to find out if happily ever after existed, it was necessary.

CHAPTER 57

Kristy searched through the stack of papers that sat on top of the battered white desk in her spare bedroom. She knew those notes were here somewhere.

She hadn't even meant to tell Mark she forgave him for leaving her standing at the altar. The words had slipped out. But as soon as she'd said them, she realized that those were the very words that might just set her free.

All last night, she'd thought about the sermon she'd heard about forgiveness. Even though it had been months ago, before she'd screwed things up with Ace, she was sure the notes she'd taken that Sunday were probably still around somewhere.

She sifted through a stack of old *TV Guides*, but it wasn't there. She found a stack of church bulletins from last month and thought she might be onto something, but didn't find the pages she was looking for. She sat down and thought about that Sunday. It had been the day Ace came over to fix the fence. The day Mark had dropped off her savings bonds. A glimmer of hope sprang forth, and she opened the top desk drawer. There, underneath the envelope with her name scribbled on it, was a little scrap of paper.

At the top, she'd written simply, "To Forgive."

She went to the kitchen table and sat down, Bible in hand. Maybe it was finally time to put the past behind her. The whole past.

◎◎

Kristy pulled the list off her refrigerator and read over it one last time. *Forty reasons why Mark and I weren't right for each other.* She shook her head. She'd meant it this afternoon. She did forgive him.

The longer she dwelled on why she and Mark were wrong for one another, the longer she was holding on to the past—letting it creep into her present and impact her life. It was one thing to learn from her mistakes. It was another to keep daily reminders of them in her kitchen.

She folded the list in half and tore, repeating the action over and over again. Talk about cathartic. The pieces fell at her feet like confetti. Gone was the pity party from previous weeks, and in its place was a celebration. Letting go felt good. She grabbed a broom and swept the tiny pieces of paper into a dustpan, dumping them into the trash with a flourish. *Good-bye, Mark.*

Kristy sat down and sighed. If only she could get rid of the other toxic relationships in her life that easily. She looked down at the notes she'd made from her studying. Colossians told her to forgive others as the Lord had forgiven her. She thought back on her life. How many times had she asked for forgiveness? Too many to count. And she believed with certainty that God had forgiven her. Shouldn't she try to do the same?

She flipped over to Ephesians 4:31 one more time. Bitterness. Rage. Anger. Were those words that could describe her? She had a sinking suspicion that they were.

She knew reaching out to Sarah wouldn't be easy. And trying to make amends with her dad would probably produce thoughts that she'd have to ask forgiveness for later. But if there was one thing any good student of history knew, it was that those who don't learn from the past are bound to repeat it. And it was time to change her patterns.

CHAPTER 58

Indian summer had turned into full-fledged fall. Brightly colored leaves adorned the trees, making a walk through the park a feast for the eyes. Deep reds, yellows, and greens meshed, forming a spectacular sight as Kristy turned the corner near Water Oaks Pond. She held tightly to Sam's leash as he inspected the base of a tree.

The past weeks had been tough. Thoughts of Ace were never far from Kristy's mind. She was startled, sometimes, by a memory so sharp it felt like it had just happened. She'd finally used the last of the bubble bath he'd given her, and just the small act of watching the remainder of the liquid dissolve into the hot water had brought her to tears.

But Kristy knew she was finally dealing with the parts of her life she'd avoided for too long. And it had taken Ace's abrupt exit to make her do so. That was the only silver lining she could find. Hopefully, someday, it would all pay off.

Sam pulled her down the road, past the Tennessee Monument. She paused briefly, remembering the moment they'd shared at that spot.

"How can you not believe in love?" Ace's words haunted her. How was it that she'd allowed herself to become so jaded? And how was it possible that she'd lost the one person who'd actually had the ability to make her believe in love again?

The ringing of her cell phone brought her to reality. Fishing the phone out of her jacket pocket, she glanced at the caller ID. Sarah. She took a deep breath. All of a sudden, the message she'd left for Sarah earlier in the week didn't seem like such a great idea. But what was done was done.

"Hi."

"Hi, Kristy." Sarah sounded flustered. "Sorry I've just gotten around to returning your call. Both kids have been sick and things have just been crazy."

"Sorry to hear it. I hope they're better now."

"I think everyone's finally recovered"—her voice faltered—"except for maybe me."

"Are you sick, too?" Kristy pulled on Sam's leash and attempted to lead him toward the parked car. For such a small dog, he certainly had a lot of willpower. He clearly wasn't ready for his jaunt outside the confines of the fence to be over.

"I have a sinus infection, I think. But I haven't even had time to go to the doctor. You wouldn't understand how it is, though."

The goodwill she'd planned for this call went out the window as something inside Kristy snapped.

"Why not? Do you think single people don't get sinus infections? Do you think that just because I don't have a husband and children, I don't know what it's like to be overloaded and overwhelmed? Because I do, Sarah." Kristy's raised voice alerted Sam, who scampered toward her with interest. "And furthermore, I'm tired of your insinuations that my life is somehow not as complete as yours. I'm happy for you. Why can't you be happy for me?"

Sarah was quiet for a minute. Then she sneezed.

"Bless you." Even through her anger, Kristy felt sorry for her sister. And for herself. Sorry that she'd let things go on for so long between them without saying anything.

"Thanks. For the blessing, not for the going-off. I don't know what you're talking about anyway. I never said your life wasn't complete."

"You didn't have to. You imply it every chance you get. It's as if you can't wait to point out that things haven't always gone according to plan for me as they have for you. But you know what I've figured out? It isn't my plan or your plan that matters. It's God's plan. And obviously He knows better than either of us, wouldn't you say?"

"Well, yes. I suppose I hadn't thought of it that way."

"Sarah. . ." Kristy trailed off. "Remember when we were kids? We were best friends. We shared secrets and dreams. What happened to us?" She sighed.

"I guess we drifted apart. We didn't have the same interests. You were all cheerleader captain and beauty queen, and I hated that stuff."

"Don't you mean you hated me?" May as well get it out in the open.

"*Hate* is such a strong word."

Kristy smiled in spite of herself.

"But maybe I resented you a little."

Now they were getting somewhere. "Resented me? Why?"

"You were good and kind and such a straight arrow. Mom always wished I could be more like you."

"Did she say that?"

"Well, not in so many words, but she thought it."

Kristy rolled her eyes. "Whatever."

"And remember that summer I got shipped off to live with Dad? Come on, Kristy. That was low. Dad didn't want me there. He told me that flat out."

Kristy cringed at the thought. "Sorry. But Mom didn't know

297

what to do with you. You were out of control at that point. You wouldn't even speak to me then. And Mom was convinced you were about to join a cult or something."

Sarah chuckled. "I was just trying to be different."

"Different from me, you mean?"

"Something like that. But I hated myself for it. It's hard to go down a road you know is wrong, just for spite."

"Well, you should at least be thankful to me for one thing." Kristy opened the car door, and Sam jumped inside.

"What's that?" Sarah asked.

"Bringing Andrew into your life."

There was a long, silent pause on the other end.

"Sarah?"

Her sister's voice was muffled when she finally answered. "Yes," she said weakly, "I am grateful for that."

"You don't exactly sound grateful." Was Sarah crying?

"Sorry," Sarah gulped. "I am. Andrew helped to save me from what I was about to become." She took a deep breath and let out a tiny laugh. "And to think, I only came home that weekend to make you mad by showing off in front of your goody-goody friends. Who knew it would change my whole life?"

Kristy wasn't buying it. "What's wrong?"

Silence again.

"Are you and Andrew having problems?"

Sarah's sigh came through the phone line loud and clear. "I don't know what we're having. Nothing big, hopefully. But we probably need to have a talk like this ourselves."

"Why don't you get someone to stay with the kids and surprise him at work for a lunch date?"

"Do you really think you're qualified to be giving relationship advice?" Sarah paused. "Sorry. I do that without thinking."

"The question is, why do you do it?"

"I guess because I'm a little jealous of you."

298

Kristy felt like she'd been stabbed with a bayonet. "How could you be jealous of me?"

Sarah gave another small laugh. "Let's face it, Kristy—I went from living in the dorm to marrying Andrew. I've never had to fend for myself the way you have. You are your own person, but sometimes I don't even know who I am."

Kristy felt tears burning her eyes. "I know who you are. You're a strong woman. You have to be. I mean, look at the way you take care of your husband and your kids. You balance it all." She felt like she needed to say more but wasn't sure what. "And you have the best-decorated house I've ever seen."

Sarah giggled. "I do have good taste, don't I?"

"You do. And a wonderful family. I'll be praying for you."

"Thanks, but we'll be fine." The earlier vulnerability in Sarah's voice was gone as quickly as it had come. "Save your prayers for someone who needs them more."

Kristy shook her head. She wouldn't let Sarah build up all the walls they'd torn down in the last few minutes. She cleared her throat. "I'll get to my reason for calling, then." Deep breath. "I'm really trying to turn over a new leaf. And I'd like for us to start over."

"Start over?"

"Yes. I'm letting go of the past. Sure, you and I have had some differences. But I'm done with them. I'm not holding a grudge anymore."

Sarah was silent.

"Anyway, I just wanted you to know. I'd like us to be friends. But if we can't be, that's okay, too. Either way, I love you. And I hope you'll consider it."

Kristy felt like the unspoken words were the most important ones. *I forgive you for the way you've treated me.* As she and a very confused Sarah hung up, she felt good about it. She was letting go of the toxic bitterness she'd been carrying around. And it felt great.

CHAPTER 59

I think it's admirable what you're doing," Vickie said. "I read somewhere that forgiving those who have hurt you is the most empowering thing you can do."

"I don't know about that. But if God can forgive us for all of the dumb stuff we do, then it's only right that I forgive others for the things they've done to me."

"Very true."

"But there is one other thing." Kristy took a sip of coffee. "I'm going to stand up for myself from now on."

"You're kidding!"

Kristy chuckled at Vickie's amazement. "There's nice. And then there's too nice. I let Sarah and my dad treat me horribly. I can forgive them for it. But that doesn't mean I have to keep letting it happen."

"Wow." Vickie was clearly impressed.

"It was becoming a pattern. The two of them, then Mark. I was so afraid of hurting them, I allowed myself to be hurt over and over. So now that I've forgiven them, I'm moving forward. I would like to be friends with Sarah. But if she can't do that, I'm not going to dwell on it anymore. I've made my peace."

"How about your dad?" Vickie had been her friend for a long time. She'd been there in college to witness every time Kristy's father had made plans with her only to cancel at the last minute.

"That phone call was a little less civil than the one with Sarah." Kristy shuddered at the memory. "He just didn't get it. I honestly think he didn't think he'd done anything wrong. But I said what I needed to say. I'm letting it go. And I let him know, in no uncertain terms, that if I got married again, my prospective groom wouldn't be forced to ask his permission." She sighed. "I can always wish that part of my life were different, that I'd come from a stable two-parent home." She shook her head. "But I didn't. This is who I am. And I'm not letting it affect the rest of my life the way it's affected me up until now."

"So you really think you can do it?"

"Absolutely. It was like knocking over dominoes. Once I talked to Mark and then threw out the list I made, it all became so easy from there."

"How about Ace?"

"I haven't gotten quite that far just yet. I'm still not sure I can trust him."

"If not him, then who? From what you told me about him, he sounds like a pretty amazing guy. Are you sure you don't want to even try to find out if he was cheating?"

"Not yet. I don't know if I want to know. What if he was? I'm not sure I could deal with that."

"Speaking of cheating. . .have you spoken to Ainsley lately?"

"Not in the last week or so. You?"

"Yes, actually. And I was going to wait and let her tell you, but since I have you on the phone, I will."

"Tell me what?"

"Those letters we found in the shoe box? The ones you and I assumed meant Brad had been having an affair? Well, come to find out, she was right all along. They didn't belong to him. They belonged to the other guy who died in the same accident. Some of their belongings got switched accidentally when they boxed them up."

Kristy drew her breath in sharply. She'd been so sure. It had seemed that there was no doubt that her friend had been wronged.

"You still there?" Vickie asked.

"I guess maybe sometimes things aren't always what they seem after all."

"Can you say 'jump to conclusions'?" Vickie replied.

"Do you think she knew how certain I was that they belonged to him?"

"You've never had much of a poker face. But I don't know that she paid much attention." Vickie sighed. "Of course, I'm not much better. I wasn't as sure as you were that those letters belonged to Brad, but I did think it was mighty suspicious. Are we horrible people for thinking ill of a dead man?"

"I do feel bad about it. But the evidence was there and seemed so clear. Most anyone would've thought the same way we did. But I'm so glad it all got straightened out."

"You know Ainsley. She didn't doubt him, even for a second."

As she hung up the phone, she realized that was the piece she'd been missing. The not doubting someone, even for a second. In all of Kristy's relationships, it was as if she'd just been waiting for the other shoe to drop. She'd been anticipating the mistakes that would be made.

Maybe now it was time for her to take a leap of faith.

CHAPTER 60

"**S**ure is quiet around here without Matthew and Mason," Owen remarked one day as they were counting the money from the cash register.

Kristy felt certain his unspoken thought was that it was also awfully quiet without Ace to liven things up. "It sure is. But it's almost Christmas. Before you know it, summer will have rolled around again, and we'll be up to our eyeballs in tourists and seasonal programs."

Owen grinned. "You have big holiday plans?"

"I'm probably going to keep it pretty low key. My sister and her family are coming in on Christmas Eve. We'll do presents at Mom's and have a meal." She smiled. "I'm excited about it, actually. Sarah and I both got webcams, and I've been talking to Emma and Walker every few days. They've given me quite a Christmas list." She noticed a gleam in his eye. "How about you?"

"I probably shouldn't tell you this." He was gleeful. "But I can't help it. I just hope I can hold out until Christmas." He bustled into his office and came back with a tiny box.

"Is that what I think it is?" Kristy asked.

Owen popped open the box. "If you thought it was an engagement ring for Dorothy, you'd be right." He held the ring out so she could see it.

"It's beautiful." And it was. A single round diamond flanked on both sides by sapphires in what looked to be a platinum setting. It was perfect.

He grinned broadly. "You think she'll like it?"

"I think she'll love it." She put the ring back inside the box and handed it back to him. "Do you think she has any idea?"

"We've talked about it. But I don't think she'll be expecting it or anything." He shook his head. "I can't thank you enough for introducing us. She's a special lady." He got a faraway look in his eye. "And you know, it's weird, but I think she and Helen would've been friends." He smiled. "I sort of think Helen is watching down over us, glad I'm not by myself anymore."

"I'm sure of it."

She gave him a hug, and he patted her shoulder.

Then he shifted from foot to foot.

"Listen, Kristy. I know this is none of my business. And I don't like to pry."

She felt a lecture coming on.

"But I've noticed that you're the one who's alone now. And I don't like it."

"I'm fine. No need to worry about me." She patted his arm.

"No. You're not fine. You might say you are. But I know better. I've seen you sitting in your office. Even that yellow doesn't cheer you up anymore. Have you thought about calling him?"

No need to ask who "him" was. She sighed. "It's just not that simple. I said some horrible things to him. And I'm afraid I probably jumped to a rather awful conclusion. Why would he even want to talk to someone who was willing to automatically believe the worst?"

"Love's a strange thing. Filled with all kinds of forgiveness."

There was that word again. Seemed to be haunting her everywhere she went.

She shook her head. "I don't even know how to get in touch with him now. He didn't exactly leave me his forwarding address."

Owen bit his lip. "What if I told you that I know where he is? Would you want me to tell you?"

She sank down into one of the blue plastic chairs just outside of Owen's office. Did she want to track him down? He could easily say he didn't want to see her or hear what she had to say. Was she ready for that? Or if his reaction was positive, was she ready for that?

"I honestly don't know." She played with the radio holder on the side of her belt. "Have you been in contact with him all this time?"

Owen looked sheepish. "I have." He leaned against the door frame. "Look, Ace is a good guy. A little impulsive sometimes, but he has a good heart. If it hadn't been for him, I know I wouldn't have started going back to church." He shook his head. "He really reached out to me, saw that I was going through a tough time. He didn't have to do that. He didn't know me from Adam. And he was the one who told me not to tell you that I knew where he was. He said that he hoped maybe, someday, you'd decide on your own that you wanted to see him again. He asks about you, though, in nearly every e-mail or phone call."

For a split second, she felt betrayed. But she didn't blame Ace for not wanting her to know his whereabouts unless she asked for them. Maybe she wasn't the only one with a little pride.

"You know, I think I would like to know how to get in touch with him. Just in case I want to send him a Christmas card or something."

"Right." Owen nodded. "He moved back up north. He's been teaching history this semester at a community college."

That made perfect sense. He would be a wonderful professor.

"Do you have a phone number or anything?"

"Actually, he's going to be in Nashville this weekend. In case you're up for a road trip."

She looked at him curiously. "Why?"

"Some kind of Civil War expo they're having at the convention center. He said he'd be there Saturday and Sunday. Thought I might want to come over." Owen shrugged. "But I've already got plans. There's a men's retreat at Chickasaw. Some kind of father-and-son thing. Zach really wanted to go, so I promised him I'd fill in for his old man." Owen beamed with pride.

"Wait a minute. Why is he going to be at a Civil War expo? He isn't that much of a Civil War buff. Those things are for hard-core fanatics."

"I guess you'll just have to ask him." Owen wrote down a number on a sticky note and handed it to her.

Kristy gazed at the phone number. Would calling it bring happiness? There was only one way to find out.

CHAPTER 61

Kristy could hardly concentrate at work on Saturday. She'd made her decision. Sam was safely tucked away at her mom's, and come five o'clock, she was Nashville bound. She'd arranged to spend tonight with Allison, an old college friend, and after church tomorrow, she'd see what the Civil War Expo was all about. And hopefully run into Ace.

She'd decided against a phone call. It would only be awkward. Not that an in-person meeting would be much better, but it would beat the inevitable discomfort of trying to make amends over the phone.

Now that she was less than twenty-four hours from actually seeing Ace again face-to-face, she had to admit the nervous feeling in the pit of her stomach was throwing her for a loop. She felt as if she were finally at the end of a long journey. There were many things she wanted to say to Ace—needed to say to him, even.

For starters, she needed to tell him that now that she'd let the blinders of her past fall away, she no longer doubted him for a second. She knew he hadn't been cheating on her. Everything about him proved to her that wasn't a possibility. But even with her new faith in him, there was still a big unknown. What would his reaction be?

So she was going to do what she'd sworn never to do again. Take a leap of faith and hope that her heart was leading her down the path God meant for her to take.

@⟳@

Kristy snuggled farther into the fluffy down comforter in Allison's guest bedroom. She'd had a wonderful evening catching up over dinner with Allison and her husband, Scotty. They'd laughed and reminisced about their college days while looking through their old photo albums.

But now, in the silence, the reason for her visit to Nashville was keeping her awake. What would she say? What would he say? What if she was too late?

Try as she might, she couldn't fall asleep. Her head was too full of potential conversation. First, she'd play it as she hoped it would go; then the worst-case scenario. She figured, if she anticipated each version, come tomorrow she'd know what to say no matter what happened.

When the clock showed 2:00 a.m., she couldn't take it anymore. She needed help.

Kristy climbed out of the cloudlike bed and sank to her knees. Perhaps if she turned her troubles over to the Lord, He would see to it that she got some sleep.

@⟳@

Kristy pulled her Jeep into the parking garage across the street from the Nashville Convention Center and turned off the ignition. Her heart had begun to pound harder with each passing mile. Now that she was actually here, she felt as if it might jump right out of her chest.

She glanced at herself in the rearview mirror. Thank goodness for good concealer. She'd woken with dark circles underneath her eyes, a sure sign of her lack of sleep. She touched up her lipstick and smoothed her hair. She'd worn it long and wavy because she knew Ace had liked it that way, but she was now regretting the decision. Maybe it was too much. She toyed with the idea of a ponytail but finally decided against it.

She climbed out of the Liberty and clicked the lock button on her key fob. Normally she liked the *beep-beep* sound her car made to signal the alarm was armed, but today it made her jump. She made her way across the parking garage and pushed the button for the elevator. *Ding*. A gray-haired gentleman emerged from the elevator, carrying an armload of books. He was wearing a kepi similar to the one Kristy wore sometimes for her rifle demonstration. She was in the right place. "Sir?" she called.

He stopped and turned. "Yes."

"Once I get into the convention center, which floor is the Civil War Expo on?"

He gave her directions, and in a minute, she was on her way. Her pounding heart was now accompanied by a swirling feeling in her stomach. Once she was inside the convention center, she ducked into the nearest ladies' room and tried to calm herself down.

She stood in front of the full-length mirror. A red turtleneck, dark jeans, and her new black high-heeled boots had seemed like a good idea yesterday when she'd packed. But today, looking in the mirror, she wondered if it seemed like she was trying too hard. It suddenly occurred to her that she and Ace had never seen each other in cold-weather clothes.

She couldn't prolong the moment any longer. She wondered if he would just be milling about, looking at the different booths. Once inside the exhibit hall, she scanned the crowd for his familiar figure. It would be her luck if his plans had changed and he'd decided not to make the long trip to the expo. But she was here and at least had to try to find him.

A poster caught her eye. It looked like a number of Civil War authors were holding a joint book signing at the expo. Every now and then, authors came to Shiloh to do their research. Some of her coworkers had even been used before as sources for books. She scanned the list to see if there were any familiar names. Even if she didn't find Ace, she could always get some books signed to give to Owen and Hank for Christmas. As she ran her finger down the list, it lingered on one. Wallace "Ace" Kennedy.

Her breath caught in her throat. Ace? Was an author?

She looked again. Sure enough, there beside his name was the title *Gentleman General: The Life and Times of W. H. L. Wallace.*

Wallace Kennedy. W. H. L. Wallace. Suddenly his knowledge of Ann and Will's love story made sense. He must be a descendant.

Why didn't he tell her? Had he been writing all summer? She thought back to all the times he'd shown up at work bleary eyed and tired. He must've spent his nights writing. And the way he lingered in the archives. And all the research books at his house. And the new laptop. Things began to fall into place.

"Excuse me," she said to a man selling "authentic" Civil War bullets. "Do you know where the book signing is?"

"Go all the way to the back. They're set up along that far wall." He pointed a stubby finger to his right.

"Thanks."

She made her way through the crowd to where she could now see tables of authors set up, stacks of books on each table. And then she stopped.

He did look scholarly in his crisp white button-down shirt, khakis, and tweed jacket. He was laughing at the person standing beside his table. Kristy stepped a little closer. A shapely blond woman touched his sleeve as she threw back her head and laughed. The tinkling sound met Kristy's ears. She'd have known that laugh anywhere. It was the woman from the phone call she'd overheard the night of the picnic.

Kristy turned quickly on her heel and all but ran out of the convention hall. She nearly knocked down two old men wearing Union uniforms as she made her escape.

"Watch it, young lady," one of them called after her.

She didn't stop until she was safely inside her SUV. She dropped her head against the steering wheel. She shouldn't have come here. It was a mistake.

CHAPTER 62

She started the engine. Her foot on the brake, she put the Jeep in reverse. As she looked behind her to make sure nothing was coming, she noticed the bumper sticker of the car parked directly behind her. *I love my firefighter husband.*

Foot still on the brake, she stared at the bumper sticker. Tears swam in her eyes. Ainsley loved her firefighter husband. So much that even in the face of what seemed to Kristy like irrefutable evidence, her love never wavered. And in spite of the fact that Kristy had vowed to have that kind of faith in Ace, at the first test, she'd wavered. She slammed the car into park and jumped out. No more doubt.

She walked back into the exhibit hall, the heels of her boots digging into the carpeted floor. This time, she didn't pause for mirrors or directions. She walked straight to Ace's table and waited her turn.

"Who should I make the book out to?" he asked without looking up.

She took a breath. "Kristy."

His eyes met hers. She'd always heard people talk about time standing still. And for a moment, she experienced it herself.

He rose from the table.

"Diana," he said, "I need to take a break for a few minutes."

The blond was at his side in a moment. "Sure thing." She nodded toward his table. "I'll put a card up that says you've gone to lunch or something."

He nodded. "Thanks."

Diana gave Kristy a once-over then stepped around the table and stuck out her hand. "I'm Diana, Ace's editor."

Kristy accepted her hand and shook it. "Kristy. A former coworker at Shiloh."

"Of course." Diana made a "get out of here" motion with her perfectly manicured hand. "Take your time."

Kristy silently followed Ace out of the exhibit hall, her mind racing. His editor. If only she'd have asked him about the call, she could've saved herself a lot of anguish. But if she was being completely honest with herself, she knew she would've found another reason to end it with him. She just hadn't been ready.

Ace finally stopped in a secluded lobby area and turned to face her.

They both began speaking at once.

"How did you know. . ."

"I can't believe you wrote . . ."

They stopped and smiled at each other.

"You first," he said.

"I had no idea you were writing a book."

"Well, I wasn't sure how successful I'd be at it. It took a lot of research. I've known for a while that I wanted to leave the park service and give teaching a try, but a lot of universities like their history professors to be published." He shrugged. "So I figured I'd spend some time at Shiloh researching and writing. Plus, the topic was important to me."

"And your name. Does that mean you're. . . ?"

"A descendant of W. H. L. and Ann Wallace. Yes." He shrugged. "Sorry for the secrets. I didn't want to make a big deal about it. I've heard you guys making fun of those visitors who come in and say they're descendants of Albert Sidney Johnston or Ulysses Grant. I didn't want to seem like one of those people."

She shook her head. "I can't believe you didn't tell us." She paused. "Not even Owen?"

"Not while I was working there. I filled him in after the fact, though. I would've told you then, too, but the last time we spoke, you made it pretty clear where I stood with you."

She nodded. "About that," she began.

"You don't have to. . ."

She covered his mouth with her hand. "Stop. I do have to. I just need you to listen for a minute."

He nodded, and she removed her hand from his mouth.

"I couldn't handle it then. It was all too much. My life had crashed around me to the point where I didn't recognize myself. I didn't know if I was coming or going. All I could see was heartache. It seemed like it was all around me. Especially after I went to Arizona for Brad's funeral. Once I wrongly got it in my head that he'd been unfaithful before his death, I gave up the little bit of hope I had that I could actually have happily ever after."

She swallowed hard, fighting against the tears that threatened to spill from her eyes. "But I was wrong. So wrong. There is a good bit of faith that has to go with love. Faith in the other person to do right by you, faith in yourself to trust them with your heart. And I wasn't ready for that. I had a journey to travel, and it had to be on my terms. I've made peace now. Peace with my dad. With Sarah. Even with Mark. But more importantly, I've made peace with myself. I'm leaving my lists behind, lists of what the perfect man will look like and lists of my expectations about love.

"And now I'm standing in front of you with a whole heart.

It isn't pieced together anymore. I'm not a shell of a person. I'm just me. And I'm looking for the kind of love you find in history books. The kind that wars were fought over, and the kind that supports people through the worst times of their lives."

He opened his mouth, and she once again clasped her hand over it. "Not yet," she said.

"What I'm trying to say is that I love you. Wholly and completely. And I'm not afraid to say it out loud. Even though I know that there is a good chance that it's too late, that my window of opportunity has passed. I don't care. This is me leaping. With no net."

She removed her hand and stepped back.

He looked at her in silence.

Her heart, which had been pumping at a surprisingly normal speed while she spoke, began to pound again.

Still silent, he handed her a copy of his book. "Open it and take a look at the dedication."

With trembling hands, she took the book from him and opened to the dedication page. The tears blinded her as she read, *To Kristy, the Ann to my Will. Yours forever, Ace.*

Without a word, he grabbed her and kissed her gently, then pulled her to his chest. "I love you, too," he whispered.

EPILOGUE

The following May

I'd like to make a toast to my beautiful bride," Owen announced. "Please raise your glasses in honor of Dorothy, the woman who has brought a light back to my life."

The crowd raised their punch glasses and shouted well wishes.

"It was a beautiful ceremony," Kristy said to the handsome man holding her hand.

"I especially liked 'Rocky Top' as the recessional." Ace laughed and gave her hand a squeeze.

Arm in arm, Owen and Dorothy made their way over to where Ace and Kristy stood.

"Glad you could make it," Owen said, clapping Ace on the back.

"I wouldn't have missed it for the world."

"And I hear you'll have a new job come August?"

He nodded. "That's right. I just accepted a position as part of the history faculty at Freed-Hardeman University. It's less than an hour from Shiloh." He pulled Kristy to him. "Which was part of the requirement as I began job hunting."

Owen chuckled. "We're glad to have you back in these parts, and especially happy to have you back this summer. But what I really want to know is have you talked her into letting you share the yellow office?"

Kristy shook her head. "Nope. The yellow office is all mine. He'll be perfectly happy sharing an office with the other seasonals." She winked. "Matthew and Mason might even let you claim the biggest desk." She patted Ace on the shoulder. "But it's only until August. Then you'll have your very own office at the university."

"There's Hank. We'd better go thank him for allowing me the extra time off." Owen squeezed Dorothy's hand. "We're going to Disney World!"

They walked off laughing.

Just as Kristy was about to go get more punch, Ace pulled her out of earshot of the crowd.

"I have a surprise for you," he said, his eyes gleaming.

"You do?"

"Yes, but your full cooperation is in order."

She gave him a mock salute. "Yes, sir."

He grabbed her hand and pulled her outside to his truck. Opening the passenger door, he helped her inside then went around and climbed in the driver's seat.

"Where are we going?"

"You'll find out soon enough." He grinned, his eyes on the road.

She sank back against the seat, wondering what he had up his sleeve.

Five minutes later, they were entering the main entrance of the park.

"Are we going to my house?"

"Patience, my dear."

Rather than driving to the residential area, he began to drive along the tour route.

They passed the Confederate Monument.

"There's where you played the hero." She laughed, pointing to the spot where Ace had tackled the monument vandal.

"I'd never have known he was there if it weren't for your brilliant detective work, though. We make a pretty good team, don't you think?"

She nodded.

He turned left before they got to tour stop three.

"We're going to the center of the Hornet's Nest?" she asked. "I'm not dressed for a hike." She gestured toward her dress and heels.

"Stop worrying."

He slowed down as they passed the center of the Hornet's Nest and turned left onto the gravel road. They passed a row of cannons and a series of monuments. Suddenly Ace stopped the truck and turned off the ignition.

She looked at him curiously. "You know, my favorite monument is right near here."

"I know." He smiled.

Ace helped Kristy climb out of the truck and grabbed her hand. "We're almost there."

They walked the few steps it took to get to the Wisconsin Monument. It had always been Kristy's favorite spot in the park. The isolated statue was, in her opinion, the most beautiful one housed at Shiloh. And since it was off the beaten path, not many people ever saw it.

Before she could ask what they were doing there, she saw it.

A quilt on the ground beside the monument. In the center of the quilt was a picnic basket.

She turned toward Ace and smiled. "What a wonderful surprise. It's perfect." She slipped her heels off and stepped onto the quilt, sitting down beside the basket.

Ace stood by the monument, watching her.

"Aren't you going to join me?" she asked.

"Yes. But first, I was thinking we should rekindle an old game."

She laughed. "Whose turn is it to ask? Yours or mine?"

"I'm pretty sure it's mine."

"Ask away. I'm an open book." She smiled.

"Come here." He motioned to the edge of the quilt where he stood.

She rose from the quilt and went over to stand in front of him.

He took both of her hands in his. "I've been planning on asking you this question for quite some time now. But I had to think of the perfect way to ask it.

"Let me preface it by saying that you make me happier than I even knew was possible. Every day is an adventure with you. I love your stories. I love that your hair gets big when it's humid. I love that you talk to dogs like they're people." He took a breath. "You have a strength that amazes me and a relationship with the Lord that teaches me how I should strive to be. In short, you make me want to be a better man."

The tears flowed freely down Kristy's face, but she didn't let go of his hands to wipe them away.

Ace knelt down on one knee. "So the way I see it, there is only one question that remains to be asked. Kristy O'Neal, will you marry me?"

She dropped to her knees in front of him and threw her arms around his neck. "Yes," she said. "A thousand times yes."

ANNALISA DAUGHETY, an Arkansas native, won first place in the Contemporary Romance category at the 2008 ACFW Genesis Awards. After graduating from Freed-Hardeman University, she worked as a park ranger for the National Park Service. She now resides in Memphis, Tennessee. Read more at www.annalisadaughety.com.